WITHDRAWN

PRAISE FOR *FLOREANA*

"Raymond's novel is riveting and revelatory, a murder mystery embedded in other mysteries—of love and regret, loss and redemption, and how we can manage to hold on to the parts of this beautiful world that were never ours in the first place."
—Karen Joy Fowler, *New York Times* bestselling author of *Booth* and *We Are All Completely Beside Ourselves*

"*Floreana* is a stunning and deeply layered murder mystery, historical novel, and environmental love letter all in one. Midge Raymond beautifully and seamlessly weaves the hidden lives of two women, a century apart, as they negotiate the fragile terrain of the Galápagos Islands along with their own troubled psyches . . . A haunting tale for our times."
—JoeAnn Hart, author of *Arroyo Circle* and *Highwire Act*

"*Floreana* is a beautiful, unexpected, and powerful novel about the fragility of life and love in its many forms . . . A powerful and totally unique book."
—Samantha Greene Woodruff, bestselling author of *The Lobotomist's Wife* and *The Trade Off*

"*Floreana* masterfully weaves together the tales of two women who escape to the same faraway island almost a century apart. Raymond's beautiful and absorbing novel kept me turning the pages."
—Karin Lin-Greenberg, author of *You Are Here*

"In this suspenseful and immersive novel, Midge Raymond offers a possible series of events leading up to infamous awful fates of a few of the settlers, while telling an equally compelling contemporary story. Come for the disastrous love affairs; stay for the careful depiction of efforts being made toward penguin conservation."

—Alice Elliott Dark, author of *Fellowship Point* and *In the Gloaming*

"This book is a triple hitter: it's a great novel, beautifully structured and woven; it's a compelling mystery; and it's a striking lesson about ecology and the importance of keeping our world intact. All three join together in one powerful tornado of a book."

—Laurie Notaro, New York Times bestselling author of *The Murderess and Crossing the Horizon*

FLOREANA

FLOREANA

a novel

MIDGE RAYMOND

Little a

This is a work of fiction. Names, characters, organizations, places, events, and incidents are either products of the author's imagination or are used fictitiously. Otherwise, any resemblance to actual persons, living or dead, is purely coincidental.

Text copyright © 2024 by Midge Raymond
All rights reserved.

No part of this book may be reproduced, or stored in a retrieval system, or transmitted in any form or by any means, electronic, mechanical, photocopying, recording, or otherwise, without express written permission of the publisher.

Published by Little A, New York

www.apub.com

Amazon, the Amazon logo, and Little A are trademarks of Amazon.com, Inc., or its affiliates.

ISBN-13: 9781662524370 (hardcover)
ISBN-13: 9781662525124 (paperback)
ISBN-13: 9781662522826 (digital)

Cover design by Zoe Norvell
Cover image: (Jungle) *Backwaters Call* and *Backwaters Teatro* by Nadia Attura; (Botanical vine, over inset) Detail from Plate XXXIII, *The botany of the Antarctic voyage of H.M. discovery ships Erebus and Terror in the Years 1839–1843: under the command of Captain Sir James Clark Ross*, by Joseph Dalton Hooker and W. H. Hood (London: Reeve Brothers, 1844–1860), via Marine Biological Laboratory, Woods Hole Oceanographic Institution / Biodiversity Heritage Library; (Waves, inset) *Crashing Waves*, 1892 (oil on canvas) by David James (1834–1897), photo © Christie's Images / Bridgeman Images

Printed in the United States of America

First edition

For John

Mallory

January 2020

As the boat approaches Puerto Velasco Ibarra, I wipe sea spray from my face and scan the arid landscape. It's been a decade since I've set eyes on Floreana, and I'm bracing myself against the waves and the memories.

Yet despite how long it's been, Floreana looks as familiar as though I were just here. I remember, suddenly, the sense of déjà vu I felt when I first came to the Galápagos with Gavin. As though I belonged here.

And now, it looks as though I'd never left. At the landing, a scattering of civilization hugs the shoreline: the Wittmer hotel's weathered two-story building presides over Black Beach as it has, in some form or another, since the Second World War. Past the black sand, occupied by snoozing sea lions, is a brightly colored church; amid the tinder-dry scrub are piles of wood and corrugated iron; and past that—as far as the eye can see—wiry gray brush, and nothing else.

As I climb up the concrete steps to the dock, a sea turtle swims underwater below. When I see Gavin coming toward the landing, I feel lightheaded, swervy, as though I'm still on the water.

I haven't seen Gavin since I'd left him and the lab ten years ago. He was thirty-eight then; I was twenty-four. We'd been together for two years.

My eyes glide past him, focusing on Floreana's *cerros*, the sloping hills covered with parched brush. The water spots on my sunglasses blur the view.

Then he's in front of me—a brief hug, a perfunctory kiss on the cheek—and when he pushes his sunglasses back onto his head, his green eyes hold mine.

"Welcome back," he says, nothing more; he simply takes my bag and turns to lead me up a sand-strewn path.

We reach a row of dark, weathered wood structures with faded green roofs. He opens one of the cottage doors and nods me inside, setting my bag on the floor. "No keys," he says, then looks at the clouded sky. "Everything's powered by solar, so the AC is a little iffy."

I step into the dim room, then peel back the curtains to let in the light. The room is long and narrow, with small windows at either end.

"Get settled and come on over to the dining area," he says. "We'll have a drink and talk about the project."

I nod and shove my duffel farther into the room. Even in the saturating heat, I don't bother with the air-conditioning but instead open both windows, letting the ocean breeze travel all the way through.

The wood-paneled room has a bureau, a desk, and a full bed as well as two bunks. On a shelf above the desk are a few paperbacks, including the memoirs of two of the island's most famous early settlers, Dore Strauch and Margret Wittmer. The windowless, white-tiled bathroom is tiny but clean. Outside, from the deck, I glimpse a covered outdoor dining area at the far end of the lodge, tucked in by black lava rock.

I sink into the canvas chair in front of the casita—my home for the next month—and stare out at the dark blue water in the distance. Though I'd been the one to reach out to Gavin and volunteer to join him here, after so long away—from both him and the job—I'm suddenly not sure I can do this: the research, the fieldwork. The proximity to Gavin. The space between this life and the life I left behind, stretching out in not only thousands of miles but in years of what-ifs.

I feel the sting of a mosquito bite and look down to see a red droplet emerge on my arm. I'm reminded of an article I'd once read, on an international flight to a conference with Gavin, about the Pirahã tribe of Brazil, whose people have no specific words for color. Instead, they would describe the color red as "like blood."

The Pirahã, I remember, also have no numbers; they live so fully in the moment that they have no need to count. They hunt and gather what they need each day because they do not think about the future. They don't tell stories because they do not consider the past. They have no collective memory beyond the present moment, and I wonder, now that I am here, what it might be like to speak a language in which there is no past tense, in which there are no regrets, in which once a moment has passed, it is gone forever.

Dore

September 1929

Before we left I asked myself: How far must one go to truly disappear? How far must we go before the rest of the world ceases to exist?

Now I find myself asking: Did we go too far, or not far enough?

It sounded so romantic to me, back in Berlin—escaping to a tropical island, sleeping in hammocks strung between the trees, tending a garden. Yet upon the first sighting of our new home, I confess I wanted to descend to the hold of the ship and stay there until it had left again.

Floreana looked as if the sun had sucked dry every last bit of life. The scene before me was like that of a badly faded painting, the island's grayish-green hills against a hazy sky. Already I was dizzy in the heat, my heart pounding. I wanted to tell Friedrich that I felt unwell, but I knew he would tell me my illness was in my mind, not in my body.

And perhaps he would be right. Perhaps I have always been more sick in mind than in body—but what I now see is that there is no difference. How can anyone be well if she is not happy, and how can she be happy if she is not well?

Yet to express any such thing as fear or regret to Friedrich would reveal to him that I am not who he thought I was—that I am not even who *I* thought I was. And I need to believe in this woman—this strong, healthy woman who is loved and in love—for as long as I can.

This is the story no one will ever know. Perhaps, if I have hidden these pages well enough, no one will ever read these words. But I have to put them to paper. A woman cannot keep such thoughts to herself, even if there is no one she can tell. The burden of secrets is made ever so much greater by the burden of loneliness.

Mallory

I make my way to the open-air dining area, where Gavin sits at one of the wooden tables with his laptop, a bottle of wine open on the table. Adjacent to the dining area is a small outdoor kitchen with a full-size fridge and an electric stove, its doorless cupboards filled with dishes and utensils, pots and pans.

Gavin pours me a glass of wine. "It's not bad," he says. "From a vineyard in the Andes."

I take a sip. It's dry and light.

He lowers his gaze to his laptop. I lean back in the chair, the wood stiff against my spine, and look at him. The lines on his face seem deeper now, and his dark hair is spackled with gray. The lights of the dining area flicker, like candles.

He glances up. "Solar," he says, shaking his head. "Too many clouds today, I guess."

He closes his laptop and raises his glass. "*Salud,*" he says. *To health.* I clink my glass to his and take a long drink. His eyes are so familiar it almost takes my breath away, even as we sit here like near strangers.

"We'll make breakfast here," he says, waving an arm toward the galley, "and we'll come back midday, for lunch and a break from the heat. For dinner we can take turns cooking or walk into town. The water's treated here, so it's potable."

We'd come to the islands together twice, first to begin a nest-building project for the endangered Galápagos penguins and again to check on them. We'd constructed eighty nests along the rocky shores of Isabela Island, and a year later, we discovered that one nest housed a newborn chick, and another had two eggs. It was a revelation: the natural nests nearby had been ignored in favor of the ones we had made.

"I hired a Galapagueño to help us out," Gavin continues. "Name's Darwin—not kidding—and his family owns the restaurant in town. Tomorrow he'll help us move lava stones to the site. We'll start no later than seven."

We'll be building this island's first human-made penguin nests—and already the routine sounds comforting, as if I might be able to step neatly back into a less complicated past. Since making the arrangements with Gavin a month ago, I'd had to dive into research to catch myself up, learning that Floreana's earliest settlers had arrived back in the early 1800s, and over the next 150 years, they'd brought with them dogs, cats, goats, donkeys, cows, pigs, even monkeys. Now, the human population barely exceeds a hundred, yet the animals had exploded in numbers and wildness—until conservationists began stepping in to undo the damage.

Finally, with the penguins' predators—the cats and rats who ate the eggs or the tiny chicks—almost completely eradicated, it's time to build nests on Floreana. Offering safe places to breed is one of the few ways we can help them, since nearly 50 percent of their natural nests have been lost to erosion and high tides. The penguins have long been on the IUCN Red List of Threatened Species—endangered, with their numbers decreasing—and we can't afford to wait.

"We'll see how many nests we can build," Gavin goes on. "I'd love to have at least a hundred and fifty to start. That's if the habitat accommodates it; we'll see when we get there."

"Are any of the Floreana penguins banded?" A flash of memory: Emily as a toddler, finding my fieldwork photos of penguins, sea lions, tortoises, and turtles, asking me about the islands. I'd taken Scott's big globe down from the bookshelf in the study, spun it around, and showed her the tiny dots of land off the coast of Ecuador. Though Emily was the reason I'd left Gavin and the lab, she was also the only one who kept the work alive for me in some small way; most of her stuffed animals were penguins and turtles.

"We haven't banded any of them yet," Gavin says. "But if the nest building goes well, you can work with my student on that."

"Your student?"

"Yeah, her name's Hannah. She's somewhere trying to Skype with her boyfriend right now. You'll meet her tomorrow."

My hand tightens on the wineglass. On the lab's Facebook page, the graduate student who was supposed to be here instead of me had posted a photo of herself both before and after a cycling race in which she'd broken her arm, cheerfully showing off her cast while lamenting that she had to give up this opportunity to build nests. "I was *replacing* your student, I thought."

"This one's new. Green as a cactus leaf—which is why I'm glad you're here." He meets my eyes. "You'll be good for each other, I think. Anyway, I had to hire her. Her family donated money—and I mean a lot of money—to the lab. I couldn't have afforded to bring you here if it weren't for her."

Gavin drains his glass and stands. "Are you hungry?" he says. "Let's go eat."

The day's light is fading fast, and solar-powered streetlights hover above the dirt-and-gravel road to the island's only town. There are more homes than I remember, many doubling as cafés and guesthouses, and a small school for the few dozen children in town. There's still no supermarket, no bank or ATM, only a few cars.

At the restaurant, we meet Darwin's brother, Jorge, who recommends *menestra*, an Ecuadorian specialty. Gavin also asks for a bottle of wine.

Despite the dark, it's hotter away from the ocean's light breath. I pull my T-shirt away from my skin.

"I'm not sure I need to be here," I say. "If you already have a student."

"It's good you're here. I need someone to teach her."

I look at him, but he keeps his eyes lowered. "You could've said no. Picked someone from the lab. I'm not a teacher, and I've been out of the field for ages."

"It seemed like you needed this. That the timing might be good for you."

Jorge brings a sweating bottle of wine, a liter of bottled water, and four glasses. Gavin pours the wine, then says, "I saw your post on Facebook." He pushes my glass across the table.

I've nearly managed to forget about the post he's talking about. Years of a dormant Facebook account, and then one night of too much wine and far too much sadness and anger, and my relationship status went from *married* to *separated* to *single* and finally to *it's complicated*. The next morning, head aching, I'd logged in, thinking I'd change it back, but I never got to it. I scrolled past smiling faces and cheery updates, happy couples and happy children. And then I saw Gavin's student's post and impulsively sent him an email asking if I could help.

He didn't ask why, after all these years, I'd reached out now. I knew I couldn't tell him in an email, so it was just as well. We hadn't spoken in the decade since I'd left, but we remained friends on Facebook, and I followed the lab. I wasn't even sure he'd write back, let alone invite me to join him here, but I can still see his email on my screen, so mundane and yet so comfortably familiar—the clipped way he writes, the lowercase *g* with which he still signs off. And because it made me feel as though I could go back in time, as though I could erase everything that happened between our last trip and this one, I'd grasped back with both hands, the way he'd taught me to handle penguins: act quickly, hold tight, don't let go.

"I wasn't sure you'd leave Emily, though," Gavin continues. "Is she with Scott?"

At the sound of her name, a part of me freezes up, creating an icy core that sends a shiver through me in the heat. I close my eyes briefly, imagining what Gavin must be thinking—*a mother leaving an eight-year-old girl behind for a month? what kind of mother does that?*—but I allow the thought to linger for only a second before I open my eyes and look directly into his, which is harder than I imagined.

"You think I'm a bad mother."

He shakes his head. "I always thought you'd be a great mom."

"I'm not."

"Why would you say that?"

In his expecting eyes I see the weight of our shared history and all that he still doesn't know. "Emily's . . ." I pause, unable to find the right words. "She's getting away from me," I say finally, thinking back to one of our mother-daughter clashes, and after this the words come more easily. "She's stubborn and willful, and I—I'm not sure what to do."

He smiles, but there's more tension than warmth behind it. "Sounds like someone I know."

I can't bring myself to smile back. And I can't bring myself to tell him why I'm really here. Not yet.

He takes a drink of wine. "Well, the cell service isn't too bad, and the Wi-Fi's intermittent but adequate, if you want to call her. Hannah might know of some hacks. She's always online."

I drain my wineglass and refill it.

"Do you ever think about it?" he asks.

"What?"

"Finishing."

"My PhD, you mean?" I almost laugh.

"You were so close," he says.

I shake my head. "It's too late."

Our food arrives, and when I look down at my plate—a lovely, thick lentil sauce circling a perfect cone of white rice—I feel a wave of nausea.

"What's the matter?"

"Nothing. Too much wine, maybe." I drink from my water glass and pick at the *menestra*, and Gavin fills the silence with chatter about the lab, people I used to know in San Diego, new ones I don't. It's almost as if he, too, is avoiding talking about himself, or me, or us, and right now I'm grateful.

Later, as we walk back to the casitas, I try to step slowly, carefully, my limbs noodly and weak. Gavin shines his flashlight ahead, the cloudy night hovering over us like scrim. When we get to the wooden walkway leading to the casitas, I stumble in the dark, and he steadies me, his arm around my waist. "You sure you're all right?"

I nod. "Just tired."

He releases his hand from my back as we continue walking, but I stay close until we reach his casita door. Being close to him again, his wine-scented breath in the air between us, gives me a sense of what might've been. "I'm glad I'm here," I tell him, and I feel as though I'm trying to convince us both.

"Me, too," he says, and steps into his room.

In my own casita, I close my door, lie on the bed, and look at my phone—a weak signal, no Wi-Fi, low battery. It's only two hours later in Boston, but late enough. I try to remember the last time Emily had stayed up past nine o'clock, my thoughts sifting through the past, searching my exhausted brain.

The Red Sox game—that had to be it. My sister had been in town visiting, spoiling Emily with ice cream and popcorn and Fenway Franks, and Megan and Emily both got mad at me when I asked a family behind us not to consume their unshelled peanuts and toss the shells in our direction. "Mom, it's *fine*," Emily said—but I couldn't tell whether the redness in her face was from embarrassment or the beginning of a reaction.

I plug my phone into the charger and drop it into the nightstand drawer. The fan swirls above me, the mosquito netting a whirling veil.

Dore

We have accomplished our goal of moving to Floreana, and yet I feel as though I have not quite fully arrived. Perhaps I am not prepared for what's ahead of us—or perhaps it is simply easier to believe in paradise when it is still a dream.

I'd met Friedrich at the hospital in Berlin—I was the patient, he the doctor—and he'd caught my eye immediately. He wore his brilliance on his face: his brow creased as if he never stopped thinking. His blond hair wild, as if ideas were racing from his brain. His eyes, deep and blue as the Pacific that would soon surround us.

I suffered from multiple sclerosis, which had stolen the ease of my mobility and, my previous doctors had predicted, my chance to ever have children. Yet I also suffered in ways that went beyond the physical. I had married, at twenty-three, a man more than two decades my senior, and even after I was told I could not bear children, my hope stayed stubbornly alive, for there was nothing I wanted more. Yet after five miscarriages I had to admit it would be impossible.

My husband claimed to have accepted this fate, but I felt his withdrawal from our marriage. There had never been much love between us, but he grew more quiet, and our bed grew cold. I was heartbroken at the thought of such a loveless existence, and I felt our marriage no longer had a reason to exist.

Friedrich ignited cinders that had long burned out in me, and after I left the hospital I began to see him at his private practice. "You shall think yourself well," he told me, and he quoted his beloved Nietzsche: "There is more wisdom in your body than in your deepest philosophy." I believed him. Friedrich had studied philosophy before turning to medicine, and in his general practice he took a psychological approach to health, believing that it took both the body and the mind to overcome illness. And, sure enough, I began to feel a new energy, an aliveness in my body, the body that had crushed my hopes so many times but now felt full of possibility. It wasn't long until we knew our relationship would become so much more.

Though I'd been working in a bank when I met my husband, I had given up work to take care of the house, as was expected of me. But the cooking and the cleaning and the managing of the household stifled my soul. It would have been tolerable if I'd had children to raise—to nourish them and watch them grow—but there I was, feeding and cleaning up after a grown man, and I began to think of him as no more than a child himself, one nearly twice my age and without promise, one who would not flourish but only stagnate.

I could not even have pets to care for, as he was terribly allergic. Though I grew up in the city, I had loved animals since I was a child. I'd once visited a farm and had a chance to meet dogs and cats, pigs and cows, dozens of chickens. It sounds like a strange childhood notion, but as I sat on the ground and spoke softly to the chickens who looked me right in the eye, I felt they listened to me, and heard me.

It changed everything. Back in Berlin, I begged my parents for a pet but was not allowed one. When I saw *Schweinshaxe* on my plate, I could see nothing but the sweet faces of pigs; when I saw *Sauerbraten*, I saw the large innocent eyes of cows. My parents would not allow me to leave food on my plate, but I stopped eating animals as soon as I reached adulthood.

Imagine my delight in learning that Friedrich, too, had loved animals as a child and did not eat them either. Immediately we had something in common that had always been important to me but that no one had ever truly understood.

I loved him for so many reasons, not least because he was all that my husband was not—worldly, exciting, intellectual, philosophical—and also because to Friedrich I was no mere hausfrau. When I confessed that I felt like a failure for not producing a family, Friedrich, who was married himself, said, "You mustn't feel bad for something that is a matter of biology. What matters as much as your body is your mind."

Friedrich and his wife were also childless; he told me he had no need or wish for children. "Though our bodies may be different, Dore, in our minds you and I are equal. You may think it is your body that controls your life, but it is your mind and spirit that has all the power."

It was the first time I felt equal to anyone, especially a man. As we spoke of books and writing, I realized he expected as much from me as he did from himself, and I gratefully accepted this challenge, to see in myself all that I could be and not merely who I was.

We would talk for hours on the roof of his office building in Kalckreuthstrasse, sheltered from the bustling streets and hidden from view. At first our connection was indeed of the mind; we spoke of philosophy and wilderness, of the ways the world was changing and losing its way—the materialism, the disconnect of humans from nature and one another. I have always wanted, and have never had the chance, to be in conversation about ideas, and here was a man who made me think. Who sparked my brain.

Most of all, Friedrich listened to me. For once, at last, I had a sympathetic ear for my anguish—for my lost babies, for my lonely marriage. "I'm beginning to fear I will never be happy," I confessed one afternoon, and that was when he took me in his arms and kissed me. In that moment, I felt a wash of the joy that had eluded me for so long, as I'd begun to believe I was undeserving of such affection.

With Friedrich, I felt a bond like no other, a meeting of our souls that felt spiritual, inevitable, as though we were meant to be all along—and I knew this connection had to be forged through our bodies as well as our minds—no matter his marriage, no matter mine.

At the same time, I felt I couldn't live up to his stature. One evening I tearfully confided, "I worry you'll leave me. You are a physician, a healer, a thinker—and I am nothing but a hausfrau."

"Dore, you are so much more than that," he told me, his arm around my shoulders. "But it is not enough for me to say it. You have to believe it yourself."

Yet how can one believe in herself when no one else has believed in her before? Friedrich was the first, the one who made everything possible.

As if to prove he would never leave me, he began to talk about going away together, and that night on the roof, we looked skyward and searched for stars, mapping constellations as we began to map out a life together. Friedrich said he wanted to take me away, to leave the "civilized" world behind—he did not believe it was civilized at all but quite the opposite. He wanted to create a new philosophical framework, and he needed to be free of the constraints of society in order to explore his ideas, to develop a new way of thinking and being in the world. He could achieve this goal only by immersion in the wilderness, by leaving material pursuits and comforts behind to focus on self-sufficiency and healing. And he wanted us to create this life together.

At times he was so passionate about this experiment, so much more focused on his work than on us, that I again worried I had no place in it. At one point I asked him, "Do you want me along with you out of love? Or is there also room for me in your work?"

He told me that he could not achieve any validity in his project by living this new life alone—this experiment had to be embarked upon with a partner. And I would be the perfect partner in that he believed I suffered in body because I suffered in mind—he would prove that his new philosophy, and not medicine or surgeries, would make me well. "Civilization is poor in every way that matters," he told me. "We shall, by leaving it, become rich."

"Where will we go?" I asked him, my heart pounding with excitement. I had not felt so vivacious in years. I think, at that time, the promise of anything new would have thrilled me.

"I don't know yet," he replied. "I'm still investigating our options."

I had not meant the question as one for him to answer on his own; I had meant for us to answer it together. But of course Friedrich is a researcher, a scientist—though I knew that I was in all ways his equal, he was better qualified for such an investigation, and so I kept my thoughts to myself and left him to it.

And when he chose Floreana, a small, roundish island on the southern end of the Galápagos archipelago—for its remoteness, its fresh water, its position on shipping routes though it was otherwise uninhabited—I was as pleased with his choice as if I'd made the decision with him. Friedrich had practical reasons for choosing this island, but I was excited about its exotic wildlife: penguins, sea lions, iguanas. Our own tropical island surrounded by clear blue ocean. No more cold, windy, dreary winters in Berlin. And, most of all: freedom from my deeply unsatisfying life, and the promise of a new one with him. Perhaps it didn't really matter where we went.

Yet I dreaded telling my family, especially my husband. Friedrich and I had kept our affair a secret, and all the while I'd played the role of dutiful wife. I attended social events with my husband, dressed in fine clothing and high-heeled shoes, while meeting with Friedrich on the pretense of being his patient. I did not need to wear such costumes with Friedrich—whenever we met, I wore my favorite, most comfortable clothing, and I think this is one reason I embraced our affair so easily; I could be myself with him. I didn't have to dress a certain way or pretend I was a happy hausfrau. Friedrich knew—and loved—the real Dore.

And because I was feeling so much better as a result of my "treatment," my husband suspected nothing other than an improvement in my health. I would rather have fled in the middle of the night than tell him of our affair and our plans, but Friedrich made me face myself, my husband, what we were about to do. He made me brave.

And so, when I could put it off no longer, I finally broke the news one evening, as we sat amid the remnants of a nearly inedible supper.

"I don't understand," my husband said to me, sitting stunned in our kitchen. "Were you never happy with me?"

"I'm not meant to be a hausfrau," I told him, gesturing toward our unfinished food as evidence. "I can't give you what you want. And I will never be able to give you a family."

He looked away, silent, and I had the odd feeling that perhaps part of him agreed with my leaving, even as he couldn't quite seem to believe it. I had confessed not only that Friedrich and I were lovers but that we were planning to move to Floreana together.

"You deserve a chance to find someone else," I said. "To have the life you want. And so do I," I added, speaking with more confidence than I felt. I believed I was channeling Friedrich then: his unwavering certainty and his total commitment to whatever lay before him.

My husband was very clear: he did not want to be publicly humiliated, he said, and my trip with Friedrich must be spoken of as a "research trip" between doctor and patient. Because I'd already caused him so much misery, I agreed.

And then—out of guilt, or selfishness, perhaps a small amount of pity—another idea was born. I had become accustomed to Friedrich as my best friend and confidant, so I spoke to him about it first.

"What if," I said, "your wife went to live with my husband in my home? She is a good hausfrau, and they both will need one another after we're gone."

For I knew Mila Ritter was as shocked as my own husband had been. Unlike me, she had willingly given up her career to be a wife—and I felt she would be comforted by fulfilling this purpose, even if it was with another man.

Friedrich smiled and kissed me. "This is why we are together," he said. "It's a perfect plan. Everything is falling into place."

Yet my husband merely laughed at the notion and wouldn't hear another word.

As the weeks passed and our departure date grew closer, I decided to host a small supper party—a chance for me to say goodbye, to make amends.

I invited my parents and my sister, and a friend with whom I'd recently fallen out. They all believed Friedrich and I were taking a trip for his work, with me as his patient, but none of them knew the extent of it. My family did not know we were lovers. None of them knew we were leaving forever.

So I planned to make it festive, with beer and fresh bread and cheeses. My friend Elise, with whom I'd quarreled months earlier, would bring homemade potato dumplings. She had been so thrilled by my invitation, so glad we were friends again, that she did not even mention the reason for the party—Friedrich and me traveling together.

That had been what we'd quarreled about—she disliked my relationship with Friedrich. She thought I was a fool for carrying on with another man, for betraying a loyal husband.

I confess I was rather hurt by her reaction, as reasonable as it was. She knew how unhappy I'd been in my marriage, and I suppose I had hoped, somehow, that she would be pleased for me, that she might even congratulate me for finding true love. I had responded to her quite rudely. "If you were not so blind to the faults of your own husband," I told her, "perhaps you'd let yourself find true love, too."

I hadn't meant it; Elise's husband was a fine man. The truth was, I envied her, their marriage, their two beautiful daughters. Elise herself was quite lovely, with glossy dark hair and sparkling hazel eyes, while I'd always been plain. My light-brown hair seemed to look dirty rather than shiny and was uncontrollably wavy. My face has an oval shape, its features unremarkable. Years earlier, I'd overheard my mother say to my father that I was fortunate to have found someone to marry. "She's not a beauty like her sister," my mother had said, "and now at least she won't be alone."

I'd never been told I was beautiful. Until I met Friedrich. Since the day we met, I knew his attraction to me was as strong as the earth's magnetic field—undeniable, as was my attraction to him.

Just a few days before the party, Friedrich suggested that he and Mila attend as well—so he could meet my family, and most of all so his wife could meet my husband. I recoiled at once—this would hardly be the occasion to thrust the two of them together, and I was hoping for a peaceful evening—but Friedrich insisted it was for the best.

By the time the evening arrived, I was sick with anxiety. I had managed to get the food prepared and the house in order, but I was so exhausted that my limp was far worse than usual and I couldn't walk without a cane. When I opened the door to my family, it felt less like a party than a funeral.

When Friedrich and Mila walked through the door, I braced myself. Yet Friedrich, who had met my husband once previously, at the hospital, greeted everyone with a gaiety I rarely saw—he was normally such a serious man—and his mood was infectious to us all. My husband, of course, was quite angry, but because he was so concerned with appearances, he welcomed Friedrich cordially, though I could see the tension under his placid expression.

Elise arrived immediately afterward, and as her friendliness and warmth further suffused the atmosphere, I drew in my first full breath of the day.

A short while later, my sister handed me a beer, and though Friedrich does not approve of alcohol, I drank it greedily, turning my body slightly away so he would not notice. I was still very anxious about Friedrich and our spouses being under one roof, and the beer flowed through me, calming my nerves.

I watched Elise serve the dumplings, being kind to Friedrich though I knew it pained her. I wished I'd confided in her about my plans, but our reunion depended on her not knowing the depth of my deception, of my intent. Her bright and cheerful presence that night made me glad I could leave peacefully but sorry that our friendship would be over once she learned the truth. The same would happen with my sister. With more than a decade between us, she and I had never been close, but I knew I would be lost to her now, as surely as if I'd died.

My father could barely look at me for his confusion; he didn't understand my eagerness to travel, let alone with someone other than my husband. My mother was more cheerful, wishing me well, speaking about when we'd see each other again. "When the novelty wears off, we will all welcome you home," she said.

I felt a flame of anger blaze up in me, and the same lifelong need to defend myself—and now, my new partner as well. "We will be doing serious work," I told her. "Friedrich is a brilliant philosopher, and I will never tire of supporting him."

I hadn't realized I'd raised my voice in the heat of my retort, and in the silence that followed, I saw that everyone was looking in my direction. I tried to recover by saying, in as merry a voice as I could muster, "I made a bread pudding," though even the prospect of dessert was diminished by the fact that I had made it, and everyone knew I was by no means a good cook.

The evening ended on a slightly better note as Mila Ritter entertained us all with a few lovely songs, and my sister added her own sweet voice. I looked at Friedrich, our connection palpable though he was standing on the other side of the parlor, and I felt rising tears of joy at the thought of our adventures ahead; my eyes shone across the room into his. There was perhaps a little bit of sadness in my tears as well, and I held them back so that no one would feel uncomfortable. This gave me a most horrific headache, but I managed to play my part until everyone was gone and I could collapse into bed.

In the past, such excruciating headaches would have felled me for days—but now, there was too much to do, too much to look forward to. I nearly bounced out of bed the next morning.

But my last days in Berlin were not without some heartache as well as anticipation. Though my need to leave outweighed my guilt, it still wounds me to think that I had hurt my husband by leaving as I did.

Before I left, he gave me money, and then he leaned close to me, his voice as icy as January, and he said, "I forgive you. But do not think of coming back."

My husband need not worry; I see no possibility of returning to Berlin. Yet I have discovered that life on Floreana will not be without its challenges. That morning after our arrival, as I stood surrounded by possibility and looking outward at the infinite horizon, I felt uncertainty wash over me, as deep as the Pacific, and I struggled to come up for air.

Mallory

In the early-morning light, as Darwin maneuvers the panga toward the rocky shore, I glimpse a flash of black in the luminous green water below. I'd nearly forgotten the penguins' underwater grace, their sleek and darting beauty.

Gavin sees the penguin, too, and he makes a deep hawing noise, not unlike the exhale of a donkey, attempting to mimic their call. The penguin swims past.

"Maybe she's just not that into you," says Gavin's student, Hannah.

I look ahead, toward a penguin perched onshore, his feet clinging to red-black lava splashed white with guano. Red-and-orange crabs scuttle around as waves crash against the rocks. The scent of salt in the sea spray lingers in the air.

Darwin slows the panga, searching for a spot to land, and eventually pulls up to an outcropping that is dock-like enough for him to secure the thirteen-foot inflatable. Thick of body, with sun-carved lines on his face and gray hair at his temples, Darwin's in his fifties, I'm guessing, and he looks youthful in shorts, a light-blue T-shirt, and a baseball cap with the Charles Darwin Foundation tortoise logo.

After he ties up the boat, he calls my name, holding out a piece of lava the size of a large pizza box and twice as thick, as if he wants me to take it from him. He can barely hold it himself, and his laugh is deep and contagious. He and Gavin carry several large, flat plates of dark lava ashore, piling them on a wide plateau of rock.

I take a few steps over the shoreline's natural lava, sharp and uneven, trying to keep my balance. I'd slept poorly, and my mind feels as thick and slow as the still, hot air. I don't realize Hannah is behind me until she stumbles into me. "Heads up," she says, as if I'm the one who'd bumped into her.

I'd met her for the first time that morning, in the kitchen, over a breakfast of toast, fruit, and Ecuadorian coffee, and I'd been focusing on the coffee, remembering how good it was, allowing its heat and flavor to invade my senses. I barely listened as she talked about joining the program.

"I just switched majors," she said. "I was in English before, but then I took this science-writing class and thought it'd be fun to work with penguins. Still not sure whether I'll do biology or science journalism. Gavin seems to think I'll fall in love with the penguins. Like you did, he said."

I looked at her over my coffee. Her family's donation must've been sizable indeed; this wasn't the way he usually hired students. Back when I'd first walked into Gavin's lab at the University of California, San Diego, he'd summarily dismissed me, without so much as looking up from his computer screen, telling me he had no room for another grad student. Only with the encouragement of my faculty advisor did I try again. During my second visit, he agreed to meet with me, a full week later, and he quizzed me relentlessly about biology, ornithology, conservation, and my work ethic before giving me a tour of the lab. I heard nothing from him after that, and so I went to his office, where he grilled me further and told me to return the following week. I was just about to give up when he offered me a job. Later, when I asked him why he'd been so tough, he told me that was how he treated everyone. "I want to make sure my people are committed," he'd said. "If they're willing to come back at least three times, I consider that a good first step."

"Maybe it's you who has commitment issues," I replied, and he laughed.

But three years later, it was me who left, moving across the country with Scott, giving Gavin no warning. And now I'm back, not only because I needed to get away but because, with the life I'd left him for falling apart, I feel I owe Gavin an explanation, an apology, no matter how belated. Except now that I'm actually here, what I need to tell him suddenly seems impossible.

What I remember of the Galápagos—Gavin and me, immersed in work and in each other—is no longer part of the hot, humid air, which now wraps me in a different embrace. I had hoped the time and distance would allow us to slip back into our easy routines.

But Gavin doesn't look at me as he and Darwin continue to shuttle lava to shore. My face feels tight and hot, my clothes sticking to my skin, my bare arms and legs burning despite all the sunscreen. With the sun half-hidden behind thick clouds, the air as heavy as my anxiety, I'm finding it hard to breathe.

I manage to steady myself and remind Hannah to watch her step on the baking-hot lava, amid the unforgivably sharp and prickly flora. Though I'd studied these birds for years, it still amazes me that they live in this rough, tropical place six hundred miles off the coast of Ecuador. How long they will is the question we can't answer. While it's been five million years since volcanoes birthed these twenty islands, the planet is not finished with them yet; the Nazca Plate is still moving, about four centimeters a year, and many of the islands' volcanoes are still active—a reminder of the precarious and unpredictable nature of life in the Galápagos.

Gavin says, "Once we unload the panga, Darwin and I will head this way. You two start over there. We're looking for shade, accessibility—" He stops and looks at me. "You know the drill."

I give him a wistful smile. "I remember."

As I watch him turn away, I think of the day we discovered penguins living in our nests on Isabela, families raising their chicks in homes we'd made for them. We'd been following our map, counting off nests, noting their condition, looking for banded penguins—then we heard the squeak, saw the tiny wriggling body. We couldn't quite believe it had actually worked.

Then, later, we kissed in the panga on the way back to Puerto Villamil, and it had somehow felt like our first kiss, the heat of it, like a smoldering ember, ignited by the spark of possibility in front of us.

But two eggs and one chick meant only that—possibility—not success.

I realized later that was all Gavin and I had ever been together: possibility. I'd wanted for us to succeed, as a couple and especially in our work. But while the birds have flourished, Gavin and I foundered.

And so here I am again, with him on another island, to try to re-create the potential I saw back then—for the birds, and for us, too, the possibility of starting over in a completely different way.

"What's wrong with this one?" Hannah points to a penguin trudging up the lava, a smattering of red across the white of his chest.

"It's just algae. He's been out there a long time, looking for food." I glance around. None of the other nearby penguins wears this indication of long periods at sea, a sign that food is scarce. "It's a La Niña year, but I wonder if it won't be as productive as we think."

"Um, okay. I have no idea what you're talking about."

When I look at Hannah, I'm reminded of the wild rabbits that used to roam the canyons in San Diego, near Gavin's house—her light-brown hair and eyes give her a plain, alert beauty, and the way she moves is quick, aloof. Gavin was right: she has a lot to learn.

"One of the reasons these penguins are endangered is climate change, right?" I say. "Two weather patterns affect them—La Niña, which we're experiencing now, and El Niño, which has become both more frequent and more severe." I wave my arm toward the water. "Normally, the cold currents bring the fish and crustaceans to the surface, which is great for penguins. But during El Niño, the water is warmer, which means this food isn't available. During the last really bad El Niño, back in 1996 and '97, food was so scarce we lost more than sixty percent of the penguins."

"It was '97 and '98, actually."

I hadn't realized Gavin was still nearby, listening. I look at him and again get the sense that none of this will be easy. It feels as if he wants to remind me of how long it's been, of how hard it will be to step back into my decade-old shoes. I remember what he said—*I saw your post on Facebook*—and wonder whether a part of him wants to punish me for having left him the way I had, to show me what I'd been missing by giving up my career and moving away.

Hannah and I gather tools and kneepads, picks and shovels, and then I begin climbing up the rocks, Hannah close behind. Just below my feet, a wave sloshes into a crevice that would have once made a perfect nest—tucked away, well covered—but now, with rising tides, it is uninhabitable. As we walk, I see a half dozen other spots that had once been nests as well—little caverns, once dry, now eroded, water lapping at the edges. Other than a few mangroves farther inland, there is little vegetation to provide shade.

"So if this is a La Niña year," Hannah says, "it'll be good for the penguins because of the cooler water?"

"Good for penguins," I say, "but it also means less rain and a rougher season for the tortoises and all the animals on land."

It's never all good news; this I remember well. In a season when one species wins, others will lose. The Galápagos penguins try to adapt—they're known as *opportunistic breeders* because they have learned to breed whenever they can. In a bad year, they might not breed at all because they know they can't feed their chicks, but in a La Niña year, they might breed up to three times. It's why they mate for life.

We climb higher, past the dry brush and shrubs, past cactus and prickly pear trees. The heat rises from the lava in a never-ending wave. The smell of burnt earth fills my nostrils, as if the lava has only recently stopped flowing. When we reach a slight plateau, no more than fifty feet from the water's edge but high enough to stay dry, I glimpse a small opening under a jagged lava rock. It's deep enough that, once we widen the entrance, it will make a good nest.

We put on kneepads, and I begin to dig dirt and pebbles out of the lava tube. Hannah watches, and after a few minutes, I rise and step back to let her continue, the way Gavin had done for me.

I look in Gavin's direction again; he and Darwin have hauled stacks of lava rocks, sheets, and stones farther inland, and now they're lowering a three-by-three-foot square of lava to cover a semicircle of large stones, creating a cavelike space underneath. Their shirts are soaked nearly completely through with sweat.

Hannah stands up. "How does this look?"

I lean down with a trowel, observing the dry, light-reddish dirt. I scoop the dirt and rocks that still clutter the opening. "We need to clear this out better."

I explain that if a bird or pair chooses one of our nests, they'll add to it—feathers, bones, leaves, sticks—but we should make it as clean and open as possible. As Gavin had told me: *Our job is to build the structure. They do the interior decorating.*

When we finish, the opening is nearly two feet wide and a foot high, and the cavern is three feet deep and narrow at the back, where the dips and swirls of the lava close in quickly.

"Good," I say. "Now, on to the next one." I motion to Hannah to follow me, keeping my eyes downward and slightly forward, examining the terrain, moving slowly. I have to think like a penguin, to imagine being less than two feet tall and searching for a cool, sheltered place to call home, to raise my kids. A place to keep them safe.

I find a big lava rock with an opening about half a foot wide and two feet deep—plenty of space for a couple of eggs. A high spot, so it will stay dry—the waves won't soak it, and water won't run in when it rains.

Hannah kneels down and, with gloved hands, brushes dirt and pebbles away from the lava tube. I feel a blinding sting as a mixture of sunscreen and sweat drips into my eyes. I rub my hand across my face and walk a few paces away, letting my eyes clear before searching for another nest site, finding one about twenty feet away.

As I dig out the pebbles and dirt, I think of the penguin couple that might live in it one day. I think of the birds when they are courting, the tender way they preen each other, the way they ardently tap bills in a display that looks like violent kissing.

I hear a scuttling and turn around. Still on my knees, I'm nearly face-to-face with a penguin who is making the steep climb up the rocks far more easily than we did—a sight that never ceases to amaze me. I've seen penguins on nearly perpendicular outcroppings, clambering up steep formations, almost parallel to the lava as they ascend. Sometimes they tumble, falling a few feet or even all the way back into the sea, but they always get back up, shake themselves, and continue on.

This penguin's white belly is clean and bright, with no sign of the algae that splotched the other bird. It looks like a male, judging by the thickness of the bill. He is small, shorter than a human toddler, and not bothered by me as I pause my work to observe him. It's been so long that I've forgotten the magic of being this close to a wild animal. A frayed band of black loops around the top of his chest, and a marbled white strap curves from his pinkish-skinned eyes toward the back of his head and under his chin. A few black spots, like flung watercolor paint, dot his belly.

I look into his black eye as he turns his head to the side, observing me as I study him, for several long minutes. I wonder if he's a bachelor searching for a mate, or whether he's here to join a female in their shared nest. I think about Gavin, whether he ever settled down with anyone after I left, whether he's still a bachelor himself. All I know about him now is from glimpses of Facebook updates and e-news from the lab; I have no idea what the last decade of his life looked like, outside of work.

But then, Gavin's life *was* his work, as our life together had been. While at first I'd loved the natural blurring of the two—we shared experiences I never shared with anyone else: traveling to the remotest areas of the world, working to save an endangered species—after a while it wasn't enough. We never once went out to dinner, never traded gifts on birthdays or cards on Valentine's Day. We didn't have much contact outside the lab, the field, the bedroom, but because back then work was everything, Gavin, too, was everything.

The penguin ambles forward, away from me, and I watch him until he's out of view.

I turn back to the nest and finish hollowing out the opening, then straighten up and walk over to Hannah and examine her nest. She has piled up several large rocks around the entrance. I tap the rock pile with my shoe, and the stack crumbles.

"What are you doing?" she protests. "That took me half an hour."

"Better me than a penguin," I tell her. "These nests have to be stable."

She lets out an irritated sigh and kneels back down.

At midday, as the glow of the sun, muted by thick clouds, moves directly overhead, we make our way back to the panga. Hannah's face is flushed red and slick with sweat. I drain the contents of my water bottle, then feel a raindrop hit my forehead. I look up as another few drops fall—and suddenly the rain goes from drops to torrents, and I put up my hands as if to cover myself before realizing the only thing I can do is surrender.

I look at Gavin, rain streaking down his sun-soaked face, his hair wet and dripping water, and he's smiling in the way I remember—that private, somewhere-else smile he doesn't think anyone sees. The smile that reveals he's right where he wants to be.

The rain comes down so hard and fast the drops feel like pebbles, and between the sheets of rain and the steam rising from the baked lava beneath our feet, Gavin blurs in front of me. I turn my face up again, letting the rain sting my sunburned cheeks and run down my tired arms. I close my eyes, willing the moment to last, this brief moment in which the rain is erasing the day's dust and sweat, washing away everything, cleansing us all.

Dore

I have wondered, since we arrived in this rugged and unforgiving place, what I am doing here. As I write this, I've finally managed to leave Berlin behind, but my mind has not yet accepted Floreana as home. The morning mist fills the air with its muggy breath, nearly suffocating me as I take in our new reality.

We have now been here for several months, but I still think back to our first night on Floreana, when our new life felt promising.

We'd landed at Post Office Bay, near the abandoned house of some former Norwegian settlers. "We'll stay here tonight," said Friedrich, looking at the decrepit old house, its roof filled with holes, every inch either weathered gray wood or angry red rust. It was so hideous, so inhospitable, I found I could not breathe. As I struggled for air, for speech, he held me up, steadied me, and looked into my eyes. He murmured, "Our dream come true," as I continued shaking, my head swimming into darkness. And then I collapsed.

No human settlers, I have learned, had ever been able to make a life here. An Irish sailor in the 1800s stayed a few years, growing vegetables and trading them for rum. Around that time, a group of soldiers came from Ecuador's mainland, overseeing a penal colony of prisoners who had been banished by the Ecuadorian government. They created a settlement and left behind most of the animals who still roam the island, feral and starving.

Over the following hundred years, Floreana was ravaged by buccaneers and whalers, and they stayed only long enough to exploit the land and its creatures. They took hundreds of thousands of tortoises, dumping them into the holds of their ships as a cheap source of meat and oil, and so now, I will never have the privilege of seeing them. Where once these majestic creatures thrived, those few who weren't taken ended up starving to death when their grasses were eaten by the abandoned cows, goats, and donkeys and when their eggs were devoured by orphaned dogs and cats.

Floreana is hardly the paradise I'd imagined. And yet, I knew Friedrich had chosen carefully, and I trusted him completely. I couldn't judge our new home so harshly on only our first day.

I recovered from my fainting spell, but it hardly mattered—night came on quickly, at six o'clock, and once again darkness filled my vision. The mosquitos swarmed us, biting like fury, and we had no choice but to retire into the hot and stuffy settlers' cabin. The voices of the wild animals came at us in the dark, such total blackness. Yet another detail I had not considered when I dreamed of reading long into the evenings under the sun.

Friedrich and I lay together speaking quietly—why, as the only humans on the island?—and at last, for a few sweet moments, I felt we were where we belonged. Our hushed whispering reminded me that we'd left our old life behind—the days when our love was forbidden and when we could only dream of the day we'd be here together. Now we were here, beholden to no one, and we whispered not due to shame or secrecy but out of passion and intimacy. In those precious moments I felt that this journey would indeed be everything I'd longed for. A chance to live in nature, among animals. A place where my physical ailments could heal, under sun and sky. A way to have love in my life at last.

My hopes were dashed the next morning. I limped across the white sand—I have not yet managed to heal my chronic limp by mere power of thought, especially here on this quicksand terrain—to the warm blue water of the bay. In the distance I was delighted to see penguins swimming, their black heads popping up above the water before they dove under again. Frigate birds and boobies flew overhead, diving for fish.

I thought I would take a swim—being in the water was soothing to me, and the only place where my body felt whole. Then I saw a large, dark shape in the water, much larger than the penguins. I waited, watched, and then I saw a fin break the surface. I stood there unbelieving as I saw another, then another, an endless school of sharks warning me that this water belongs to them, not to me.

It was no matter; Friedrich was eager to go. We left the beach and walked inland, in search of a place near one of Floreana's natural springs at which to make our home. I reached for his hand, in a gesture of affection but also because I was still unsteady on my feet. He gave my hand a loving squeeze, then released it. "It's time to begin the healing process, Dore," he told me. "You can't make yourself well by leaning on me."

I struggled a bit to keep up with him, but I knew he was right. I was determined to overcome my ailments, but it would take time, perhaps weeks or even months in the balm of the sea breezes, for me to begin to walk more easily.

After a trek that took hours but felt like an eternity, we found our way to a series of small caves nestled into the hills. The caves had clearly housed other settlers before us, with their natural shelter and a gushing spring nearby.

We spent our second night at the caves, and it was there that I hoped we might build our home. Though some parts of the caves had been carved by the hands of men—and the fruit trees were planted by previous settlers—it felt so much more natural than the Norwegians' rough settlement. While I could not delude myself into thinking that we were the first to spend time there, I did feel as though, right then, the caves existed just for us.

But Friedrich had other ideas. "These caves are too small," he said. "And look at this land." He waved his arm around the steep terrain surrounding us. "How can we plant and tend to gardens here?"

"It may take a little extra work," I said, "but it will be worth the trouble. It's so beautiful."

He looked around, studying the landscape. "We are not here to make things beautiful."

"Aren't we?" I asked, surprised. Perhaps I had misunderstood his entire philosophy, but this was, I believed, precisely why we were here. If we were to give up all material things, what were we to replace them with other than the glory of nature? If I was to seek healing without medicine, how could I do so without beauty?

Distracted, he did not answer.

I found myself confused by this version of the man I loved. I knew, of course, that he was focused, perhaps too focused at times—but his intensity was among the qualities I loved best.

Perhaps this was because, in Berlin, the object of his attention had been me.

I told myself that we had much work to do before we could feel settled enough to concentrate on each other again. I told myself that it was out of his great love for me that he wanted to get our home established quickly.

And so we kept exploring, and Friedrich found another spot that was suitable to him, and that also had a spring—and yet preparing it was no less work, I thought, than a home at the caves would've been. In the island's sticky and unrelenting heat, we had to clear the thick, dense vegetation, move boulders, cut down a tree. And then, when Friedrich saw me examining the hoof and paw prints of the animals who came to drink at the spring, he said, "We must build a fence."

"Why?" I said. "They were here before us."

He gave me a strange, brief look. "They'll trample everything," he said.

"But they need this water as much as we do," I told him. "It's not fair to cut off their access. It may be the only spot they know."

"Then they'll have to find another spot."

I felt my hands clench, felt a fire combust within me. I wanted to leap at him and shake him, remind him that he loves animals as much as I do.

Instead, I told myself that he was only trying to provide for us, and he must have felt tremendous pressure to make our new home livable. The stress was getting to us both, and though he was acting quite unlike himself, I resolved to be patient; my dear familiar Friedrich would reappear in due time. Yet to know that these poor creatures would suffer for our actions nearly drove me mad.

But there was no time for madness. We had to transport all our belongings from Post Office Bay, dozens of trips under the steaming sun, using a pitiful old abandoned horse Friedrich had captured. The lava fields shredded our shoes—they were flayed as if by knives—and even the shortest journey required a machete. We have worked from dawn to dark every day, and still there is never enough time.

We brought way too much, I realized as we worked so hard to transport it all—the building materials and accessories, the bedding and the kitchenware, the books and the stationery—and at the same time, we did not bring nearly enough. Friedrich did not bring enough medicine, enough tools. And perhaps I did not bring enough fortitude, enough patience.

But I had brought enough optimism, enough faith. Even as we toiled under the sun, the stifling heat felt like nothing compared to my stifled life back in Berlin, and despite the exhausting job of moving our supplies, I realized I would not trade this adventure for anything. Here I was, on a tropical island with my love, creating a new life for ourselves.

Our home would not be built in a day, but we have bestowed it a name—Friedo—a melding of our names, the only marriage we have. Though we had left our spouses, neither of us divorced, and we ourselves did not marry. Our previous unsuccessful marriages, Friedrich claimed, were proof that we had no need to make our union "official." We were, we agreed in a passionate moment back in Berlin, married by heart and by soul, and we did not need the seal of church or state to build a life together. For the first time in my life, I felt rebellious—both of us outlaws in love—and I was thrilled to reject all that I used to be so that, here on Floreana, I could become someone new.

And yet, I was realizing, everything would take time. Even as we began setting up our homestead, it did not yet feel like home to me. I was quite taken aback one day when Friedrich admonished me for putting sugar in my tea as we were taking a much-deserved break. I needed the energy—and, more than anything as I tried to adjust to our harsh new surroundings, I needed a touch of sweetness.

"Am I not allowed one small luxury?" I asked.

"But this is not a life of luxury, my dear Dore" was his answer. "Anything worth doing comes with sacrifices. You know that, surely." He gave me a reassuring smile.

His equal, he'd claimed I was, in every way, and yet I seem to have little say in matters of our new home, our new routines. I try to understand his anxiety—but my heart sinks when I think of how much more difficult our paradise is than I'd imagined.

I busied myself organizing our books, setting up my kitchen. Though I'd escaped my domestic life in Berlin, I am playing the same role, in many ways. But here, at least, I have Friedrich's help.

He took charge of setting up our bedroom—little more than a sleeping area—and I found myself puzzled when he hung two hammocks. Not one.

I'd brought plenty of bedding, but that was not the point. "Why," I asked him, "did you not set up one bed for us to share?"

"It's far too hot to sleep together," he said.

"I wasn't referring to sleeping," I said.

He understood me then and came over, taking me by the arms, as it was too hot for the sort of embraces we'd enjoyed in Berlin. "There will be time for everything," he assured me, "once our work is done."

Of course, I did understand the importance of rest, as our days were so busy, but despite our best efforts, we have not slept well since being here—nor have we made love. Though we have been working nonstop, though the heat is oppressive, I still long for intimacy. Yet there is too much work to do, and I fear it will never be done.

Every evening, when night falls, I feel a sense of relief—knowing the day's toiling will cease, that my tired body can stop—but I never feel fully rested. I don't know what feels longer, the days or the nights. They are both exactly twelve hours long, and endless in different ways.

The sun vanishes so quickly, I feel as though it's teasing me. Our fleeting equatorial sunsets. Our paradise lost.

Mallory

The next morning, just after six o'clock, daylight streams in through the lightweight curtains. I open my casita door to let in the morning air. Hearing nothing from Hannah's or Gavin's rooms, I busy myself by organizing a day pack—binoculars, field notebook, water bottle, protein bar, sunscreen, insect repellent—and unpacking my clothes, arranging them in the bureau in the same order as at home: underwear in the top right drawer, socks on the top left.

I plug in my laptop and wait for the very slow internet connection. No email. Not that I expected anything. I hear the echo of Scott's voice in my head: *You're going to have to let go, Mal. You're not the only person who's capable of caring for Emily. You won't be able to parent her forever.*

I had never wanted to admit that he was right, and I still don't.

My fingers hover above the keyboard. Scott was always admonishing me to take a break from what he saw as overparenting, and I've never been able to let go, my every moment all about Emily. Yet now that I'm here, without them, my sense of time has shifted, and it feels as if I've been gone forever and, at the same time, as if I'd never left. I remember having read that Margret Wittmer, the only mother among the early settlers on Floreana, once went home to Germany for a visit, and, because no ships went by, her husband and son waited nearly a year without a word from her—not knowing whether she was alive or dead or ever returning to them.

A hundred years earlier, those who lived here were accustomed to the stretching out of time—and now that I'm back, though we have our devices and our schedule, I feel as though time is suspended somehow, as if the world isn't still spinning on elsewhere. Or maybe this is only because, deep down, it's why I'm here—an attempt to stop time because I can't turn it back.

I look up to see Hannah standing in the doorway, and I wonder how long she's been there, watching me stare at my laptop screen.

"Time to go," she says.

"I'm ready." I pick up my day pack and follow her to the boat landing.

~

As we get out of the panga, Gavin asks me to work with him for the morning, then leads me to an area where he and Darwin have stockpiled lava for nests. Twenty minutes later, as we kneel next to each other to work on the first nest, the silence between us feels more companionable than awkward, and for a brief moment it's as though I'd never left.

"Do you think you'll work things out with Scott?" He doesn't look at me, keeping his attention on the stacks of stones he's stabilizing so we can add a lava roof.

I remember reading a book about teenagers—I was getting a head start because at only eight years old, Emily was already stubborn and rebellious, and I didn't know what we were in for in a few more years—in which the author wrote that the best time to talk to a teen or tween was in the car, when you could both face straight ahead and not have to look at each other. I find this is easier with Gavin, too.

"I don't know." Scott moved out six months ago. It will be seven by the time I return from Floreana, and I'm still not sure what will happen.

"Why didn't you just tell me?" Gavin asks. "I mean, back then."

I knew Gavin had not wanted a traditional life—a wife, children, anything that would get in the way of his work—and it should've been easy to tell him that we simply wanted different things. But I was so young then, with so much to learn about life and love and what I wanted. I think Gavin may have sensed me drifting away, toward the life I saw for myself—but for me, it was more complicated than that. I wanted a family, and I was falling in love with Scott—but I never fell out of love with Gavin. A part of me had never wanted to leave him and still wonders whether I'd done the right thing.

And so I hadn't told Gavin I was seeing anyone else until I gave him my notice, resigning from my job and our relationship all at once. He was shocked at first, but in the end he'd focused more on the job transition than on what had happened to us. Overwhelmed with guilt, I was grateful he'd made it easier on us both, though I'm still haunted by twinges of regret.

And now I owed him so much history. "I met Scott at a party," I said. "My sister introduced us. Megan didn't know about you and me—she thought I hadn't been out with anyone in years. It was mostly to shut her up that I even went out with him."

During the time Gavin and I were together, I felt as though I had two lives: the one I lived, and the one everyone else perceived I was living. I couldn't tell even Megan—who I knew wouldn't understand—how much I loved everything just the way it was: My days in the lab, crunching data with Gavin, worn linoleum under my soles and yellowish fluorescent lights overhead. Nights at Gavin's apartment with its floor-to-ceiling windows overlooking the tops of eucalyptus trees in the canyon. I'd often thought of Freud's famous saying: *Love and work—that's all there is.* For a long while, I thought I had it all.

Until I didn't. Until I wanted to talk about something other than research, to read about something other than birds or climate change. Until I began to envision my life five, ten, twenty years out—and realized I wanted little humans in it.

Scott was many things Gavin was—a traveler, devoted to his work—and many more things he wasn't. He had a big family on the East Coast and was close to his siblings and their kids. He always took time off for the holidays to bring his nieces and nephews to theme parks and zoos, neither of which Gavin would ever set foot in. Being with Scott felt like the promise of a whole new life—an optimistic one, filled with kids and fun rather than facing down extinction and climate catastrophe on a daily basis.

"What's he like?" Gavin asks now.

The question shouldn't surprise me, but it does. "Um, he's . . . a workaholic, like you. We moved to Boston for his job—I think I told you that—and he travels a lot. Though not as much as before Emily was born."

Gavin settles a large slate of lava over the cavern of the nest. "A family man."

There's more I need to say, but my voice freezes in my throat. I think of the night Scott and I met—it wasn't actually *at* Megan's party but afterward, around midnight, outside her apartment building, my Uber arriving just as he was trying to take my number—and how so much of our time together felt this way, hurried and fleeting, because his job kept him on the road when it wasn't keeping him at the office. And I think of the night I told Scott I was pregnant, how his face lit up, how he said all the right things. Among them was that he had a chance to move to the Boston office—which meant, to him, being near his family, and which meant, to me, making a clean break from the life I'd slowly been unraveling. Which meant, finally, being on the path I'd wanted all along. Even if it was a path without Gavin and the penguins.

Gavin hands me a trowel, and I dig out the entrance to the nest. I'm relieved when he says nothing more, and we continue working in silence.

∼

By late afternoon, the heat has abated somewhat, but my clothes are soaked, my skin hot to the touch. As I finish a nest, I brush away the loosened rock at the entrance, shoving it over the tufts of grasses coming up through cracks in the lava, green and brown and dying.

Hannah is working nearby, Darwin helping her with the larger lava rocks. At lunch, Gavin told us he was staying behind to work on the data, and without a word Hannah had aligned herself with Darwin instead of me.

I turn toward the water and begin to walk, slowly, eyes downward as I look for another nest site among the lava folds. I stop short when I see a penguin carcass.

The shape of the bird is unmarred, the body bleached white, tail feathers still intact, the curve of the neck turned toward the shore, as if searching for something. Next to the body is a pile of bones—scattered but still clearly those of a penguin. They might've been a pair, these two, raising a child together, starved when the cool La Niña waters had not arrived in time to feed them, unaware, as most of us are, of the unexpected fragility of life.

I tear my eyes away and move on.

When I find a possible nest site, I peer into the dark lava tube, hovering there to let my eyes adjust well enough to tell whether it's deep enough for two penguins, two eggs.

Over the years I've tried not to think too much about my past with Gavin, but now, looking into that narrow darkness, I'm transported, more by body than by mind, to a night on the west coast of New Zealand's South Island, where Gavin and I had traveled after a conference in Christchurch. I can feel again the blackness of the night, the day's warmth rising from the asphalt as I walked with him, nearly blind, down an empty highway in the dark. Gavin led the way—he was always leading the way, and I loved learning from him, and I felt myself expanding around him—but at the same time, I had a faint awareness that our roles might never evolve, that I was destined to follow him, that I would never have the chance to lead him down new paths as he did for me because he didn't want to go where I imagined I'd be headed.

That night, my eyes gradually adjusted to the dark, and soon I could see the shadows of trees, the broken white line of the road's center divide. Gavin stopped near a steep bank towering above the roadside and turned me toward it. The entire forest was glowing with bluish-white lights, blinking like fireflies. "Glowworms," he said.

They looked, as the ferns rustled among them in the night breeze, like twinkling stars, rivaling the sky above us. "Why do they glow like that?"

"To attract insects. It's how the females attract mates, too."

I leaned against him in the dark. Despite my nascent doubts, it was moments like this when I couldn't imagine a life without Gavin, without the wonder of discovering new things every day. "Animals are so perfect," I said with a sigh. "Why do we humans just seem to mess it all up?"

"That's why we're trying to make it right again."

He was talking about the penguins, about our research, but right now I'm thinking of why I'm here, of all the things I thought I might be able to make right again by stepping back into the past.

I punch the pick into the lava hole, pummeling through the thick black stone, savoring the shattering ache that jars through my bones. My muscles melt into the day's fiery heat as I shut my mind to let my body take over, lost in the steady rhythm of the work. Later, when I look at the nest, I study the entrance to the cavern and barely remember creating it. My back aches, and I can feel the exact spot on the back of my neck I missed with sunscreen, but I have no recollection of the last hour.

∼

When I return to the panga, Darwin and Hannah are waiting, laughing together. "What's so funny?" I ask.

"Nothing," Hannah says, as if she doesn't want to include me.

Darwin makes a drinking motion with his hand. "She got into the gin," he whispers, nodding toward Hannah.

"Shut *up*," she says, laughing again.

I feel left out, a step behind, reminded of the challenges of picking up where I left off—with the work, with Gavin, with anything.

But then I look up and see the sky afire with imminent sunset, and as Darwin starts up the engine, I hear a splash and look over to see a blue-footed booby in the water, another one close behind, diving from thirty feet above. And it's a comfort, then, to know that for all that has changed, some things here have remained the same.

I put my hand on Darwin's arm, and he cuts the motor. I lean over the side of the boat and look down, the blue-green water awash with fish and seaweed, the colors so vivid it looks like molten glass. Just a few feet below, hundreds of fish dart away, followed by two penguins, scooping up what they can in their bills before resurfacing.

"Do you mind staying a minute?" I ask, and Darwin shakes his head, sitting down on the panga's rubber edge.

"The penguins try to herd the fish together to make them easier to catch," I say to Hannah. She doesn't seem all that interested, and I wish I could make her see how beautiful it is, this intricate ballet of animals above and below the water. "And when food is abundant like this, they all go after it in a big feeding frenzy. The flying birds dive into the penguins' fish, and if they catch any, the penguins will steal the fish right from their mouths."

The feeding behavior of Galápagos penguins in conjunction with other seabirds had been the topic of the last paper I'd written before disappearing from the world of science. I remember when it got accepted—I'd just found out I was pregnant—and I knew then it would be my last.

Above, a dozen blue-footed boobies are circling, and every few minutes one dives into the water. The penguins swarm below them—I count somewhere between eight or ten; it's hard to tell, they're swimming so fast—to catch the scattering fish.

As I stand swaying in the panga, again I feel a strange sensation of time, as if it's slowing and rewinding, unfurling lazily in the heat, as if I'm in a different reality altogether, one without history or memory—nothing but sea and sky and squawks—and for a brief moment, I'm immersed in the surprising peace of this timelessness.

Then, out of the corner of my eye, I see Darwin stand, and he taps his watch. I nod, and he starts up the motor, and we return to Black Beach.

Dore

The drenching rains have come, and the insects swarm us, then linger afterward. The ground is so wet and swampy it breathes moisture. And then the rain is so soft sometimes, such a light mist, and the soil so saturated, that it can be hard to tell from where the water emerges—only that it surrounds us, like a thick, biting cloak.

The mosquitoes are the size of raspberries, and the ubiquitous cockroaches march on in relentless armies, but the biggest atrocity are the ants. Their bites are worse than the mosquitoes', and they attack not only our bodies but our food supply and our garden. They gnaw through the mosquito netting, and sometimes I wake to find my bedding crawling with them.

And evenings are difficult enough—one might mistake the island for a tranquil place if it weren't for the nights that come alive with wildness. I lie awake waiting for the next sound—the next crackle of brush, the next hoof-step on the ground. The howling and braying. The fights and stampedes. The hooves gathering at the fence Friedrich has built.

"They will not bother us," I insist, but Friedrich doesn't listen to me; a week ago, he procured a rifle from one of the passing ships.

I'm not afraid of the animals, and I don't believe Friedrich is either. What he feels is worse than fear; he feels nothing but rage. They break his fence to get to the spring. (The water was always theirs.) They forage in our budding garden. (How are they to understand boundaries?)

They tell us, in their way, that this land belongs to them. (As it does. As it should.)

Sometimes at night, I hear sounds I do not recognize as earthly. I hear voices in the night air; I hear the animals' movements not so much as noises but as whispers, as if they are trying to tell me something.

During our journey here from Berlin, Friedrich and I heard rumors of ghosts on Floreana, tales passed along from visitors who'd claimed to hear otherworldly sounds while staying here. On many nights, I awoke to the sound of shrieking—so high-pitched that the first time I heard it, I thought I might have imagined it, that it should have been inaudible to my human ears. I immediately thought of one of the earliest settlers, the Irish pirate who was described to us in the most horrifying way: a sun-blistered, ragged drunk with a sinister countenance and a murderous disposition. I remember hearing a tale of him freeing prisoners from the penal colony, only to enslave them himself, unleashing his machete upon those who didn't obey his commands. I cannot recall what happened to the pirate, but in those moments I felt his captives were still here on Floreana, crying out to me in the night, when I am most vulnerable but also most open. I found myself wondering whether these ghosts were trying to warn me of something I did not yet understand.

When I mentioned to Friedrich being frightened by strange nightly sounds, he laughed. "You heard nothing but the storm petrels," he said.

"At night?" I challenged him, but he only shook his head.

Perhaps he was right—but it would not surprise me that this island may be haunted. And because the island's biggest victims have been its animals, I wonder if I am imagining the wrong species. Am I hearing the animals' spirits in the night, in my dreams? I know in my heart that we are not entirely alone out here in our shared darkness, that there are indeed souls all around us. I sense that, like me, they are seeking tranquility but do not know where to find it, or whether such calm exists at all.

Friedrich—in order to keep us safe, he claims—has taken to hunting. It is under this guise that he shoots these poor pigs and cows and then insists we eat what he kills so it does not go to waste.

It is nothing short of murder, in my mind, and I try, for both want and necessity, to keep our meals appealing so he will not continue hunting. Yet my skills are limited, my kitchen primitive. Fruit and eggs. Fried sweet potatoes. I do not know how much longer I can abide the killings—I will not partake of their flesh, not ever—and yet I am powerless to stop Friedrich. I have always admired his tenacity in all things, but this means I have to accept this trait even when he does things I do not like.

But I am determined as well. Yesterday, when he picked up his gun, I followed him, sneaking among the trees and thorns, out of sight. He was, I knew, after one of the creatures who had trampled our garden the night before.

As I crouched behind a bush, I watched Friedrich take aim at an innocent boar who was grazing, completely unaware of either of us. In that second I looked to the ground and found a stone, and I threw it as hard as I could. It landed at the boar's feet and sent him flying in the opposite direction, away from us. Safe.

When Friedrich turned to face me, his gun was still raised. I stood and held up my hands as if to say *Don't shoot*, but then I lowered my arms back to my sides, as if daring him to do just that.

"I'm not a savage," he said, seeming disappointed in me, just before he turned away.

Yet in that moment, he'd looked the part, with a ragged beard growing in to match the chaotic mass of his curly hair, his beautiful eyes flashing with anger. He hardly resembled the dashing doctor I'd met in Berlin.

I want to beg him to stop the killing, but I fear he will not do as I ask, and then where does that leave us? It's hard for me to witness Friedrich behaving so differently.

How can a man be one person in one setting and someone else in another?

We came here seeking freedom, yet we do not sit on our porch eating papayas and coconuts; there is too much work to do. We don't relax in ocean breezes but swelter in the equatorial heat, slapping at insects. We still have not taken a single swim in the crystalline, shark-filled waters of Post Office Bay, and we would not have time to swim even if we could.

I envisioned tranquil days of harvesting vegetables, with the warmth of the sun on our backs. Yet while the ground here is rich—when I'd first dug into it, I felt its fecundity so vividly I could practically see the leaves and colors of our garden swimming before my eyes, like a dream—I soon realized the soil is in fact very shallow, and I worry little will ever take root and grow. That we will never be able to lay down roots. That we will never thrive. It feels like an apt and foreboding metaphor for us trying to make a life here. For the hopelessness of my ever making another life with my own body.

I can't stop thinking about babies. I'd always believed I failed my first husband by not giving him children. Now, I feel as though my second so-called marriage is failing, too, not because Friedrich wants a child but because I find *myself* wishing for one: Floreana has renewed this yearning in me. My connection with Friedrich is becoming as ephemeral as the morning mists, and I wonder if having a baby is my only hope to avoid drowning in isolation.

Friedrich, when we met in the hospital, told me I could think myself well. And now I wonder, despite my illness and miscarriages, whether I might think myself pregnant.

My heart is full of love, but who to receive it?

My husband did not accept or return what love I had to give, and Friedrich, at times, is as cold to me as the dead ash in my kitchen stove. It occurs to me that this is why women have children—how can we depend on men to return the abundance of love we have to give?

I feel as though the animals are my only true companions here. I have begun speaking to them, the living animals as well as the ghosts, in the day as well as the night—but instead of whispering in their ears as I'd done as a child, I must do so from a distance, and often silently, so my voice doesn't carry. And still all I can do is apologize—for the blazing hot bullets of Friedrich's gun, for the terrorizing shots that ring through the air. For myself and our fences and our repetition of the brutality they've already endured. "I'm sorry," I murmur as Friedrich bathes in their water, splashing in their spring as the light disappears from the sky and they hover in the distance with a thirst they cannot quench.

Among the vegetable seeds we brought from Berlin, I'd hidden some carnation seeds. I will plant a flower garden, though Friedrich doesn't know yet and surely won't approve. *We are not here to make things beautiful.* But I need something to raise, something to nurture, some beauty to behold. Some new, colorful life. Something to love.

I am hoping my Friedrich will return to me, that the man I fell for in Berlin will reappear as we become more settled here. "We will know ourselves better outside of civilization," he'd told me in Berlin, and back then I didn't think this would be anything but good. It's hard to consider that who he is becoming may be the real Friedrich, and I try to ignore the feeling that I have made an irreversible mistake.

I am not alone here on Floreana, yet I find that being so utterly dependent on another, to put one's life in another's hands so completely, is worse than being alone. It would be a blessing to choose loneliness.

Mallory

Gavin calls a dinner meeting, and we meet in the kitchen after sunset. Despite a cooling breeze, the air remains steeped in heat, and my hair, wet from a shower, clings to my neck and shoulders, the strands curling as they dry. Bugs fly around the flickering lights.

Gavin, chopping an onion, pauses to stir the contents of a large pot on the stove. "I thought we'd try our hand at *menestra*," he says.

I lean over the breakfast bar that separates the kitchen from the dining area and peek into the pot, simmering with lentils, its heat and spices rising in the humid air.

"I'll make some rice." As I step around to the small cooking area, squeezing past Gavin, I remember how closely we used to work and live together: his hand on my back, my fingers touching his. Now we're careful, in a way we've never been, not to touch.

"Four nests," Hannah says from across the room, leaning across the dining table to peer at Gavin's laptop. "Is that a good day?"

"Five would be better." Gavin sprinkles cumin into the pot, then looks around. "I left the wine in my cabin."

"I'll get it," Hannah says.

I can feel Gavin watching me as I add water to the rice on the stove, and I think of our conversation earlier that day, which is still unfinished, though he may not realize it. I stir the pot and then ask him, "Why'd you stay behind this afternoon? Are you avoiding me?"

"No." He finishes the onion and begins to chop a red pepper. "It just seemed like there was nothing more to say."

He's still focused on chopping, and I can't read him like I used to. I want to reach out and touch him, to close this gap between us. Something about the heat in the air, the sun's burn still stinging my shoulders and neck, the ache from a day's hard work—it reminds me that I have never truly let go of Gavin, that it's impossible to be free of all that we've shared, between us and among the penguins: life, hope, promise, despair. I'm not sure either of us knew where we might end up, but I never meant to leave so suddenly, and without telling him how much he meant to me.

But now, as I look at his posture, turned slightly away from me and focused downward, I'm not sure he'll welcome anything I have to say. I glance over my shoulder to be sure Hannah isn't back yet. "Were you angry that I left you," I ask, "or that I left the lab?"

He adds the chopped pepper to the simmering lentils. "Both, I suppose." He stirs the stew without looking at me. "They were one and the same, really."

I have always known this, but for some reason it feels like a slap. A sizzle rises from the stove; my rice is boiling over. Quickly I turn down the heat. Gavin's face relaxes into a smile. "Your cooking skills haven't improved a bit."

Hannah returns, carrying two bottles of wine, which she puts on the breakfast bar. Gavin opens a bottle, and Hannah pours three glasses.

I pick up my wineglass and think of all Gavin doesn't know. How my cooking skills have actually become impeccable, as they must when your only child has a deadly food allergy and every meal has impossibly high stakes.

The first time Emily had a reaction, when she was nine months old, I didn't know what had actually caused it. It wasn't until three months later that I put two and two together, realizing I'd cut up a soft pear for her using the same butter knife Scott had used for his toast. It had traces of peanut butter on it, so little that I had no idea it was there, and when Emily put the pear into her mouth, her face turned red.

At first I thought she was choking, and I rushed over to her, trying desperately to remember what to do with a choking baby—Emily was too little for the Heimlich maneuver, and I could end up hurting her if I didn't do it right.

But when I reached her, I saw that she could breathe. By then, she was crying and rubbing at her eyes, her face puffy and her skin blotched with hives.

Lifting Emily from her high chair and holding her close, I found my phone and called our pediatrician, bouncing Emily on my hip and trying to stay calm. The doctor instructed me to give her a couple of drops of children's Benadryl—fortunately, as an anxious new mother I had a pharmacy's worth of over-the-counter children's medications—and soon after I did, her symptoms subsided. An hour later, it was as if nothing at all had happened. I never gave Emily pears again, even after learning they weren't the real cause.

"Almost done," Gavin says, pulling bowls from the cupboard. His *menestra* and my lumpy rice look less appetizing than the beautifully presented meal we'd had at the restaurant in town, but the exertions of the day have given me more of an appetite than I've had in ages.

As we eat, Gavin turns to his laptop and punches in some numbers. "So, four nests today," he says. "Let's work up to five a day, at least, and see if we can do even better by the end of the week. Some days will be slow, so we should move faster whenever we can."

"How many Galápagos penguins are there?" Hannah asks.

"We don't know," Gavin says. "Anywhere between twelve hundred and four thousand, which is half of what we had in the '70s. But we can only guess."

"Other penguin species are easier to count," I add, "because they nest in one place, at the same time every year. But Galápagos penguins don't have just one breeding season, and they don't gather in large colonies. Some are banded, some are microchipped. We count some by boat, some by land."

"The numbers could be higher than we think, but my guess is that they're lower—or soon could be," Gavin says. "This is why we're nest building. Even in a good breeding year, their population won't increase if there's no place for them to lay their eggs."

It's a relief to be talking about penguins, and, to keep the conversation focused on Floreana, I ask Hannah if she's heard about what's known as "the Galápagos affair." She shakes her head.

It's the islands' most famous human story, and by far the strangest. I'd told Emily about it years ago, as if it were a bedtime story: A hundred years ago, one German couple, and then another, went to live on Floreana Island, and then an evil baroness showed up and plunged their lives into chaos before disappearing and never being seen again. Scott thought the story might give Emily nightmares, but it was no scarier than *Snow White* or *Hansel and Gretel*—and besides, Emily loved it, with her flair for the dramatic, and she especially loved stories about where I used to work.

I hadn't needed to embellish much. As I'd learned by reading Dore's and Margret's memoirs, two German couples did move to Floreana in the early twentieth century—first a doctor, Friedrich Ritter, and his lover, Dore; then Margret and Heinz Wittmer and their son, Harry. They were followed by a self-described Austrian baroness and her two lovers. Within a year, two of the men were dead, and the Baroness and one of her lovers disappeared and were never seen again. To this day, no one knows what happened.

"I wish we knew," I say after telling Hannah the story. "Especially the fate of the Baroness. She's the best character."

"Except she wasn't just a 'character,' she was all too real," Gavin reminds me. "She created such havoc when she arrived here—flirted with the men, ignored the women. She stole supplies the ships were delivering and even took everyone's mail." He shakes his head as he takes a drink of wine. "What made it worse was that she wanted to open a luxury hotel here for rich Americans—everyone's worst nightmare. She started building right away, calling it 'Hacienda Paradiso.'"

"She was allowed to do that?" Hannah asks.

"There were no building codes then," Gavin explains. "No police. People could do whatever they wanted, and no one could stop them. The islands had a governor on the mainland who gave them land grants, but there was nothing like law and order. The Baroness took what she wanted, and everyone else was helpless, especially when they learned she carried a gun and was a good shot. She also had those two young German guys with her. The others seemed relieved when she and one of her lovers vanished without a trace."

I've just remembered something else. "Apparently no one ever searched the island for them," I add. "Dore and Margret wrote different versions about what happened in their memoirs—but there was never a formal investigation. It was as if someone knew what happened, and all the others knew they knew, and everyone just moved on."

"Holy shit," Hannah says, and I see her making the connection between the invasive species and our work. "So that's why it took so long to do nests here. Because the settlers had animals?"

Gavin nods and explains that the Wittmers had brought their dogs, but there'd already been donkeys and cattle and feral cats living on Floreana when they arrived, from previous visitors.

I take a sip of wine and let my mind drift as Hannah asks Gavin another penguin question. I'm thinking about the animals and how long it's taken the national park and conservation groups to eradicate these nonnative species so that, one hundred years later, we can be here making room for penguins again.

I snap back to the present when Gavin turns toward me, saying, "Ten years, just about," apparently in response to Hannah's question about how long I've been out of the field. I can tell by Hannah's expression that it's a number she, at twentysomething, can barely comprehend.

"So why'd you quit?" she asks me.

I reach for the wine bottle to refill my glass. "Personal reasons," I say, a bit more sharply than I intended.

"Ah," she says, looking from me to Gavin, as if suddenly understanding something. Then she stands. "Well, I should get some sleep. Looks like you guys have lots of catching up to do." She takes her plate to the sink and drops it in, then leaves the dining area.

Gavin washes dishes, and I dry them. We're quiet, but I'm aware of our closeness. When we finish, he pours the last of the wine into our glasses, then looks at me. "I'm not angry with you," he says.

"I wouldn't blame you if you were. *I'm* angry with me. Not only for leaving you but for the way I left."

"Well," he says, "obviously you found someone who gave you what you needed. I couldn't have done that."

"But what I did wasn't fair. Maybe I should've given us a chance."

I sense bitter edges around his short, tight laugh. "It probably wouldn't have turned out any differently."

But what if it did? I think but don't say.

"You wanted a life outside the lab," he continues. "I never could've given you that."

I swallow some wine. "Have you ever managed to have a life outside the lab?"

He shakes his head. "It's been far more work than play. But you know I'm okay with that."

"So, you're the quintessential bachelor penguin," I say, using Gavin's term for males who don't find mates.

"And you're the opportunistic breeder."

"Ouch," I say, but he's smiling, and I feel as though the bitter edges may be wearing away.

"What's Emily like?" he says.

The smile fades on my lips as I grow wistful. "Nine years old. Such a handful."

"I thought she was eight."

I look down into my wineglass. "No, you're right. A parenting thing, I guess—always looking ahead."

He nods. "Does she look like you?"

I've never posted photos of Emily on Facebook or anywhere else. Gavin wouldn't have seen her cinnamon hair, her fair skin, her little features sharp even in her young face. So much like me, in almost every way, except the eyes. "Almost exactly."

"Do you have any photos?"

I shake my head. "No one likes to look at photos of other people's children."

"Try me."

I hesitate, my phone heavy in my pocket. "Maybe later. My phone's out of juice."

He nods. "It happens. You have to put it in airplane mode or you'll drain it in a matter of hours."

"Tell me more about you."

As we sit here, alone again, in the humid air and fluttering light, I wonder if Gavin invited me here for the same reason I wanted to come—to have that sense of possibility again, that feeling that we could change the world together. That we could be unstoppable. And at the same time, this bit of longing is mixed with sorrow: that I don't deserve to have a second chance at this, at anything.

"Me? You're looking at it." He shrugs. "Sometimes I wish I hadn't devoted myself completely to work. Every once in a while I wonder: What's my legacy going to be? A guy who spent his entire career trying, unsuccessfully, to save ill-fated birds?"

As he drinks the last of his wine, I study him. The lines on his face have deepened, radiating from his eyes, crossing his forehead. He's still lean, but his skin looks tougher, redder—from years in equatorial sun, or maybe from all the wine. I don't remember him drinking quite so much years ago.

Before I can say anything, he lifts his eyes to meet mine. "You were my best student," he says, and I feel a flutter—of what, I can't tell: hope? desire?—but it's good to feel something again, other than numb.

"I haven't found anyone with the same passion for the work," he continues, "and in the meantime the penguins are disappearing."

And so we are back on the same page, as we always were, inseparable from our work. Maybe this time, it will be enough.

I cut off thoughts of the past and think of the IUCN Red List, on which Galápagos penguins are listed as "endangered"—not yet "critically endangered," "extinct in the wild," or "extinct." But these penguins have been endangered since I've begun working with them; even when Gavin began, nearly twenty years ago, they were in this category.

"Was there ever a time when the penguins were a species of least concern?" I ask, referring to the only category that comes before "near threatened," the only category that offers a modicum of hope for an animal.

He lets out a short laugh. "Humans are the only 'species of least concern' that I can think of," he says. "That's what worries me."

And that's why, I remember, he never wanted children; he always said there were far too many of us humans in the world already.

For a moment I think about the categories, about how humans are animals that never come up on the Red List. "The language of extinction is so misleading," I say. "The idea of humans as a 'species of least concern'—for the IUCN, this means not worrying about them. But if you turn it around, it's like saying humans are least concerned about penguins. About any species other than our own."

"That's exactly what we're dealing with," he says. "It's what we'll always be dealing with."

"I'm glad I'm back," I tell him. "I know we can't pick up where we left off, but—"

He raises a hand, and in the lambent light I can't read his eyes, glassy with heat and wine. "Let's not, Mallory, okay?"

"But—"

"Not tonight. I'm tired, and I've got data to crunch and you've got nests to build tomorrow."

He stands, and as I follow him I feel an ache stretch within me, like a torn muscle, the discomfort of being here when I should be at home, of wanting to be everywhere and nowhere, and not knowing how else to exist.

We walk back to the casitas together, and when we reach Gavin's door my phone beeps, and he steps back, surprised.

"I thought you said it was dead."

"I thought it was." I look at the phone. A text from Scott. **How's it going there? Let me know if you want to talk.**

"Everything okay?"

"It's fine. But . . . I should respond."

"Of course. I'll see you in the morning."

I watch him close his door. Instead of going into my own casita, instead of responding to Scott, I sit in the canvas chair outside the door. Other than what's necessary, I've barely spoken to Scott since he left our marriage, and I know I'm repeating the pattern that brought me back here, that I'm running from something I will eventually have to return to. I think of Gavin calling me an *opportunistic breeder*, which makes more sense than he knows. Like the penguins, I try to wait for the right timing, to juggle all the circumstances life presents and do the right thing—but the birds are so much smarter. They've found a way to create their families and move forward, while I seem to keep going backward.

But going backward also allows me to forget, and the sense of timelessness I've always felt here is soothing. I think again of the settlers and wonder what it was like to live back then, with no schedule, no sense of time other than where the sun was in the sky. Did they feel it as an absence of time, or was time in fact more precious?

And for a moment, I imagine being among the penguins and sea turtles, the frigate birds and flamingos, to become who I used to be, before I'd had anything to hide, truths I still can't say out loud. I wonder what it is about Floreana that has made so many of us believe it can save us.

I look toward Gavin's window, seeing his shadow moving around inside. I turn away and shut my eyes, listening to the ocean roll the beach's rocks against the shoreline.

Dore

Months more have gone by, with little to report but more of the same. Yet today I write with a bit of news that makes my heart sing: a little cat has found her way to me.

One day while in the garden I heard the sweetest sound—a tiny mew—that was as beautiful to me as any music. I held out my hand, and she came right up to me, nuzzling my hand, and then jumping into my lap. Though she had been, like so many, abandoned by previous settlers, she had not gone feral. She was thin but seemed healthy and clearly had been managing well for herself, other than for a lack of human company, which she so obviously craved.

She took to me instantly and followed me around the garden and into the house. I learned quickly that she did not like Friedrich; she would not approach him and kept her distance when he was near. He didn't notice or care, and he allowed me to keep her because I told him she was an excellent hunter and would help with the rats that were constantly creeping into our food stores and gnawing at our budding garden.

My cat fills me with wonder—to think that, despite being orphaned, she has learned to trust again, to let me care for her and offer me affection in return: the nudge of a soft furry head, the flick of a tongue, a purr. She has had to survive like a wild thing, yet she turned herself over to me so easily, so willingly, when I opened my arms to her.

She is a wise creature and knows to visit when I am alone here at Friedo. At first I worried that I had too little to offer her, but affection is all she seems to want from me. I do save for her the meat I do not eat and feed it to her when Friedrich isn't nearby. I hide the scraps in a napkin, folded into my skirt pocket, and he is none the wiser. We rescue each other, in this sense—she saves me from arguing with him over my unwillingness to eat flesh, and I offer her a free and easy meal. She has put on some weight, and her fur—brown and gray and black, with stripes along her back—is glossy.

She makes the long, hot, sleepless nights more tolerable. When I hear her soft mew near my hammock, I open the mosquito netting to let her jump in. Despite the heat, she settles near my chest. Her purring quiets the restless nighttime voices I hear all around me, and with her by my side I am able to relax into sleep.

I have named her Johanna, which was to be the name of my first child. With each of my miscarriages, I did not know the gender of the babies, so I chose two names for every child who did not come into the world—a girl's and a boy's. Johanna Theo. Elsa Viktor. Anna Michael. Elisabeth Leo. Gisela Max.

And in this way, and in so many others, Johanna became my first child.

And, since Johanna showed up, I have been blessed with more children—though of course I would never tell Friedrich about my way of thinking of them. When we discovered four starved, abandoned chickens wandering around, we created a coop for them, and I named them all. The rooster, Leo. The hens Elsa, Gisela, and Anna.

After the losses of my unborn children caused me so much helpless grief, I had tried to convince myself I didn't want or need children at all—and Friedrich helped convince me of this; it was so important that I believe it. Yet as I feel Friedrich and I growing apart, I can see again that I have always wanted children more than anything and that I have been using all my energy to suppress this unbearable grief. It's no wonder I feel so weak I am often unable to get out of bed.

But as I adopt these animals into my life, I feel a certain lightness of being. Johanna and the chickens soothe me, especially with Friedrich so busy with the hard labor required to live here. Even when I toil alongside him in the heat, we are working too hard to talk like we used to, and at night we are too tired for love or deep conversation.

But whenever I am near Johanna or one of the chickens, they acknowledge me with a nudge, a purr, a cluck. I feel, once again, as though I am needed. As though I am loved.

Meanwhile, I have taken charge of the garden, which suits me well. I have planted vegetables (and flowers), and despite my worries about the fertility of the soil I am eager to see what might sprout.

Despite everything, I am still hopeful.

The trees, planted by settlers years before, are dripping with fruit: lemons and oranges, papayas and guavas. Due to this abundance and our other supplies, I still cannot fathom why Friedrich persists in eating animals.

"Do you not remember?" I asked him one evening, grimacing as he skinned a calf he'd shot. I could barely watch his abuse of this tiny creature. How cruel a fate he'd suffered, to be taken from his mother by a cowardly man with a rifle, then torn apart, desecrated.

"Remember what?" he replied, in a tone of annoyed impatience.

"In Berlin, when we discovered we were both vegetarians. You told me how much you hated hunting with your father as a child. And you were happy we were both living an enlightened life, free of cruelty to others."

He continued his gruesome work. "Our needs are not the same here as in Berlin."

"Nothing is the same as it was in Berlin." I spoke quietly, disappointment muffling my voice. Now that we were here, I'd hoped to feel more connected to Friedrich, not less—and yet I can see that he is changing.

And I wondered if I noticed this because I am not changing enough. I had dreamed that Floreana would make me well; I truly believed Friedrich when he said I had the power within my mind to heal myself in body.

But now I worried: What if I don't become who I believed I could be here on Floreana?

"That is the whole point," Friedrich said. "For our lives to be different."

I turned my thoughts back outward. "But it's you who is different." I'd never said such a thing aloud. "All you do is work, and we have no time for each other."

"The work is not going to get done by itself," he said. "And you choose to spend your time with those animals instead of helping."

"I'm not as strong as you are," I insisted. "I can't do everything you can do."

He paused before he answered, the earth red all around him, and he came close to me with his bloody hands. "You're as strong as you want to be, Dore," he said.

I looked into his eyes and felt a hint of the warmth I knew so well, which he rarely exhibits anymore, and also a touch of his new coolness. I felt both encouraged and criticized at once—and then I wondered whether perhaps my consternation was not because Friedrich was changing but because I was seeing him clearly for the first time.

I turned away, my dismay as thick as the perpetual mist in the air.

Can we ever forgive one another for not being who we each thought we'd be?

In the gaps of our silence, I remind myself I am not alone. I take comfort in the voices of the wind, the trees, our chickens. I feel as though our island is newly inhabited, populated by a love I had not expected—my sweet new pets, a new appreciation for the land that feeds them and the canopies that shelter them and the breezes that cool them. They are my children, the closest I will ever have to my own.

Mallory

The next few days pass in a haze of heat, dirt, and sweat, and amid the grueling work my mind goes offline. It's a welcome relief to focus only on the tasks at hand—digging, scraping, stacking.

Even the penguins are hot, doing their best to cool themselves. They stand facing the sun so the heat can reflect off their pale bellies. Many are hunched over to keep the sun off their sensitive feet.

Late in the afternoon, as I climb into the panga, my body aches so much my brain registers nothing else. I relax into the unexpected mercy of being unable to think, of being temporarily free.

As we ride back to our lodgings, Gavin's absence feels as strong as a ghost. He hasn't joined the nest-building fieldwork in days, and I've seen him only briefly, only in passing. He hasn't even eaten dinner with us—he's busy with data and grant writing, he says. I imagine I feel like a ghost to him, too, showing up after ten years, looking like a mirage out in the hazy heat of the lava rocks. I want to be close to him again, even though I know it will never be the same. I miss my closest friend, my field partner, the penguin bachelor who couldn't give me a family but who still gave me so much. I miss the person I was with him: a woman who didn't carry around so many regrets, who had everything in front of her instead of wishing she could start over.

When I reach my casita, I pause outside to take off my shoes, grimy with seawater and black sand. My legs are marbled with dirt, sweat, and sunscreen, my clothes thick with lava dust. When I straighten up, I notice my door is ajar, but I don't remember opening it. I push it open and step inside. I can hear the shower running.

"Hello?"

The water stops, and a woman appears around the edge of the door, a tiny white towel pulled tight around her body, her long blond hair dripping over her shoulders and onto the floor.

"Oh, hi," the woman says. "You must be Mallory. Are you looking for Gavin?"

I wonder if the heat has gotten to me, if I've walked into the wrong room. But my laptop is on the desk, the T-shirt I'd slept in on the still-unmade bed.

"I didn't have any hot water," the woman says, "so Gavin offered me his shower. He doesn't have any hot water either, it turns out."

"None of us has hot water," I tell her. "And this isn't Gavin's room."

I hear footfalls against the wooden planks of the long deck.

"I said the third door from the end." Gavin is standing in my doorway, addressing the woman in my room. "At least, I thought I did."

He turns toward me. "This is Calista Keehn. She's a photographer here on assignment. Callie, this is Mallory, the researcher I was telling you about."

Callie crosses the room, gives my hand a firm shake, then smiles up at Gavin as she squeezes past him in the doorway. Then she swings her head back around, droplets of water from her wet hair sprinkling his clothes.

"Sorry for the misunderstanding," she says. "Let me make it up to you both. Join us for dinner. My assistant makes killer *patacones*."

"Sure," Gavin says. "We'd love to."

I wait until she's gone before raising my eyebrows.

"She's here on a job," Gavin says, "but she's also a freelance videographer looking for penguin footage. This could be just the PR we need."

"You haven't been out building nests all day. I'm too exhausted to be social."

"Just for tonight, Mal." He turns away.

I take a cool shower and put on a loose white blouse and a long cotton skirt that will give my arms and legs a reprieve from the bug spray, though I still have to spray the backs of my hands, my wrists, my feet and ankles. I soak my palm and pat the repellent onto my cheeks, forehead, and neck.

I tie my wet hair back and, in the tiny bathroom mirror, take in my florid face, drooping eyes. I've avoided mirrors for months, though I have to admit that donning a skirt has as much to do with being seen next to Callie as avoiding bug spray. It feels indulgent to care what I look like—almost like a betrayal, if I let myself think of Scott and Emily—but I'm relieved to see the mirror's reflection is not quite as bad as I thought. In the equatorial light, flecks of gold emerge from the brown of my eyes, and, thanks to the sun, my normally brown hair is sprayed with highlights.

When I open my door, Hannah is on the deck. She's already met Callie. "I thought her name sounded familiar, so I googled her," Hannah says as we walk toward the kitchen. "She's shot wildlife documentaries for the BBC. She's kind of a big deal."

I say nothing. I don't have the energy to spend the evening entertaining another Galápagos newbie, especially when I've been hoping to talk again with Gavin. And given both his and Hannah's interest in Callie, I'm beginning to worry our fieldwork could turn into some sort of overcrowded reality show.

In the kitchen, food, cookware, and utensils cover every surface. Gavin stands at the breakfast bar across from Callie, who's at the stove. She wears loose green pants and a skin-hugging tank top, as well as a hat, even though the sun is down and the kitchen-and-dining area is covered. Pots and pans occupy all four electric burners.

Callie hands a spatula to a tall, lean man standing next to her. "This is my assistant, Diego Aguirre."

Despite the heat, Diego looks cool in his long pants and shirt, which seem as though they came from the same REI catalog as Callie's. Gavin fills wineglasses on the breakfast bar. Callie takes a long drink and licks her lips, slightly reddened from the wine. Then she looks down at the cookware in front of her. "I hope you're hungry. I made fish stew. I've also got fried rice with *pollo*, and of course Diego's making his famous *patacones*."

"Just the *patacones* for me," I say, and Callie looks at me. "I don't eat fish," I add.

"You don't eat fish?" Callie repeats, as if I'd said I don't breathe air.

"It's what happens," Gavin says lightly, "when the animals you study are endangered due to fishing."

"I love fish stew," says Hannah.

Diego piles *patacones* onto a large platter and takes it to the table, along with an overflowing bowl of guacamole. The green plantains have been thinly sliced, fried, and battered, then fried again to a golden, flaky crisp. He catches me staring.

"It's a family recipe," he says. "The trick is in the seasonings, which, of course, remain a family secret."

"You're from Ecuador?"

"Native Galapagueño," he says. "I grew up on Santa Cruz."

"Diego's done stints at the Darwin Research Station, working with the tortoises," Callie says. "He's amazing around animals, but it was his photographs that made me reach out to him. That, and his knowledge of the local history. He knows where all the bodies are buried, quite literally."

"How long are you on Floreana?" Gavin asks.

"Two, three weeks," Callie says. "It'll depend on the footage we get."

"Are you shooting an unsolved mystery?" Hannah asks, then says to me and Gavin, "She's covered the Great Sphinx and Stonehenge."

"Nothing nearly so interesting," Callie says. "But what my project lacks in drama, it makes up for in dollars. We're here to get highlights of the local flora and fauna for a travel company."

Diego is quiet—I can't tell if it's by choice or necessity—but he's listening, with an expression of vague amusement on his face.

"While you're here, you should investigate the murder," Hannah says.

Callie pauses, wineglass in the air. "The what?"

"The Galápagos affair," Gavin says. "The other day we were telling Hannah about the Floreana settlers."

"Oh, right, of course." Callie waves her hand as if to shoo away a fly. "Ancient history, don't you think?"

"It's a great story," Hannah says. "Maybe you should pitch it to the BBC."

Callie shrugs and takes a long drink of wine. "Do you ever imagine what it would've been like back then?" She sighs and looks around, turning toward the darkness beyond the lodge, the rush of the sea in the distance. "All alone. Like Adam and Eve. No need for clothing. Nothing else to occupy your time but—"

"No air-conditioning," Diego says.

"No medicine," Gavin adds. "Very little water."

Callie laughs. "You men take the romance out of everything, you know that?" She pulls out her phone and begins to take photos of the empty plates on the table, the two empty bottles of wine. "I should've 'grammed this before we dove in—the food looked sublime." She leans in close to Diego to take a selfie of the two of them. Callie flips her hair, then purses her lips, while Diego's mouth turns upward in a tolerant smile that doesn't quite reach his eyes.

Callie looks up from her phone. "Let's crack open another bottle," she says, but no one responds.

The barking of a sea lion floats toward us on the slow breeze. I stand up and begin to clear the table as Callie taps away on her phone. Diego rises and picks up a couple of plates as well, but Callie waves him back over. "Diego, stay here. You, too, Gavin. I need your help identifying this bird before I post it. Diego, we're going to need to get footage of this one tomorrow."

I finish clearing the table, and Diego is already washing up. Like Callie, he looks as if he's in his late twenties. His black hair is flattened around the crown by the day's pressure of a hat, and though his hair is short, it's also a little wavy, with one lock that keeps falling across his forehead.

As we're finishing the dishes, I hear Callie say to Gavin, "Why don't Diego and I join you tomorrow. I'd love to get some footage of the penguins."

"Sure, why not," Gavin answers.

I'm surprised—it's unlike him to let anything, or anyone, get in the way of our work. But it's not *our work* anymore, which he seems to be making clear. When I look at him, he doesn't meet my eyes. "We meet Darwin at the landing at seven," he tells Callie. "You're welcome to join us."

I don't bother protesting but say a quick good night and return to my casita. Inside, I lie on the bed and pick up my phone. Though Scott had moved out six months ago, my fingers tingle with the muscle memory of texting him, of scrolling through my phone to call him. We used to be in touch constantly, even before Emily. His traveling and the vastness of time zones often made it difficult to talk, but I loved waking up to his emails and pictures, and sending off goofy selfies or photos of Emily before going to sleep. Despite the busyness of his schedule, Scott always had a sense of fun, with everything, as if he'd never stopped being a kid. Though his work encompassed corporate terms like *content management*, *geolocation*, and *internationalization*, he made it fascinating; catching up with Scott after one of his trips was like sitting in on a cultural lecture, or watching the Discovery Channel.

I learned from Scott that in Russia, it's bad manners to shake hands over the threshold of a door. I learned that in Asian countries, wedding dresses are red, never white, because the color white symbolizes death, as does the number four. *Most executives don't know this either*, Scott told me, *and this is why I have a job*.

He told me this not long after we'd met, as we spent an afternoon walking along the beach on Coronado. "Did you always want to do this job?" I asked him, linking my fingers through his.

Scott's job involved helping companies translate their websites—linguistically, culturally, geopolitically, technically. He doesn't speak any languages other than English but knows the foundations of dozens; he can tell the Cyrillic alphabet from the Greek and identify a bidirectional text like Arabic or Hebrew or Persian at a glance. He knows that in Russian, there are no words for *privacy* or *efficiency*; there is no translation for the phrase *take care*. In Italian, there is no word for *wilderness*.

But, as interesting as it was, Scott's work dwelled on the face of things. He knew a little about a lot but didn't take deep dives into any one language or culture. It reminds me now of Callie, who is here to tell stories and take photographs—she'll skim the surface of what we do but will not actually effect change.

Which was why I loved working with Gavin. Which is why I wanted to be a mother. Conservation, like parenting, gives us a chance to change the future. To *create* the future.

Yet at times Scott's parenting felt much like his surface-level expertise. Though he traveled less after Emily was born, he was still away enough that most of the work fell to me, and the stress of managing Emily's allergy, even once I got into a routine, never truly diminished. Scott grew into the role of the cool dad, and I became the hyperattentive, overly anxious mom, someone I barely recognized, someone Scott barely recognized—and someone Emily was beginning to rebel against. Scott's encouraging me to just let go of all the worry, as if it were that simple, only made me hold on to it more, and this rift splintered and widened as Emily got older.

What I remembered about my time in the Galápagos was that birds had been easier, and now I'm hoping I can somehow recapture that sense of purpose, of hope. Yet despite the hard work, I feel more like Callie—that I'm not really a part of what we're doing but somewhere outside it.

Back then, I'd been eager to help the penguins, to change their future. But now I can see the downside of living too much in the future, as I had with Emily. Too anxious a mother to enjoy the present, I'd missed out on the moments of her childhood that, once gone, were lost forever. And now, with Gavin, I'm not sure how to exist in the present, how not to worry about where we go from here. And I have absolutely no idea how not to regret where we've already been.

I'd never told Scott about my relationship with Gavin. He knew we had traveled together, that we spent a lot of time working together, but he didn't know that by the time I met him, Gavin and I had been having a two-year affair. And when I left, the story of me and Gavin became something I tried to forget.

No longer able to trust my sense of timing, I put my phone on the nightstand and turn to face the window. The breeze fills the curtains like a sail.

Dore

When the rains come, there is nothing Friedrich and I can do but sit inside, in nearly unbearable closeness to each other, listening to the downpour and watching the island turn wet, from soil to sky.

We focus on our reading and writing. I write short stories, including tales about my animals that I would love to read to a child one day, and Friedrich writes articles about our life on the island, sending them to magazines he hopes will publish them, as if to prove how clever we are.

And, of course, we write letters home, in which I keep up the facade of contentment, of optimism. I can't bear to admit, even to my family, even to Elise, that my coming here was a mistake.

And so this diary—my saving grace, the only place I can share my truest feelings—has become a companion of sorts, one who listens to my worst thoughts and takes them all in without judgment. Yet I worry even this is not entirely safe. One day, as I was scribbling my thoughts in these pages, I was so engrossed that I did not notice Friedrich standing nearby. My heart nearly stopped with the notion of him reading all the thoughts I've carefully kept to myself. I need a hiding place for this journal, I fear, and soon.

Despite the dreariness of our days and the weather, I've found delight in another new child who has come into my life—a donkey.

He was the sole survivor of a group of short-lived settlers here on Floreana recently—I hardly find any of these human visitors worth mentioning, as they last no more than a few weeks, at most. They see our life here and think they themselves will stay, usually with some monetary gain in mind, like hunting the cattle on the pampas, the wide plains in the middle of the island. Friedrich and I are admittedly inhospitable toward them—only in this, it seems, are we united—offering little help or company, and once they realize how harsh the conditions are, they ultimately give up and move on. Sadly, they often leave their animals behind—or kill them outright, which is horrific but at least it is merciful.

By the time these latest settlers were gone, we presumed all their donkeys had perished, until we discovered one of them wandering around, skin and bones. We immediately led him to Friedo; Friedrich was amenable to our adopting him, since the animal could be of use to him one day. I fed him grasses and plants, and Friedrich set up an enclosure. I named him Viktor, after the second child I might have had.

My Viktor soon grew stronger, and his coat became thick and beautiful. Fortunately Friedrich had nothing to haul, no use for him as yet, and I was grateful that Viktor did not have to endure any further punishment at the hands of humans.

He and I went out each day for a ride. I am slight and knew my weight wouldn't be a burden to him, especially compared to what he was used to—heavy loads and heavy men—and I did want him to take some exercise, for his own enrichment, and also so he wouldn't grow fat. I feel as though he enjoyed this time we shared as much as I did—just the two of us, free of human demands and obligations. I relished the chance to take a short journey without stressing my body, and for once I began to feel a sense of healing. We never wandered far, but it still felt, to me, as though we'd truly gotten away.

Yet soon I began to feel guilty about confining Viktor. While I was certain he had been used for hard labor by his previous caregivers, and I knew the life we gave him was a better one, still, he was not free. And I believe all animals—human and otherwise—want to be, and deserve to be, free.

And so one day I left open the gate to his corral so Viktor could decide for himself. And, much to my disappointment, he fled. I knew there were a great many other wild donkeys on the pampas, but I'd believed that

Viktor was happy with us. With me. I thought we had a special bond. I felt nothing short of heartbreak when he left me and did not return.

After Viktor ran away, I myself considered escaping—but to where? I could not easily seek passage away from Floreana, though the thought has begun to cross my mind. But we never know exactly when the visiting ships will arrive, or who will be on board, or where they are going—they could be cargo ships or pleasure yachts or research vessels. We may glimpse them approaching the island and hurry to meet them, or we may visit the bay and happen upon them, anchored offshore. We are often invited on board—though even if I were tempted to stow away, what do I have to return to? Especially after writing letters home about my new life in paradise.

And, despite all the difficulties, I am not yet ready or willing to admit defeat.

Besides, I have to look after Johanna and my chickens. I can't imagine leaving them behind; I worry about how Friedrich might treat them. How could I leave them to a life I don't even want for myself?

I must learn to find happiness in the things that are good. I discovered an egg in our chicken coop today—I believe it was Anna's. Our first island-grown egg. I felt it was her way of thanking us for taking her in, keeping her safe. And our garden has yielded cucumbers and radishes, a few tomatoes. I can hardly believe this dirt has brought forth such wondrous rewards.

And so, life continues on. I have thus far neglected to mention that the house is finished at last, just in time for the rainy season. I'm grateful, though the idea of a home suggests permanence, and this rattles my nerves to my very core.

Completing our house wasn't easy, as nothing here ever is—Friedrich found only one wood suitable for building, and so our house is made from acacia trees, with walls of tarp and corrugated metal that we acquired from visiting sailors. It feels airy and large, with plenty of shelves for our books and papers. And now that the rains have come, these curvy-branched, thorny trees have come to life once again, sprouting new branches.

Our house is alive—yet inside it, I am slowly dying.

Yet another new season is upon us, and it has brought many travelers to Floreana. The island's visitors help me forget what my life here is really like: we paint them a picture of pure heaven.

Every time a ship arrives, my heart lifts. The crew and passengers bring us gifts of seeds, soap, flour, tools. We receive mail and news from home. Over these past weeks, we have received many vacationers, drawn by the beauty of the Galápagos Islands and specifically to Floreana. Thanks to Friedrich's articles and the tales from those who have visited us, news has spread around the world that Friedrich and I are living here in an Eden we have built ourselves.

After touring our homestead, the passengers often invite us on board their yachts for a meal or to spend an evening listening to music—Hayden and Mozart, Beethoven and Schubert. The sounds of the cello, violin, and piano soothe my ears and my soul. Music is one of my greatest pleasures, and one we do not have on the island.

I had not fully considered all the things I would miss, as I had believed that Friedrich and I would have all we needed if we had each other. But everything changes when there is no stage, no music, no costumes, no props, no other players. As usual, when others are present, Friedrich is gracious and doting, as if he is the perfect husband—and we do pretend we are married, as it seems too complicated to explain otherwise. We become actors in a theater of visitors, who create for us a lovely but make-believe set.

We dine with Europeans and Americans, answering their questions and getting news of the world we left behind. I am not accustomed to the company of other women—other than my old friend Elise, I've had no other female friends—and I have little in common with them.

One evening, after the sharp nose of a gleaming white double-masted ship, long and graceful as a whale, glided into the bay, I felt how futile my life here is when I saw something I could not have seen had I not been on the deck of that magnificent American yacht. We were watching a flock of blue-footed boobies dive for fish, and I glimpsed a small, sleek body leaping and swimming through the water—then another, and another. "Penguins!" I exclaimed, so delighted to see them I barely noticed I was speaking out loud. I had not seen these elusive creatures since our first days on the island.

"Oh yes," said one of our hosts. "We've seen dozens of them."

I was surprised and a bit saddened. "Why is it I never see them on shore?"

"How could they survive, my dear Dore," said Friedrich, "with all the cats roaming the island? Including yours."

He said it in a kindly voice—a performance for the others—but I heard the reproach underneath. We were ushered inside for dinner, but I longed to remain on the deck, watching the penguins as they shared the feast of fish, from underwater, with the flying birds.

In the dining room, I found myself next to an American woman who asked me if we had children, and in that moment, I was tempted to say, *Yes, I have six: Johanna, Viktor, Leo, Elsa, Gisela, and Anna.*

But I simply smiled and shook my head; I do not wish to give anyone fodder for rumors. Back home, I had always known I did not fit in, and perhaps that is why I came here—to feel as though I might belong somewhere. If only I had known that I could come to the ends of the earth and not fit in here either.

Yet I'm grateful for their presence, if a little self-conscious. They are well groomed—the yachts have private cabins and bathrooms, such a luxury—and well dressed. The American women I dined with wore ankle-length dresses with flouncy sleeves, and sandals with heels. The woman who asked me about children—I believe her name was Mary—wore long, billowy white trousers and a smart sleeveless top. They all wore jewelry that sparkled and shone—earrings dangling like flowers from their earlobes, polished stones on delicate strands around their necks. They looked refined and elegant, and by comparison I look like one of the island's feral animals. I pay my appearance no mind on most days, living in the same unvarnished comfort I so enjoyed when I had first met Friedrich. When we rush from Friedo to meet a ship, we don't have much time to tidy up. I cannot help but wonder what these women think of me, with my hair wild and sun-kissed, my skin darkened by the equatorial sun and mapped with cuts and scratches, my smile revealing our primitive existence (several weeks ago, when the pain in my mouth became too great, Friedrich had to pull the infected teeth). In a way, when we board the yachts, I feel as though I'm back in my old life. But although I always don my nicest, cleanest dress, I know my clothing must seem plain, and my homemade haircut unkempt.

But they seem to be in awe, filled with curiosity and admiration. Our meals on board are cherished but also quite overwhelming in their stark contrast to my daily life. We sit on plush seats, the comforts of which I have long forgotten. Our meals are served on tablecloths so smooth and white I must pay close attention to avoid spilling anything. All the wood glowing with candlelight in the dining room is a deep, burnished brown, the carpets a rich navy as blue as the sea.

I'm constantly receiving questions as I'm presented with an array of foods I haven't seen in so long and that seem so foreign now: deviled eggs and aspic, finger sandwiches and scalloped potatoes, fresh cheeses and baked olives. Despite the extravagance, despite the offerings of wine, whiskey, and brandy, I have found no greater luxury than glass after glass of ice water.

I avoid the main dishes—roast beef and rack of lamb, claiming my stomach is unaccustomed to such rich foods—and while Friedrich greedily digs in, the staff serves me extra helpings of navy beans and corn, asparagus and fried potatoes.

As I navigate all this abundance, I'm also navigating their queries. Mary leaned forward during our dessert of rice pudding and Neapolitan ice and whispered, "They say you and Friedrich live in the nude, when no one is visiting."

I looked at her, shocked, but she was smiling. I confess that on the hottest of days I can hardly be bothered with donning clothes, nor can Friedrich, but how anyone but us can know this, I cannot say.

I did my best to smile back at her, to reflect the coy twinkle I saw in her eyes. "That will always be our secret," I said.

It is because of this curiosity, I am certain, that the next day she and her group came to our homestead to witness our daily life. We disappointed them, surely, by being clothed and doing our chores; we gathered our food and water, worked the sugarcane mill Friedrich built. They watched us as if we were animals in a zoo.

I must admit I am proud of what we have achieved. We do not have the fancy meals served on china with silver that they enjoy on their yachts, but after much anxious waiting, we have filled our kitchen with food from the garden; we have built a cooking stove of gathered stones. We grow beans, peas, beets, radishes, cauliflower, cabbage, onions, celery, potatoes, spinach, tomatoes, sugarcane. We have also been able to harvest bananas, papayas, coconuts, guavas, pineapples, lemons, and oranges. It's hard not to take pride in our bounty, the riches we are blessed with, especially when I see awe in the eyes of these visiting strangers.

Friedrich likes showing off our home and gardens, for once giving me credit for my share of the work. With our wide, shady porch and sleeping hammocks, our life here looks romantic. The visitors have no idea that life here is not what it seems. I play the role of Eve as well as Friedrich plays Adam. We show off our Eden, and we fool them all.

Sometimes I believe I could be happy here if only I could be on my own, just me and my sweet Johanna and the chickens. I wonder sometimes how much longer I can endure this place, this life.

Is it wrong to wish we had failed?

Mallory

At five thirty, when I peek out my door, the rain I'd heard on the roof overnight has lessened to a mist. I lie back down, still tired, and feel more tired when I think of trying to build penguin nests with Callie's chatter in the background and Diego hovering with a camera.

I think of Gavin in the casita next door, and suddenly he seems farther away than ever. Maybe I'm not meant to inhabit his world again, after so much time. I was another person then, and I've been several more since; even in the past year, I've become versions of myself I'd never wanted or imagined. How many personas can a woman embody in a single lifetime?

I'm reminded of a day, years ago, when Emily was about three years old and we were at my brother-in-law's house in Marblehead, a quaint coastal town on the North Shore, about forty minutes from Boston. Scott's brother, Jason, took off his glasses, and Emily said, "You don't look like Jason." Jason replied, in a voice deeper and more serious than his usual tone, "I'm not Jason. I'm Fred."

And so it began—a game in which Emily would demand to see Fred, and Jason would walk away, pretending to look for him, then return, sans glasses, to her delight: "Hi, Fred!" Then she would demand to see Jason again—and so it went, all summer long. She never questioned why Fred and Jason couldn't be in the same place at the same time.

One day, a few months later, Emily and I walked through Boston Common after preschool and then stopped and sat on a bench to have a snack. We ended up talking about the summer in Marblehead; Emily reminisced about the beach, the sandbox in the yard, Jason and Fred. For the first time, she seemed to make the connection. "I like it when Jason is Fred," she said. Then she asked me, "Who are you when you're not Mom?"

"I'm always Mom."

"Who are you when you're not Mallory?"

"I'm always Mallory." I was confused, partly by Emily's sudden acknowledgment of having known the game all along, and partly by the question itself. It was a good one, a legitimate one: Who was I, really?

I think back to before she was born, when I was traveling the world, counting penguins and building nests, when I was blithely happy in a love affair with no future. When I met the man with whom I did see a future. When Emily became that future. When life became a lot less carefree but a lot more precious. I'd become a different person—one whose job as a parent was more meaningful but also more stressful. It had not been up to Mallory to keep alive an entire species, but it was up to Mom to do just that with a vulnerable little human.

Emily's question made me wonder: Was there any Mallory left at all, or was I now completely and entirely Mom?

To change the subject, I asked, "Who are you when you're not Emily?"

Emily replied, "I'm a green girl with purple hair and giant butterfly wings, and I live in the forest . . ."

I should've known my tenacious daughter wouldn't give up that easily. Not half an hour later, as we walked toward the T station, she asked again: "Who are you?"

Finally I answered her. I told her I was a mermaid who lived on an island in the Pacific and swam with penguins and sea turtles. Emily was transfixed, and I described every Galápagos animal I could think of—the blue-footed boobies and the flamingos, the finches and the lava lizards—realizing only later, as I put Emily down for her nap, that I was not so much telling a make-believe story as I was remembering a lost dream.

And now, amid the haze of memories, I wonder whether it's possible to get what I came for, to reclaim the Mallory of all those years ago, or at least a part of her. Whether there can be any reconciliation between Mallory and Mom, after all this time.

One thing I do know is that today won't be that day. It will be hard to build nests with a photography team following us, and impossible to spend any time with Gavin.

As the sun lightens the sky, I wash my face and put my day pack together—and as I pass the bookshelf, I see that one of the books is sticking out more than the rest, as if someone had just reshelved it. I absently push it back—then recognize the book, the memoir of Margret Wittmer.

I pick it up and flip through the pages, glimpsing an illustration of the pirate caves, where every one of the settlers had spent their first nights on the island—and that's when I know what I'll do today.

I send a quick email to Gavin, then don my pack. The casitas are quiet as I hurry past the closed doors and toward town, to the road that stretches up to the highlands.

I've never been to the caves—it's a tourist site, not a research one, at least not for penguins—and while I feel a little guilty, I suspect it'll be a wasted morning anyhow, far more about Callie getting good footage than about us building good nests.

The caves are about five miles up the dirt road, at 1,500 feet elevation, but I've got all morning. The hike might even help loosen some of the tight muscles in my legs and shoulders. The road is mucky from last night's rain, and I feel mud spatter and cake on my bare calves as my shoes kick it up behind me.

It takes three hours to reach Asilo de la Paz. I stop at the parking lot, drink some water, then follow the arrow on the weathered wooden sign toward the trail. There's an open-sided chiva bus parked nearby—a tour group—but I don't hear any voices.

The landscape is utterly different here, a microclimate all its own, with moss-covered rocks, ferns sprouting from the ground, the *garúa* misting the air and saturating verdant hills. I take a deep breath and smell fresh grass and wet stone.

As I reach the caves—carved out by eighteenth-century whalers and buccaneers before being inhabited by the settlers of the 1930s—I stop and look into a face sculpted into one of the bigger stones. The stone towers over me by several feet, almost as wide as it is tall, and there's something peaceful about the closed eyes, the head's gentle tilt backward. Ferns grow from the top of the head like hair, and the face has a mossy eyelid, a green five-o'clock shadow.

I walk through the wild, overgrown landscape, acacia trees curving overhead, blocking the light, the ground damp and spongy under my feet. I push aside leaves and vines, seeing only a hint of white sky through the gnarled branches above.

I see a giant tortoise ahead and stop in my tracks. Though they'd been wiped off the island entirely by the early twentieth century, they're now being reintroduced to the highlands by the national park; they'd been gone for so long it's amazing to see this individual crossing the trail right in front of me. I wait, watching his face—wrinkled and wise, tiny dark eyes, flared nostrils, a subtle overbite. The lines on his carapace are clear but fading, not terribly worn, and I'm guessing he's probably a few decades older than me—well into his sixties. He'll live at least another hundred years.

He stretches his neck to attack a patch of grass, staring back at me as he chews, long strings of grass hanging down his chin, like a sloppy little child. Finally, he ambles forward, step by leisurely step, until he's off the path.

When I reach the largest cave, I can see why it was so inviting to the settlers. A wide entrance leads to a cavern of soft lava stone, with patches of white basalt carved to create benches and shelves that line the walls; a little stove; storage nooks. It isn't very deep, but I go all the way to the back, where it's cool, and sit on one of the hand-formed benches. Outside, the day glows white, a few twigs and branches silhouetted by the sharpening sunlight.

Though it's cooler in the cave, it's no less buggy, and I slap away a mosquito. A sudden shiver runs through me, from the chill of the cave, or perhaps something else—I feel an odd, hair-raising sensation, as if someone's watching. I turn, but no one's there. I stand up and listen, for a tour group or a straying visitor, but hear nothing.

I sit back down, in a different spot this time, and—maybe it's the new angle, or because the sun has shifted—I see a dark gap I didn't notice before.

A closer look reveals that part of the lava has crumbled away. It looks as if, long ago, someone had tried to carve another nook and failed, giving up—but now something has come loose, perhaps from the heavy rains, or from a leak that sprouted somewhere deep in the hillside.

I reach in, and a huge piece of the facade tumbles down, giving way to an opening large enough to stick my head into. It's a lava tube, but unlike most, this one goes deep down into the earth, probably formed thousands or millions of years ago, the lava slowing and hardening as molten liquid continued to pour through it, creating a channel into the depths of the island.

The walls of the shaft are wet but still rough; the introduction of water here is recent. I wedge my phone in, light on, and shine it around. Not seeing much, I push myself up onto my toes to get a better view, but there's barely enough room for my shoulders, and I don't want to get myself stuck. I'm working my way back out when I see it—something wedged into a crevice about three or four feet down.

It could be a pile of dead leaves—brownish, with thin, discrete sheaves of something—but some are lighter and straight-edged, like the pages of a book. I pull my hand out, pocket my phone, and reach back in, trying to get my fingers on it. It's too far away, so I stretch my upper body into the tube until I'm nearly upside down, my hips the only thing keeping me from falling all the way in. My arms and face scrape against the stone, but I'm still not close enough. I dangle a little farther in—and then I'm slipping, tumbling.

I throw out my arms, bracing myself against the curved sides, and fling my legs wide to hook my feet at the entrance, my heart slamming against my chest. After I catch my breath, I see that the object is now within reach, at least—it's wet, slimy—and once I have a grip on it, I begin to worm my way backward and up, a reverse rappel out of the narrow space.

Once I'm out of the tube, I look around, listening again for voices. It's still quiet.

I wobble over to one of the carved benches and sit down, waiting for my heart rate to return to normal. I'm trying not to think of what might have happened had I fallen, alone, having told no one where I was going.

After a few moments, I'm calm enough to examine what's in my hands—two slender, leather-bound journals—and with shaking fingers I untie the sturdy leather string holding them together.

The paper is damp and moldy in places, though the leather has preserved it well—and it's only wet on the outside. I turn the pages, gently unsticking them from one another; the ink is well preserved, too, if a bit blurry in spots. The handwriting is ornate, cursive, difficult to read. I can't decipher any of the words, but the language mini-lessons I've received from Scott over the years helps. Based on the spellings, the number of uppercase words, a few special characters, it looks like German.

I straighten up and hold the book out, as if it might offer more clues. Dore and Friedrich had stayed here at the caves only a day or two when they arrived on Floreana, but the Wittmer family stayed for longer before building their own house. Even the Baroness stayed here at one point. Could these journals belong to one of them? The date on the page in front of me is 1933—a time when all of them were here.

I go back to the lava tube and lean in, shining my phone light all around, but I don't see anything more. When I emerge, I feel a wave of dizziness—the rush of not only having been upside down but of something else.

It takes me a moment to figure out what it is, this jumble of emotions, a tangle of so much that I wished for in coming here but didn't truly expect to feel. The unexpected discovery of something important—these journals seem unrelated to penguins but could change history nonetheless. And, even more, the guilty relief of several hours passing in which I haven't thought of Scott and Emily—a few fleeting moments in a space in which I might have a chance, finally, to answer Emily's question: *Who are you?*

I walk to the mouth of the cave and take a breath of the cool, misty air. A Galápagos sulphur butterfly—*Phoebis sennae marcellina*—flits past me on wings as yellow as the tropical sun. Again I think of Emily—*I'm a green girl with purple hair and giant butterfly wings . . . Who are you?*—and I remember a cool late-autumn day in Boston, when Emily was about six and Scott and I had taken her to a special butterfly exhibit at the science museum. We went through two doors to enter a room in which at least a dozen different species flew freely in a hot, humid enclosure, landing on our clothing, our heads, anointing us with bright spots of orange and yellow and blue, colors shifting and blurring as they moved their wings. I'd glimpsed what I thought was a sulphur and pointed it out, but Emily and Scott hardly noticed, they were so entranced by the whirring of tiny wings, smiling as butterflies flitted among us. As we left the exhibit, between the two exit doors we all stood still while a museum employee inspected our clothing, then turned us around in front of a mirror to check for stowaways. It was then that I noticed a small, black butterfly on my shoulder, unwilling to move at the wave of the employee's hand. Finally, I gently shook my sweater.

Now, as I hold these two journals at the entrance to the cave, I remember that butterfly's rapid fluttering, its reluctant escape, and I feel a glimpse of recognition in my presence here on Floreana, in my attempt to cling to a past that seems determined to shake me free.

Dore

I have neglected to write for so very long, and I've missed this diary, the only place I have to unburden my soul. Even as I write, I wonder to whom I am confessing all these inexpressible thoughts. I do imagine someone reading it one day, someone who might understand the terrible burden of getting what you thought you'd always wanted.

Does a life exist if it doesn't get recorded? I am beginning to wonder.

We came here seeking solitude, and yet we eagerly await news of the world from passing ships. We eagerly hand over letters to be delivered to the very civilization we longed to escape. We eagerly show off the life we are creating here, as if we need witnesses to make it real.

Can one experience paradise if no one is watching?

We like to think we are invincible, but I know we would certainly have failed if it weren't for the ships that supply us with all that we'd neglected to bring. They have given us everything from seeds and building supplies to tools and medicine. Friedrich does not admit that we came ill-prepared, or that we are living every day on the edge of failure. Here we are, at the birthplace of Darwin's theory, and yet how little we humans have truly evolved. How far we have yet to go.

As if to prove this notion, visitors continue to arrive, to try and then fail to make a life here—and yet I suppose I knew the day would come when settlers came to Floreana and did not leave.

It's been quite an adjustment—and I am still getting accustomed to having neighbors.

What has surprised me is how different all of us are—there is no one type of character who comes here, no thread that connects us, no way of knowing who will fail and who will stay.

We have not yet had longtime companions on the island, and it's been so long since I have felt I have anything in common with other humans anymore. When I first met the Wittmers, I felt disappointed that their family was here to stay. I feared that, as with the women on the yachts, I would have nothing in common with them—and the Wittmers would not be sailing away. They would stay, and remind me that there is no place in which I feel at home.

It is one thing to wonder how I look to others who are merely passing through—quite another to see myself as our new neighbors do. In what they observe in my outward appearance, I can't help but see a reflection of my inner self. My face, dappled with the dirt and sweat of hard labor, always seeking approval. My mouth, sunken with missing teeth and swallowed words. My dirty white dress, a seamless transformation from bride to ghost.

Yet I also felt hopeful about the Wittmers. Since leaving Elise in Berlin, I've missed having a close friend. I also realized that I could be of help—that, for the first time in my life, I could be a teacher; I have knowledge that few others possess. I have become an expert in something merely by surviving here.

So imagine my surprise not to be needed—to be in the presence of newcomers so self-assured that they set about their lives as if they weren't in the middle of the ocean. It leaves me to wonder, yet again, what is wrong with me, why I struggle so where others do not.

Friedrich sees them as intruders on our idyll. Yet for me there is some comfort in their presence, the knowledge that he will be kinder to me in the midst of their company—I trust this will ease some of the tension between us.

The members of the Wittmer family are bright-eyed, clean-clothed, fresh as the morning—a woman, a man, a boy of twelve years. Their arrival awoke in me something lost, forgotten, or simply buried.

The child, Harry, turned out to be Margret Wittmer's stepson, and then I learned she was pregnant. Pregnant! I could not believe it, and Friedrich was furious when Margret told him the reason they'd chosen Floreana was because they knew a doctor lived on the island. Friedrich was most unwelcoming toward the suggestion that he could help them with their medical issues, as this was precisely what he'd longed to escape back in Berlin.

But I found myself eager to hear more about the baby to come, and I whispered to Margret, when Friedrich was busy elsewhere, not to worry—that despite his petulance, Friedrich's ego was such that he would gladly prove how helpful he could be. She laughed and thanked me.

I must admit I felt an odd yearning upon meeting these new settlers. The young family seemed completely prepared for what greeted them here, completely happy. Friedrich showed them to the caves and suggested they settle there, much to my chagrin—but I was happy to hear later that they planned to build their own home somewhere else.

We expected, based on their choice to follow us to Floreana instead of finding their own island, that they would be needy. Yet they were independent, self-sufficient, apparently needing no one but one another. They seemed to feel a sense of adventure, and at the same time a sense of purpose—they appeared to be filled with wonder and excitement on one hand, and on the other, they knew exactly what to do, as if they'd lived here all along. They had everything I wished for when I came here. And I considered that maybe I had more to learn from them than to teach them.

Margret was pretty, with a friendly, open face and a bright, welcoming smile. As a pregnant woman she looked fit and healthy and capable. I could not help but wonder: Had I looked so fresh when I first arrived on Floreana? (I also had to wonder if I might have looked just as robust and happy if any of my own pregnancies had survived as long as hers.)

We soon welcomed them for a visit at Friedo, and Margret and I had a chat. She admitted that when she first saw the island, she thought it looked desperately frightening—"What am I doing here?" she said she asked herself—and we had a laugh about that. She also confessed that, like Friedrich and me, she and Heinz had told no one of their plans in advance so that they could not be talked out of it, and we bonded over this, too. I felt a surge of hope at this first meeting, in the promise that we could be friends.

Yet it wasn't long before I had to acknowledge that Margret and I have very little in common, despite us being so close in age. For one, she has a child—Harry is not her own, but she loves him as if he is—and she has the even greater fortune to have another on the way. They'd told us the boy, Harry, was sickly, and that he is the reason they'd come to the islands—for the sunshine and fresh air—but he looks healthy to me. And Margret is in love with her husband—or so it appears. At the very least, it's obvious that she and Heinz share a warm and companionable relationship, and it reminds me of how Friedrich and I used to be.

Heinz seems to have none of the struggles that Friedrich and I had; he takes to his chores with enthusiasm and vigor, and he is kind to Margret; when we see them, they laugh together often. They have settled in remarkably faster than we did. They'd brought far more supplies than we had—of course, they'd read about us in the news stories that had appeared in Europe, and they'd prepared far better. We had not done it best, but we had done it first. I felt proud of all that we'd achieved but wished I could be more helpful, that I had something to offer them.

Yet I didn't linger on such thoughts for long. Amid the flurry of the Wittmers' arrival, I've had a spot of great joy, as my Viktor has returned to me. He came to Friedo one evening just before the sun set, and at first I thought he was an illusion. He was covered in wounds, which were in turn covered in insects, likely from a fight with another male donkey on the pampas.

I cleaned him up and led him to his pen. Again, I left the gate open to allow him to choose freedom, and to my delight, he stayed. I fed him a variety of grasses and treated him to some bananas and cucumbers, and a precious orange. I whispered in his furry donkey ears, "Welcome home." And I think he understood.

Viktor timed his return quite well—one day when the Wittmers visited Friedo, while Friedrich was showing Heinz and Margret our sugarcane mill, I followed the boy Harry to Viktor's enclosure, where he stood looking at my beloved donkey, whose wounds were already healing. I gathered some greens and opened the gate.

"Would you like to feed him?" I asked, and Harry eagerly agreed.

He stood very close to Viktor, with absolutely no fear, and it wasn't until months later that I realized Harry did not see very well and had to get close to everything.

I enjoyed Harry's company that day and loved the attention he gave to my animals. When Johanna came strolling over to us—perhaps envious of our affections toward Viktor; she liked very much to be the center of attention—Harry reached down and picked up my little cat, holding her at eye level. Johanna nuzzled his face with her own, purring loudly, and the look on Harry's face was one of pure bliss.

The Wittmers had brought along two dogs, which I suspect were more working dogs than pets, but Harry spoke of them with great affection. I was glad he had animals of his own, as he was bound to get lonely. I was mystified as to why the Wittmers would bring an almost teenager to live on an island in the middle of the sea—I am hardly one to question such a choice, but I had come of my own free will, however I may have misjudged it, and Harry was just a boy, with no say in the matter.

I masked this uneasiness as I asked Harry how he felt about being here. He replied that he is greatly excited for his new adventure, and his response seemed genuine. Unlike adults, children do not yet know how to lie, how to tell people what they want to hear.

Because Harry loved animals, I asked him if he'd like to read my stories, the little tales I've written about the adventures of Johanna, the chickens, and my dear Viktor—all the things I imagined my creatures got up to when they weren't with me at Friedo. Though I had dreamed of one day reading these stories aloud to a child, I knew Harry was too old for this. But though the stories may be simple, I thought they could teach him a bit about the island, and he has such affection for my pets. Harry's eyes widened when I brought him a notebook filled with handwritten pages, and he held it as though it were a treasure. "Keep them as long as you want," I told him. "Maybe you'll be inspired to write some stories of your own."

Yet it seems Harry is kept too busy to write. I do hope he is finding adventure in all the work—despite apparently being ill, he certainly does a lot of the labor of building a homestead, alongside his father. He is as tall as Margret, and growing fast; after several months on the island, he is now nearly thirteen years old. I admit I envied Margret, having these two strong males to do all the hard labor, while she could content herself with cooking the meals and setting up the house.

And though she was surely more domestically accomplished than I was, I visited one day, bringing her some bananas and offering tips for cooking and storage in the tropical heat. I suppose I had a vision of the two of us trading recipes, drinking tea together in the afternoons. But Margret was independent, confident in her abilities, and while she was pleasant to me, it seemed she had no need or desire for friendship. Perhaps she had enough company in her own family.

Once they settled in, we saw very little of them. We did the neighborly things for one another, like bringing mail from Post Office Bay or delivering supplies that had come in. But I felt quite wistful about what could've been—and, strangely, more alone than before they had arrived.

Mallory

It's quiet when I return to the casitas, and already past two o'clock. I take a quick detour to the landing and see that the panga isn't there; they've already gone back out. I hadn't meant to skip the entire day.

I close and lock my door, then pull out the journals. They feel a bit drier now, and I riffle the pages, making sure none of them are stuck together. I look at the words again, picking out the name *Friedrich*, and wonder if the diary belonged to Dore. But of course any one of the settlers could have written about Friedrich Ritter.

I think about Friedrich and Dore, how her published memoir blamed the Baroness for the fate that befell them on Floreana—though I've always wondered whether their presumably idyllic life went sideways even before then. Dore probably left out so much in her memoir, keeping up the appearance of normalcy, just as I'm doing here. These journals, if they're hers, could hold all her secrets.

And as for my own secrets—I've never kept a diary, my life comprising field notes and academic papers, replaced later with nut-free recipes and shopping lists. But for the first time I understand the compulsion to write, to set secrets free in a place that feels safe when nothing else does.

I lean back on the bed, and the next thing I know I'm jolted awake, hearing and feeling at the same time a loud thump that reverberates across the deck, rattling my casita.

I open the door to see Gavin, righting the small table he'd knocked over. He sinks down into his chair and gives me a look I've never seen before. "This job doesn't come with vacation days, Mallory."

I shut the door to my casita, suddenly not wanting to share the journals with him. "To what job are you referring?" I ask. "Tour guide or babysitter?"

"If you can't be flexible," he says, "maybe you shouldn't have come."

"I came here for the penguins."

"This *is* about the penguins. Did it occur to you that some positive footage in the right places might help us raise a few more dollars for the program?" He runs a hand down his forehead, rubs his eyes, then sighs. "All I think about anymore is money. My life is a three-year cycle of worry. A spreadsheet whose numbers always suck."

I pull my chair closer to his and sit next to him. We're silent for a few minutes, and then I ask, "So, how was it? Do you think she'll help?"

He doesn't look at me but out toward the ocean. "We'll see."

I, too, look toward the ocean and feel my gaze stretching and reaching, deep into the Pacific and beyond, to the South Pacific, to New Zealand, the place where I'd truly fallen for Gavin—a deep, all-consuming plunge. But it was also the place where a small part of me realized he and I weren't going to fit, and I buried that knowledge as deeply as I could. I wanted us to fit; I wanted us to mate for life, like the penguins we were devoted to.

At that time, I'd not yet been to Ecuador, had never seen penguins in their natural habitat, and Gavin was determined to show me. "Seeing penguins in the wild changes everything," he said.

We hiked through a dense rainforest to a two-hundred-yard-long crescent of beach, with steep cliffs on either end tucking in its golden sand. Rock outcroppings rose opposite the shoreline, obscuring the area where the rainforest met the sea. Unlike the beaches of San Diego, here there wasn't a scrap of detritus—no aluminum cans, no water bottles, no cigarette butts, not a shred of plastic. The sand was littered only with shells and kelp. The tide had washed away any hint of the previous day's visitors, and it felt as though we were the first people ever to walk on this spot.

We sat for two hours on a pair of adjacent boulders, waiting for the tawaki—the Māori word for what scientists call Fiordland crested penguins. Though it was mid-November, springtime, when penguin parents would be feeding their chicks regularly, no penguins emerged from their nests or the sea, and I worried this meant they weren't breeding.

"Not necessarily," Gavin said. "But it probably means there aren't more than a couple of nests around here. Which isn't a surprise, with the public access." He nodded toward the hiking trail. He seemed to think for a moment, then asked, "Do you have your camera with you?"

"Yeah, it's right here."

"Good. Come with me."

We returned to the eco-lodge where we were staying and walked past our cabin to a shed filled with bicycles. Gavin handed me a helmet and said, "Let's go."

"Where?"

He gave me a wink. "To the beach we're not supposed to go to."

I followed him down a back road, away from the lodge, until we reached the highway—a shoulderless two-lane road: narrow, curvy, unforgiving. And busy at this time of year, the beginning of the tourist season.

"Are you crazy, Gavin? We can't bike this. We'll be killed by the first car that comes along."

"If you want to see tawaki, it's the only way."

And there it was—that little flash of recognition that this would always be Gavin's life: penguins above all else.

As if to highlight the risks of his devotion, a car whizzed past, at more than a hundred kilometers an hour. I hesitated—but only briefly. In that moment, I was all in. And for most of our time together, I would be all in, ignoring what I hadn't wanted to see, that I could never come first for Gavin. That nothing could, other than the birds.

We rode single file, Gavin in the lead. The road was so narrow that cars had to move into the opposite lane to pass us, and each time they did, I felt a rush of air that made me wobble on my bike.

At last Gavin pulled off the pavement onto a barely perceptible gravel shoulder and dismounted.

"Hurry," he said. "We can't let anyone see us."

I followed him into the bush, struggling to pull my bike through a tangle of ferns and vines, over exposed tree roots and slick, sharp rocks. After a few yards we came to a small clearing, and Gavin slid his bike, handlebars first, between two rows of tall ferns, then positioned mine next to his. When he stepped back I couldn't see the bikes, and I wondered how we'd find them again.

Gavin led me along a narrow, nearly invisible trail through the rainforest. Rain fell in a light mist, lingering in the air like a living entity. When we reached a wide creek—about twenty feet across, three feet deep, with a brisk current—Gavin pointed down the trail to where a cairn, positioned at the edge of the trail, rose above the creek's muddy edge.

"I built that a couple of years ago, as a decoy," he said. "If anyone does find their way here, they'll think the trail continues this way, across the stream."

"And they'll get totally lost," I said with a laugh. "I love it."

Then he turned, continuing through a thick copse of ferns, mati, and silver beech. The trail appeared once again under our feet. We walked for at least forty minutes before the dense vegetation began to thin out. The increasing brightness gave way to a wide white-sand beach. The sky was grayish-blue and still drizzling.

"There are three colonies we know of here," Gavin said, pointing to where the stream was flowing out to sea. "One nests up that stream, and the other has its nests in the scrub up the beach. The third is over here."

He took my hand and led me to a boulder field at the far end of the beach. The tawaki, he'd told me, climb up the slick rocks and build nests in the rainforest, in the bush, under the roots of trees.

We sat on a large, flat boulder to wait. "They usually come ashore in groups," he said. "There are about seventy, eighty nests here above this bank, and with the chicks eating constantly right now, we'll definitely see at least a few of them." He indicated the trail the penguins would take up to their nests, about thirty feet from where we sat. "We have to stay low and not move too much. They'll notice the shape of us, but if we're still, we won't bother them."

I moved close and leaned against him, our rain jackets already soaked, my feet cold and wet. I had one hand on my camera, inside my jacket, and my other hand was tucked into Gavin's, his fingers closed around mine.

I nudged him when I saw a small body riding a wave to shore, then popping upright. The penguin waddled over the seaweed toward the bank, his round white belly glistening with seawater.

As we watched, another penguin came ashore, and the two stood about five feet apart, though neither acknowledged the other. Their yellow eyebrows were slick against their heads, and as they shook their bodies and preened their feathers, the crests burst free, flung out to the sides of their heads.

All of a sudden, three more birds appeared from behind a tall rock, and all five penguins hustled toward us. "Don't move," Gavin whispered, nodding toward the water, where a fur seal had hauled out onto the rocks. The seal was enormous, his milk-chocolate coat sleek from the ocean, and when he turned languidly toward the penguins, his light whiskers looked as sharp as teeth.

I didn't dare pull out my camera. If the penguins were frightened back into the water—whether by us or the seal—the chicks in their nests would go hungry.

Eventually the seal turned away and lumbered over the rocks—it takes a seal far more energy and effort to go after penguins on land than at sea—and the penguins began to make their way toward their nests, taking their time now, the moment of danger gone. They stopped to preen and shake off more water, their leisurely grooming giving me a chance to take a few photos.

They continued on, jumping from rock to rock, occasionally stumbling and falling onto their stomachs or slipping backward and trying again, often nearly horizontal as they balanced their squid-stuffed bodies over slippery boulders, as the rocks turned from porous black lava to round, dense gray stone amid the bright-green scrub grass. The penguins' feet seemed to wrap around the curves of the stone, gripping as they made their way forward. One by one, they disappeared into the thick brush.

"Listen," Gavin whispered.

I could barely hear it over the sound of the wind and the waves—the trumpeting call of the birds reuniting.

"In about fifteen, twenty minutes," Gavin said, "their mates will come down. It'll be their turn to forage."

We waited, and less than thirty minutes later, I saw the first orange beak, the first yellow crest peek out from between two vinelike branches. The penguin looked around for several minutes before beginning her painstaking descent down the rocks, toward the sea.

"A lot of work, feeding those babies," I said, raising my camera again.

"It is," Gavin said. "And only one of the chicks will actually get the lion's share of the food. The other one will eventually starve."

I lowered my camera and looked at him, thinking he was joking.

He explained, "The tawaki only raise one chick."

"Then why do they lay two eggs?"

"The second chick is like an insurance policy. In case the first one doesn't make it."

"They actually let one of their babies starve to death? That's horrific."

"That's nature," he said. "They simply can't afford to raise two. That's why this place is such a secret. There are only fifteen hundred pairs of tawaki left in the world. This is one of the few places where they can breed in peace."

"But if the birds themselves let half their chicks die . . ."

"They're doing what they have to do to survive. Chances are, if they raised both chicks, one or both would die anyway. Having one strong chick at least gives the species a shot at survival."

Later, as we made the trek back to our bikes, I thought about what Gavin had said—*Seeing penguins in the wild changes everything*. He was right, though not in the way he thought. For the first time, I began to wonder how he could do this work, be so detached—and whether I would need to become the same way. To survive not only the work but the two of us.

By the time we returned to the lodge, it was raining steadily, the temperature a few degrees colder. I slipped my bicycle into the shed behind Gavin's and took the towel he handed me. We toweled the bikes dry in silence.

"You okay?" Gavin asked as we walked back to our cabin, the sky growing darker. I had no words for the sudden confusion I felt, the doubts I wanted to ignore, but Gavin seemed to understand. Inside, I couldn't stop shivering, and he turned on the shower and slowly, gently removed my wet clothing. The warm water stung as it hit my skin, and when it poured my hair down into my eyes, Gavin reached over and smoothed my hair back, soaking his sleeve. Before he could take off his clothes, I caught his hand and pulled him into the shower. He held me for a few moments, the water streaming between us, and I felt myself relax. After a few moments he turned me away from him and washed my hair, his fingers massaging my scalp, my shoulders.

As I look at him now, in Floreana's fading light, I remember how his hands on my body elicited comfort, and desire, and a stirring within that, despite our previous encounters, was entirely new. I didn't know exactly what it was, only that it was connected to what we'd seen that day, and that we'd crossed a threshold together, into a new world where despair and hope fused and became one. This was what Gavin could do for me that no one else could.

Last month, when I had told Megan I was leaving for Ecuador—by text, so I wouldn't have to talk to her about it—she texted back, simply, WTF? I knew exactly what she meant: *Why there, why now, how can you just leave like this?* At the time, I didn't respond. But now, sitting next to Gavin and thinking back, I realize something I could never have articulated to her, to Gavin, or even to myself, until now—that I'm seeking that feeling again, the fleeting moments in which despair meets hope, and, for a very brief while, hope wins.

Dore

It is a struggle to write about what has happened—even to think of it—but maybe by writing I can let go of some of my anguish. I have noticed for weeks that Johanna was looking fuller, heavier; I thought perhaps she had gotten into some of our bread.

But then, one morning, I went out toward our chicken coop, having heard tiny mews. I followed the sound and found my lovely Johanna, sprawled out in a hollow she'd made under a thorny bush, nursing six kittens. They were a few days old, at least—I could not get past the briars to see them up close, nor did I want to alarm Johanna—and they had her beautiful markings. "Well done, my smart girl," I told her, observing that her hideaway in the brambles would ward off predators and keep her family safe. I went to get her some food—we still had some cured meats stored away—and Friedrich caught me near the chicken coop as I was returning to her.

"Meat? For the chickens?" he asked.

I was bubbling over with happiness and couldn't contain myself. I regretted my words as soon as they left my mouth, and I will never forget that moment, one of my gravest mistakes. "It's for Johanna," I said. "She has had kittens, and they are all nursing away, hungry as can be." And only then did I notice the look on his face.

"Where are they?" he said in a most menacing way.

"What do you mean?"

"It's a simple question, Dore," he said. "Where are they?"

At that point, I was very frightened, and I refused to tell him. But their location could not remain a secret for long; the little creatures were mewling, and the high pitch of their cries led him directly to them.

"Friedrich, don't you touch them!" I ran after him, pulling at his shirt but unable to stop him.

"You are distracted enough with this cat and that donkey and all the chickens," he said. "We are not here to raise pets, Dore."

"But they work as well," I told him. "They will grow up and help us with the rats."

"We don't need more than one cat at Friedo," he said. "They will never leave and will only continue to multiply."

I implored him to let them alone, but he refused to listen. He knelt down at Johanna's little hideaway, and I saw her ears go back. "If you don't want to see this," he said, "I suggest you leave us."

I yanked hard at his shirt again. I begged and cried. At last, in shaking me off, his hand landed with such a blow to my cheek that I stumbled and fell back onto the hard dirt. And, knowing what would come next, I turned away and covered my ears with my hands. Even through my fingers I heard Johanna's hiss, her howl of protest, and I pulled myself to my feet and ran back to our house. I flung myself into bed and remained there for the rest of the day. Sweat and tears mingled to soak my bedding.

The next day, I saw Johanna wandering around her hideaway, sniffing and meowing, as if still unsure where her babies might have gone. She let me pet her, but I know it brought her no comfort.

I noticed with some degree of pleasure that Friedrich's arms were covered with marks, bright-red scratches against his suntanned skin. I could not tell whether the injuries were from the thorns around Johanna's den or from her claws, and it didn't matter. They were deep and painful looking—but still not nearly enough.

I will never forgive him for this.

Since that day I have tried to tell myself things will get better, to ignore the hollowness expanding inside me, even when I feel I could burst from it. I had no one in whom to confide about what happened to Johanna's kittens, and I longed for the warmth of Elise's forgiveness and friendship—for the comfort of familiarity. But even the familiar was out of my reach: I had not packed any photographs, or anything that represented what had been my former life. I had not imagined how much I would one day need them.

Johanna kept her distance from Friedo for a while after Friedrich killed her babies. Eventually, she began to return—she avoided Friedrich, as usual, but she spent time with me as I worked in the garden, letting me stroke her fur, as if she'd forgiven me for being unable to help her. She felt thin again, even more so than usual, and I knew she'd been grieving.

Finally, the need to speak of this to someone overwhelmed me, and I sought out Margret. I visited her at her homestead, bringing her some oranges and a few fresh eggs. Harry was there, and, not wanting to distress him with what had happened, I waited until he left before confessing to Margret what Friedrich had done. How I had been helpless to stop him.

"Oh, what a shame," she said, in her practical and somewhat soothing way. "They would have made such lovely pets."

"It was just so cruel," I said, and began to cry again.

She put a hand on my shoulder. "Men," she said, as if it were so simple. "Heinz and I had a disagreement about setting traps for the wild dogs. I told him not to bother, that it's not as if our two will run away and join the pack. But men do what they must do."

She was not as sympathetic as I'd hoped. Did life on this island harden everyone? I did come here hoping to become stronger, but becoming numb to pain, to cruelty, was not a strength I wanted.

Still, speaking my anguish out loud did ease some of the burden I carried, and when Margret brought me a cup of tea, it was sweetened with so much sugar I could have hugged her.

We sat quietly near her garden, and I commented on how lovely it was, filled with vegetables and bright with flowers.

"I planted carnations in my garden," I confessed to her, "but Friedrich destroyed them. He doesn't believe in unnecessary indulgences."

"How could flowers be unnecessary?" She nodded toward her garden. "Pick as many as you'd like."

I was delighted and left that day with my arms full of flowers. Already wilting in the heat, they would never be the same as growing my own, but placing them in my hammock, where I slept alone, I could at least remember my intention and know that someone else here understands me.

Margret Wittmer's presence is validating, but I also know I must prove to Friedrich—to myself—that I can find beauty here, or create it despite him.

Yet it feels that so much is standing in my way. Is it this place in particular that is hindering my will to grow?

Is it this body, which has failed me in so many ways and yet which always must come with me?

Is it this soul of mine, which seeks happiness relentlessly, and which somehow keeps turning in circles, always ending up back where I began?

Or is it the person I came with? Because, like my body, like my very soul, I fear he will be with me forever.

I comfort myself with the grace I can still find. I look into the eyes of my animals. I study each blooming wildflower, the flight of every mockingbird, the passing of cloud after cloud, wave after wave. I surround myself with things that have no other purpose than to nourish the soul.

Mallory

Yesterday's rain remains in the air, not in drops but as a thick shroud of humidity. From the panga I see a sudden, swift movement along the shore—something bigger than a crab or marine iguana but far too quick to be a penguin. I put my hand on Gavin's arm. He sees it immediately and lifts his binoculars to his eyes. Darwin slows the panga.

"Shit," Gavin says, lowering the binoculars. "It's a fucking cat."

It isn't possible. Or shouldn't be.

I reach for his binoculars, and through them I see a brown-and-black tabby scooting along the lava rocks, moving hastily but carefully over the sharp stones. Looking for eggs, or baby iguanas, or penguin chicks.

"I was afraid this might happen." Gavin scrambles to pull out his phone, and I hand the binoculars to Hannah.

"I thought the cats were gone," she says.

"They're supposed to be." Gavin's words are clipped, his jaw tight, and despite this immediate and troubling problem, I like seeing this glimpse of the Gavin I knew so well: passionate, even angry at times.

I look over toward the cat and remember reading, back when conservationists were working on eradicating cats on Isabela, that a single cat could reduce the island's penguin population by 50 percent a year.

With his phone raised to take a photo, Gavin directs Darwin closer to the spot where we'd seen the cat, but already the tabby has disappeared somewhere within the lava tubes and crevices.

"Will you contact the national park?" Gavin asks me. His voice is low and grim. "They'll take care of it."

Hannah lowers the binoculars. "What does that mean—take care of it?"

Gavin doesn't answer, and Hannah gets the point.

Anxiety snarls in my chest. Not only are the penguins vulnerable to changing weather and fishing boats but now also to this feline predator, who looks almost exactly like the cat Emily had picked out at a local shelter in Boston when she was two. He was an older cat—even the shelter staff were surprised that a child would choose an adult cat over a kitten—and lived with us for only three years before succumbing to kidney failure at the age of twelve. I think of how hard it was for Scott and me to give Emily this first lesson in life and death, and how accustomed Gavin is to all of it. I have not been in the field long enough to not want this cat to live.

But there's no time to think about it now. We disembark and get to work. The clouds are still low, still trapping moisture in the air. I'm a little sore from my journey into the lava tube in the cave yesterday, but if anyone's noticed the scratches on my arms and face, they must've assumed I got them from building nests.

After finishing a nest, I step up onto a plateau to take a drink of water. Ahead of me is a natural nest with a penguin inside. I step forward, slowly. The penguin—a female, I think—looks at me and lowers her beak. Her feathers are clean and new—she has recently gone through a molt—and my heart skips a beat when I see an egg, which the bird nudges closer with her beak, tucking it under her chest. I lean forward, looking for a band—there is none—then jot down the location. I don't have a scale or caliper to weigh and measure her, but I can see that she's in good condition, about three or four years old. Her nest is filled with feathers and bones, leaves and twigs—a sign that she has a good partner to help her raise her chick.

I wave Hannah over to show her the nest.

"Penguins lay eggs in pairs," I say, "so there may be another we can't see. Or maybe it's still on its way."

"Will we get to see it hatch?"

"It depends on how long she's been here—incubation takes about a month. We'll check on her and see."

As we quietly step away, Hannah asks, "Why are you still wearing your backpack?"

The journals are inside. Without knowing what they are, exactly, I didn't know where to keep them, other than not in rooms that don't lock. A greasy mix of sunscreen and sweat slides between my shoulders and the pack's straps. "Extra water bottle."

It's a decent excuse, but I'm not sure Hannah's convinced. In the distance, a pair of penguins, their ivory bellies facing the sun, are bent over in the heat.

Two hours later we head back toward the landing site, hugging the shore, where the waves splash up, misting our faces. Three penguins are down near the water, preening, shaking water from their feathers; two are bobbing in the sea.

"If it weren't for cats," Hannah asks, "would penguins have any predators on land?"

"Not the adults, but they always have to worry about their eggs and chicks. Hawks, owls, crabs."

"And in the water?"

"Sharks. Sea lions and fur seals."

"Shit," Hannah says, shaking her head. "It's amazing they're able to survive."

I can't help but think of the journals in my backpack—what a miracle that they, too, managed to survive—and perhaps this is why I'm clinging to them so tightly, carrying them around much the way I once carried Emily in her BabyBjörn: protectively, as if they are as precious. But I don't even know what these books are, what I'm protecting. And I need to find out.

I look at Hannah and sigh. "Sometimes it does seem impossible," I say, "but they just keep surprising us."

Dore

It has been months since I've written, and—so soon after the Wittmers arrived—we have received yet another group of settlers on Floreana.

And with them, life as I know it on this island has been forever changed.

While I looked upon these new arrivals with dismay, I reminded myself: I had *wanted* this life to change, hadn't I? In some odd way, perhaps I was getting what I'd wished for.

There were so many things about the Baroness that stood out. I cannot recall her real name, but it hardly matters; it seems appropriate to use the title, even if her claim to it has yet to be proven. Her manner is so grandiose, so expectant, that it's obvious she believes it, even if none of the rest of us do.

She arrived at Friedo on a donkey. She wore a full riding costume and carried a long whip in one hand. Bright-red lipstick showed off her wide mouth, and she smiled as if she were a queen and we were her subjects. Her blond hair was tied back with a sleek black ribbon. She was accompanied by her companion, a young man named Rudolf Lorenz, whom she treated like both a lover and a servant—*darling* this, *darling* that, as she asked him to do just about everything for her but breathe. I began to wonder whether she used the whip on the donkey or on the man.

"We've heard so much about you," she said as we gave her our usual tour of Friedo. "You have provided a wonderful example of what life can be."

She spoke to Friedrich, as if I wasn't even there. I expected Friedrich to react with the same irritation he'd had with the Wittmers upon learning they'd followed us to Floreana, but instead he seemed quite taken with her.

She has a certain glamour, I admit, with her red lipstick and her dyed hair, with her attitude that says *Worship me*, and it's easy to see how this might lure him in. I wondered how Rudolf Lorenz felt about this, and indeed he looked quite uncomfortable. (I did not know at this first meeting that he was not the only lover she'd brought to the island.)

The Baroness behaved as though she owned Friedo and we were merely her housekeepers. She wandered through our garden, asked Mr. Lorenz to feed her donkey some of Viktor's food, and walked through our house inspecting everything. Even without being asked, Mr. Lorenz fetched her one of our chairs so she could sit down on the porch—apparently all her snooping had been quite exhausting. They stayed so long that it grew too late to go back to the beach—it would be nearly impossible to navigate the trails in the dark—and Friedrich and I had no choice but to invite them to stay the night.

We were very hospitable, setting them up with blankets and hammocks, but it was not enough for the Baroness, who complained of the cold and kept everyone awake with loud coughing, which I am quite certain was exaggerated if not downright fake. In the morning, I prepared hot tea and a nice breakfast of fresh eggs and fruit, of which she refused to eat even a bite.

It wasn't until they left that we eagerly went to open the mail they'd brought us—only to discover it had all been opened. She had read all of our letters.

Friedrich and I had a moment of understanding between us, in our shared disgust. Finally we could agree on something: our dislike of this so-called baroness.

In the coming days, we would talk to the Wittmers about her as well, discovering that they liked her no better than we did. Margret told me with undisguised horror how the Baroness, despite having not walked a step to get to the Wittmers' home—she still went everywhere on her donkey—complained that her feet hurt, and Mr. Lorenz promptly settled her down at the Wittmers' spring to bathe and massage her feet.

"Her feet—in my drinking water!" said Margret.

I confess I had to repress a smile, succumbing to a little schadenfreude as well as understanding. This was the first time Margret had seemed to struggle with anything on the island, and it made me feel closer to her. We had something in common now.

"They didn't even ask," she continued, "and so I had no chance to refuse them—not that they'd have paid me any mind. They do whatever they like, as if they own the whole island."

Margret was right; they did behave as though they'd been here first, as though we were all here for their own convenience. They had brought with them quite a lot of supplies—and animals, including birds, cows, and donkeys, which made me instantly wary, as I have yet to see anyone treat animals with any compassion or fairness on this island.

And then there is the mystery of her two lovers: Rudolf Lorenz and the other, Robert Philippson.

They are both German, both about thirty years old, though they look younger, Mr. Lorenz especially, by at least a decade. They are both very good-looking, slender and fit, with bright eyes and thick, lustrous hair. I wonder what it is about the Baroness that makes them so faithful, for she is appallingly rude, her contempt unmasked even when words drip like honey from her mouth. And yet they fulfill her every wish, obey her every command.

I can't stop thinking of Mr. Lorenz washing the Baroness's feet—the act of both a lover and a servant. What unsettles me is the reminder of a day, more than a year ago, when I had asked Friedrich to help me bathe my feet, after I'd been trudging all day on the hot, sharp lava and my back ached so badly I could not reach down to clean them myself. Of course, he refused me—after how hard I'd worked to help him!—though his refusal of either help or affection no longer comes as a surprise. And then, to envision Mr. Lorenz kneeling at the feet of this so-called baroness, his loyalty and adoration—it is almost too much to bear.

I myself became a bit obsessed with her as well. Her radiant smile, which could turn from charming to dangerous very quickly. Her eyes like storm clouds. Her gay, infectious laugh, accompanied by a coquettish flip of her hair. The sound of her voice lingers in the air like the calls of the mockingbirds, a constant echo rousing my curiosity and occupying my thoughts. When she turned her attention to someone—always one of the men—she was impossible to turn away from. I studied her, wondering how she did it. Was it something innate, this confidence, this assurance that her every glance would be met with adoration? Or was it something learned?

I had felt this attention upon me only once—so long ago, and so fleetingly—with Friedrich, and it has disappeared so completely I don't know if I'll ever feel it again. I do not know if I have the spark within me, as the Baroness does, to ignite passion in a man ever again. I cannot flip my hair, which barely moves with the wind, for it is as short as Friedrich's. My smile is jagged, filled with the broken teeth of an aged shark. I rarely laugh.

It may not be very modern to say this, but it is what all women want—to be adored in this way. But is behaving like the Baroness the only way? She is pretentious, demanding, condescending, and mercenary. She orders these two men around, and they leap, eager to do her bidding. I wondered whether it was fear that caused this behavior, whether she held something over them—but then I came to see it is something much more obvious and just as powerful, perhaps even more powerful. Sex.

Mallory

I wake before dawn and tune my ears to the silence. I think of home, of the ambient noise inside and around our house in Boston—the fridge and the boiler, the cars and the trains—and how familiar it all is. As with anxiety, you get used to the constant hum until you don't even know it's there.

Now, I find myself sinking into the morning's quiet, as if I could disappear into it. I let myself wonder if I've made a mistake coming here, if it's impossible to bridge the past and present in the way I hoped would allow me to move forward.

Or maybe I need to take Scott's advice, for once. *Let it go.*

Maybe that's the only way. For now.

I put on my wet suit and head to the beach, just as the sun is coming up. The beach is empty.

Standing at the shoreline, I zip up my suit. My first few steps into the water are icy, but I warm up as I swim past the gently breaking waves, watching the early light glimmer on the water as the sun breaches the hills. Below me, fish and turtles swim past. No penguins and, fortunately, no rays. As I swim back to shore, the sun is a giant, blinding yolk rising above the hills.

I sit down in the coarse black sand. A few minutes later, a sea lion ambles up the shoreline. He comes within about ten feet, pausing to study me. I don't move—here, there's no need to worry, even though he outweighs me by a hundred pounds, though his teeth could rip through my wet suit with more efficiency than a sharpened kitchen knife. He moves a few more feet—parallel, neither closer nor away—then flops down on the sand, shutting his eyes.

I hear a sound—or maybe it's more of a feeling, the sensation of something moving toward me—and turn, expecting another sea lion. It's Diego, wearing swim trunks and nothing else.

"I didn't mean to scare you," he says.

"You didn't."

"Surprise you, I mean. You look surprised."

"I thought I was the only one up so early."

He laughs. "It's not early. It's almost seven."

"Really?" I had no idea I'd been out here so long. I turn toward the casitas but can't see whether anyone is waiting. "I should get going," I say, but I don't get up.

As if he understands, he says, "This is my favorite time of day. Quiet, no people."

"Really? It's that much fun working with Callie?"

He laughs again. "She's all right. It's a good job, but . . . she's here for one assignment, and always looking for the next thing. She wants to go to Fernandina now. To search for the formerly extinct tortoise."

"Hasn't that discovery been well covered by now?"

"She thinks she can do better. She doesn't even know we can't go there without permits."

"I can see why you try to find a bit of quiet. She's keeping you busy."

Diego sits next to me in the sand. "It's good money, and I'm applying for PhD programs at this moment."

"In what?"

"Conservation," he says. "The Darwin Foundation likes PhDs—that's my dream job."

He leans back on his elbows. "I grew up watching cats hanging out on the pier next to sea lions. It seemed natural to me; I didn't know any better. When I got older, I learned there is nothing natural about it at all. We didn't have a veterinarian on Santa Cruz until 2010—all we had was the center for invasive species."

"Ah, right," I say. "Because here, pets are invasive species."

"It's weird, no?" he says. "Most people don't see their pets that way. I used to want to be a vet—but now I feel like I need to study how we can all survive together."

I tell him about the cat we'd seen near the penguin nests. "Gavin asked me to call the park service. They euthanize cats, don't they?"

He nods.

"It doesn't seem fair. To choose one species over another."

"We don't have room for both."

It feels as though the planet no longer has room for in-between, for compromise. But I don't want to think about the cat right now, so I ask Diego, "What are you focusing on for your PhD?"

"I'm thinking of the tortoises. So many species fascinate me, I haven't decided, but I'm drawn to them."

"Why, exactly?"

"Many things," he says. "That they live so long we don't even know what their lifespan is. All that wisdom in their wrinkled faces. They're so much smarter than humans. They've got their priorities right."

"What do you mean?"

"They sleep twelve hours a day. They mate for four or five hours at a time. They're vegetarians." He grins. "Maybe one of those is the secret to their longevity."

I laugh. "If you can figure that out, your future's looking brighter by the minute."

"We'll see. There's so much we still don't know."

"That's how I feel about the penguins. I worry they may be gone before we can learn everything."

"I have that same feeling," he says, nodding. "That *Torschlusspanik* is setting in."

I look at him. "What did you say?"

"Sorry," he says. "It's sort of an untranslatable word. It's a type of panic, having the feeling that time is running—"

"No, I mean, the word itself," I interrupt. "It wasn't Spanish."

"German," he says. "*Torschlusspanik*, literally translated, means 'gate shut panic'—you know, the fear of the doors closing on you. On your opportunities."

"You speak German."

"*Ja,*" he says with a smile. "My grandmother came to the Galápagos from Germany. She was married to a German at the time, but he died. She married again, an Ecuadorian. They had four children, including my father. I studied German and English in secondary school on the mainland, and after my grandmother died I spent a couple summers working in the kitchen at the Wittmer place"—he nods toward the hotel beyond the beach—"practicing my German and learning to cook German food." He laughs. "I don't even eat meat, but I can make a five-star schnitzel."

I laugh, too. "So, your German is limited to schoolyard lingo and cooking terminology?"

"No, I got my bachelor's degree at the University of Munich." He shrugs. "But I don't use it much anymore, so it's fading."

I lean toward him. "If I gave you something written in German, do you think you could tell me what it's about?"

He gives me a curious look. "What is it?"

"I'm not sure. That's why I'm asking."

He hesitates for so long that I'm about to tell him *Never mind* when he says, "Okay."

"Thanks. I won't be too much of a bother, I promise." The warming sun reminds me of the time. "I'd better go." I stand up, but then, before walking away, I think of his hesitation and say, "Maybe don't tell Callie."

"Okay." He doesn't seem fazed by the request.

"Great. I'll find you later?"

"Sure. Good luck with the nests today."

The other casitas are still quiet, so I shower off the salt water and prop open my door as I compose an email to the park service, with details about the cat and the location.

But just as I'm about to hit send, I pause, my finger hovering above the keyboard. I realize my hand is shaking, and I hit save instead.

Dore

It's nearly impossible to believe we have been on Floreana for three years. Perhaps we survive simply because there is no other option. While we now have good shelter and an abundant food supply, it is my heart, my soul, that I fear will not survive.

Our island has changed so much—all because of one woman, whose ego is larger than the entire Galápagos archipelago.

The Baroness is not, apparently, content to live a quiet life on Floreana like the rest of us. She has launched a public-relations campaign on a scale we could not have imagined. Thanks to the numerous letters and articles she has sent abroad, we are now receiving more visitors than ever, whose interest is solely in meeting her. Friedrich and I and the Wittmers are invited onto their yachts as an afterthought, if at all.

One day, Friedrich and I met a group of American visitors at the shore, and as Friedrich was talking with the captain about our mail, a woman asked me, breathlessly, "When do we get to meet the Empress?"

"The Empress?" I was confused and about to ask if she meant "the Baroness" when the woman pulled out several newspaper clippings whose headlines included such phrases as *Empress of Floreana*, *Queen of the Galápagos*, *Empress of the Islands*.

"We can't wait to meet her." The woman babbled with excitement, and I asked to see the papers, as casually as I could, and managed to skim a few headlines and paragraphs before she took them back. Clearly the Baroness herself was responsible for these stories. They told tales of all of us settlers being under her command—I even glimpsed a drawing of two men resembling Friedrich and Heinz—in chains, like prisoners! At least one article was about the Baroness opening a grand hotel here on Floreana, to be called the "Hacienda Paradiso," in part to showcase the exotic animals she has captured to create her own zoo.

Of course, I myself write fiction when sending letters home, but it is only to appease my family, not to be sensational. These news stories filled me with a terrible dread. Obviously the Baroness is not in charge of any of us, as much as she likes to believe it—but I do worry about her other ideas. She has been receiving a great amount of building materials, and because we've all begun to avoid her as much as possible, there's no way of knowing whether she is building a hotel or caging the island's creatures or both.

The visitors that day headed straight for the Baroness's homestead, and Friedrich and I were left on the beach. I told him about the newspapers, and he frowned, muttering something about talking to Heinz before the Baroness got too out of hand. I knew he felt slighted that she was getting more international press than he was.

But what could we do? We could not force her to leave, though Friedrich vowed to contact the authorities on the mainland to try to do just that.

The next morning when I woke, I thought of home, of what my life might be like had I stayed in Berlin. The day before, we'd received news from Germany—my husband and Friedrich's wife are living together in my former home, fulfilling for each other that which Friedrich and I could not give them. My husband now has a competent hausfrau, and Friedrich's wife has a staid provider.

Though now there is no hope of going back, I can't help but wonder whether it would have been better to stay miserable in Berlin than to be miserable here. Would I have been happier back home, believing I could one day have a brighter future, than to be in that future only to realize it was not so bright after all?

Despite my efforts to control them, my emotions seep through anyhow—and a part of me feels envious, not relieved. I picture Mila in our home, wearing my clothes, cooking in my kitchen, lighting my candles, eating off my plates. I picture her making love to my husband. I picture her belly round and full, bearing him a child.

Perhaps my feelings are complicated by the presence of the Baroness and her two lovers—witnessing yet another life lush with romantic abundance, as my own loneliness deepens.

I did not expect what happened as the three of them settled here—the awakening I feel in me upon seeing them all together. Underneath the loathing and anxiety, I also have an insatiable curiosity about them, particularly their sex life: Do they all engage in sex together? Do they take turns? Are the two men involved with each other as well as with the Baroness? Would she even allow such a thing, given her need to be the center of attention? I find hours of my day, vast portions of my thoughts, fixed on these questions. I lie in my bed at night, awake and alone, listening to the animals make savage love in the night, their cries reaching my ears like a ship on its way out of harbor without me on it.

It does not help that my life with Friedrich has grown ever more intolerable. Though we do share a distaste for the Baroness, everything between us remains a battle, or a chance to berate me. I fear he dislikes the Baroness far less than he admits, just as I do.

And I fear that I have created my own inexorable fate, that I have tied myself inescapably to Friedrich. Forever. Until death do we part.

Mallory

I'm lying in bed, trying to stay awake, and I check my phone again, still hoping Diego will text me. I'd given him my number earlier, in the kitchen before everyone else arrived for dinner, and now I'm wondering whether I typed it in wrong, or whether he's changed his mind. I lower my head back against the pillow and close my eyes.

I wake with a jolt when my phone buzzes. **Meet me on the beach, under the Southern Cross.** It's almost eleven.

With the porch lights still on, I can't see the sky. I tuck the two journals under my arm and slip on my sandals. At the end of the deck, I pause to let my eyes adjust to the dark and then make my way toward the beach, toward the blackness just beyond the weak, solar-powered path lights.

I bring a flashlight but don't turn it on, even when I reach the sand. The sky is clear. The stars are bright, winking and sometimes skittering across the sky, like sand fleas on the beach.

Diego is waiting on the southern end of the beach. When I reach him, I crane my head upward. "I can't actually see the Southern Cross," I say.

"You will, once your eyes adjust." His voice is like velvet in the darkness.

I hand him the books, then take a quick glance back toward the casitas. I can no longer see the lights.

"I think they're journals," I say. "As in diaries."

He uses the light on his phone to examine the writing, flipping pages slowly. "Very old journals."

"Can you tell who wrote them?"

He continues paging through one of the notebooks. "Some of the pages are dated," he says. "Look—1932, 1933. Where did you get these?"

I hesitate. "I found them."

"Here? On this island?"

I nod. "Only a few people lived here then. The Ritters. The Wittmers."

"And the Baroness." He keeps turning pages, so focused it feels as though he's forgotten I'm here.

I look upward again, searching for the Big Dipper and not finding it, then realizing it's upside down. I let my eyes trace the night, glimpsing the bluish light of a bright star, then searching for the other stars of the Southern Cross. The sky is so luminous it begins to swim before my eyes.

Diego's voice brings me back to the moment. "This is Dore's journal," he says, with an excitement in his voice I've not heard before.

"Are you sure?"

"Pretty sure. I'm only skimming, but Friedrich's name comes up more than anyone else's." He pauses. "Did you notice this?"

"What?" I lean over to see.

"Scribbled here, on the inside cover." He reads it silently, and a few long moments later, he says, "It seems like she wrote it afterward. 'This is the story no one will ever know. Perhaps, if I have hidden these pages well enough, no one will ever read these words. But I have to put them to paper. A woman cannot keep such thoughts to herself, even if there is no one she can tell. The burden of secrets is made ever so much greater by the burden of loneliness.'"

I draw in a sharp, quiet breath at hearing these words. Written almost a century ago, by someone who once walked the very beach where we're now sitting, the words sink in deep and fast—and not only because I could have written them myself.

He looks at me. "Where did you find these, exactly?"

Again I hesitate. I see something eager in his expression, but it's too late to keep the journals to myself—if I had, I still wouldn't know what they are—and so I decide to trust him. I tell him about the pirate cave, the fallen stones, the lava tube.

"So, they were really well hidden," he says.

"Which means there's something in these journals that Dore didn't want anyone to see."

"We won't know until I read them." He stretches, then stands up. "I can take them with me."

"No," I say, a bit too quickly. "I mean, thanks, but . . . I can't ask that of you. I'd love to meet again, though. When you have time."

"Sure."

I stand up and fold my hands over the books, their leather surfaces sticky in the humid air. "Thank you. I appreciate this."

I can't gauge his expression, and I lift my eyes skyward again. "I found part of the Southern Cross," I say, pointing.

He laughs. "No, that's Alpha Centauri." He puts his hand over mine and guides it toward the right. "There," he says. "That's Alpha Crucis. And"—he continues, leading my hand with his own—"there's Beta, Gamma, and Delta. The Cross."

His dark eyes reflect a soft glow from the night sky, and I slowly untangle my fingers from among his. "It's beautiful."

"It is," he agrees.

I can't help but wonder what his showing me the stars has to do with the journals, with what I may have discovered. I hold the books close to my chest as we return to the casitas.

Dore

I have almost given up keeping track of time. If it weren't for this diary, the only thing affording me a few moments to be my true self, I'd hardly care what year it is.

We are doing our best to avoid the Baroness, but she makes it impossible. While Friedo has always drawn visitors, the Baroness's incredible stories bring even more nosy people to Floreana, and she has posted a sign at Post Office Bay inviting them all to visit her grand abode. Many of them walk right past Friedo—we are old news, it seems—and straight to the Hacienda.

Friedrich and I have not visited the Baroness since she moved from her landing place near the Wittmers to her new homestead, about halfway between the Wittmers' home and Friedo. I have no intention of calling on her and her two lovers and will not admit to anyone my curiosity. Not only about what they are building but how they are living. Do they share a room, a bed—or do they sleep separately, as Friedrich and I do? How much of their day is devoted to work and how much to pleasure? What do they eat, wear, talk about?

We received a bit of information from a small group of travelers who stopped at Friedo on their way back to Post Office Bay, after they'd visited the Baroness. Upon arriving there, they said, they'd been greeted by two men—Rudolf Lorenz and Robert Philippson—and offered sugarcane-pineapple juice. Then they were escorted to a large sitting room in which the Baroness lay stretched out on a divan, in her riding costume, her whip at her side.

"It was a most bizarre sight," said one of the women, who clung to her husband's arm as though the visit had frightened her.

"She talked endlessly about her aspirations and her hotel," the husband told us, "though the work doesn't appear to be progressing much. It looks as though they've added rooms to their house, but there are still piles of building materials lying about."

"Then she commanded the two men to serve us," his wife broke in, "and I honestly kept waiting for the crack of that whip!"

They'd endured a quick snack of cured meats—the woman shuddered when recounting the taste, and the greasy plate on which the food was served—and they left as soon as they could. When they arrived at Friedo, we invited them to sit on our newly renovated and expanded covered porch, and I felt a certain smug satisfaction as they looked around with admiration. If nothing else, our home is surely more lovely than that of the Baroness.

Over the past year, Friedrich had worked hard to renovate our house, using more curving acacia wood, along with large sheets of corrugated iron we'd bought from a passing vessel. With supplies he bought from the captains of various ships, Friedrich set up a piping system from our spring to create an outdoor shower. We must use it sparingly, but on those nights that I am able to bathe, my entire being is soothed by the fresh, cool water that pours over me. Friedrich next extended the piping system to bring the spring water directly to our new kitchen, which feels expansive compared to the former one. The bedroom now has a solid floor, allowing for a bed instead of hammocks—though again Friedrich has made us two beds instead of one.

My only qualm is the toll this work took on my sweet donkey; Friedrich insisted on using Viktor for hauling supplies from shore. I was powerless to stop him; despite all my protests, he did what he wanted. I know Viktor would have run away and never returned had Friedrich not installed him in his pen and tied him there with a rope. When at last he had no need for Viktor, Friedrich left the gate open, and my darling pet disappeared.

I was bereft, and I despaired that he would ever return. And then, a few weeks ago, I saw him at a distance—with another donkey and a foal. He had a family! I think he had wandered as close as he safely could to Friedo to show me he was well and happy. Then he was gone again.

Of course I did not mention such things to our guests as I served them fresh fruit and listened to their stories and questions about the Baroness. Friedrich assured them that the Baroness was not typical of the settlers on Floreana.

"We expect her to grow bored and move on," he said. "Not everyone can endure the challenges of life here. Even someone with servants at her beck and call."

Yet I knew in my heart it would take much more for the Baroness to leave.

At the same time, I recently felt that perhaps her allure was fading—not two weeks later, visitors stopped to see us at Friedo without continuing on to the Hacienda. Somehow the Baroness learned of this, and the next day she showed up at our gate—on her donkey, as usual, with Rudolf Lorenz in tow—with her face and posture as cold as stone.

She wore a dark scarf over her hair, with only the blond ends showing, and as usual she wore makeup and the same bright-red lipstick. Her lips were sealed so tight I thought for a moment they'd been stuck together, until she spoke.

"Rudy, remove my glasses," she commanded, and he rushed to her side to remove the dark glasses from her face, apparently so that Friedrich and I could receive the full force of her glare.

"Why are you keeping people from seeing me at the Hacienda?" she demanded of Friedrich. As usual, she acted as though I were not even there.

Friedrich scoffed. "We've done nothing of the sort."

"It is not our fault visitors prefer our company to yours." The words escaped my lips before I could stop them.

A long and uneasy silence followed. Then, gazing directly at me under the heavy lids of her eyes, the Baroness said in a steely tone, "Rudy, darling, there is a pebble in my sandal." She raised her left foot from the donkey's side.

Immediately Mr. Lorenz removed her sandal and shook it. I saw no pebble fly out, but he massaged her foot and ever so gently slipped it back into the sandal. The Baroness kept her eyes on me the entire time, a small smirk on her face. As if she were reminding me that she still has what is important. That despite it all, I am the one who is lacking.

"Come, Rudy, we are done here." She leaned down, and her servant obediently placed her sunglasses back on her face. Without another word, she turned her donkey around, with Mr. Lorenz following next to them. I saw him cast a quick glance backward before they disappeared down the trail.

Friedrich watched them leave and then he, too, disappeared—returning moments later with a machete.

I let out a gasp. "What are you doing?"

He did not answer, and I followed him out to the path—the main trail from Post Office Bay that brought visitors to Friedo and, beyond, to the Hacienda and the Wittmer homestead. Yet instead of following the Baroness and Rudy, Friedrich took a few strides toward the bay and then began hacking away at the vegetation near where the trail curved toward Friedo.

"Friedrich!"

He wore the same bone-chilling expression as the Baroness, and a few minutes later I realized what he was doing. He was creating a new trail, a path that visitors could take to the Hacienda without passing our gate at Friedo.

I turned away and left him to his task. It's for the best, I know, to have as little contact with the Baroness as possible, and perhaps even to avoid those who seek her company.

Yet despite how much I despise the Baroness, I still find myself oddly lured, intrigued by her influence, something which I have never felt even with Friedrich. Despite my wariness about her, I want to learn from the

Baroness more than I'd ever wanted to learn from Friedrich. I think of Rudolf Lorenz and the way he responded to her—in a way Friedrich has never responded to me. The power she wields over everyone she meets is somewhat intoxicating, even as she makes our lives hellish.

I am beginning to hear a constant conversation within my own mind, one in which I ask questions that go unanswered, about this life and my role in it. About being loved and worthy of love. About how much of a woman can exist without the mirror-eyes of love looking back into her own.

Mallory

I wake feeling as though I'm drowning. As consciousness returns, I remember my dream—sitting on the black sand of the beach as waves came in, only they were not made of water but of paper, page after page in an endless tide.

It's the first time since I've arrived that I've dreamed of something other than home. Of Emily. Of Scott's small, bachelor-size apartment downtown, and our three-bedroom house standing empty.

I sit up, reaching under the bed to pick up the notebooks. If these are what Diego thinks they are—Dore Strauch's private journals—it is an incredible discovery. Dore's published book is more mystery than memoir—it doesn't reveal what really happened among the settlers, and it's filled with contradictions about her own life on Floreana that have always made me wonder how she really felt, what things were really like here. Her memoir portrayed Friedrich as the love of her life, but there were also snippets of true misery with him. And her memoir differed from Margret Wittmer's, revealing completely different accounts of what happened to the Baroness, as well as Friedrich. That these journals were so well hidden raises the question of whether this could be Dore's real story—not what she wrote up in her published memoir but the truth.

I turn carefully through the pages, trying to decipher some of the words. A part of me wants to hand them over to Diego right away so he can make faster work of the translation—but I also don't want to risk it. There was something odd about his reaction to the journals last night, something I can't quite put my finger on—his hesitation when I asked him to have a look, almost as if he were trying to resist some sort of temptation. Or maybe it was his offer to take them with him that triggered my instinct to keep them close.

I realize I don't know Diego well enough to speculate about his motivation—and at the same time, I like that we are new to each other. I like the freedom of being simply a researcher, not an incipient divorcée, a bad mother, a repository of regrets.

But as much as I enjoy the comfort of being unknown, this also means that Diego could, too. That he could have as many secrets as I do. And perhaps this is why I feel the need to be careful.

I hear Gavin's door open and the sound of him walking away, toward the kitchen. I close the journal and stow them both in my backpack, zipping them in before opening the door. I sit in one of the chairs outside our casitas.

Gavin returns with a thermos of coffee. He sits and hands it to me.

"What did they say about the cat?" Gavin asks.

"I wrote an email"—this part is true, at least—"but I haven't heard back."

He looks at me as if he knows I'm lying. "We need to prioritize this," he says. "Call them. Today."

I don't answer, and as I fumble with the lid of the thermos I can feel him watching me.

"Our work is for nothing if that cat gets to the nests," he says.

"I know. I know. I'll take care of it." I take a drink of coffee, and it burns my throat.

∼

The sun is almost directly overhead when the clouds move in low. We've finished our third nest this morning, and before we head back to the landing site, I take a detour to check on the penguin with the egg, gesturing to Hannah to follow.

She's surprisingly excited about the egg; until recently, she's seemed bored with nest building, and when we're not here, she's glued to her laptop—social media and email and Skype, no doubt—uninterested in Gavin's data or in completing notes from the field. Part of me wants to convert her to this life, the way Gavin had converted me. I still grapple with the question of which life, if I could do it all over again, I would have chosen, and it's probably because, even now, I want them both.

Hannah and I find both penguins at the nest, the male and the female, standing next to each other. "See how fat the male is?" I say to Hannah, pointing to his belly. "He's been out feeding, so he's stuffed and ready to incubate the egg for a while so she can go out to forage."

But for now, they are together, and we step back to watch the male bring new twigs over to the nest, using his beak to nudge them toward the egg. It occurs to me for the first time that penguins are instinctively good parents; they seem to know everything we humans have to try so hard to learn, usually the hard way. By making mistakes.

Both birds have a lot of pink around their bills and eyes, the shedding of feathers to lose heat. The female reaches out and grooms the plumage along her mate's back.

∼

That night, I sit on the beach, just past eleven, the black sand still holding the heat of the day, and slap at sand fleas as I wait for Diego. I'd sent him a text earlier, during our break for lunch—Same time tonight?—and just before leaving again, his reply came: Same time, same place.

I stopped in the kitchen looking for something to drink. After taking two water bottles from the fridge, I also picked up a liter-size bottle of Ecuador's popular Pilsener beer. It was probably Gavin's, which meant I'd have to replace it, but I wanted to offer something to Diego for his help.

The clouds of afternoon have gone, clearing the sky and revealing its glittering light. When I hear the flip-flop of Diego's plastic sandals on the sand, I stand up and give him the beer first, then move over on the towel I'd spread out on the sand and hand him the journals. "Thanks again for doing this."

"Let's see how much I can actually translate," he says. "Like I said, it's been a while."

He sits next to me on the towel, and he turns on the light on his phone. He opens one of the journals, reading the words to himself before translating them aloud. "'I have wondered, since we arrived in this rugged and unforgiving place, what I am doing here.'"

Diego pauses.

"What is it?"

"Just a word I'm trying to translate," he says. "*Weltschmerz.* It is something like how you feel when you compare what you dreamed about to real life. It's like disappointment."

"This is what Dore felt, you mean?"

He nods. "You could say it's when reality doesn't meet your expectations."

I try to sound it out myself. *"Weltschmerz."* I've never heard the word, but I'm thinking: Scott would know this. And, after nearly a decade of being married to me, he would know not only the word but the feeling.

I'm also thinking: There should be a word for this in English, too. There should be a word for this in every language.

Diego takes a drink of the beer and continues reading, to himself at first, and then translating aloud for me. He speaks slowly, with long pauses between sentences, and as he describes Dore's first days and weeks on the island, I close my eyes, remembering the long-forgotten pleasure of being read to. Back when Scott and I took turns reading to Emily, she'd sit between us, and more than once, if Scott was reading, I'd fall asleep along with Emily.

Diego reads only a few more sentences before he stops again. "Sorry," he says. "There are a lot of words that are difficult to translate into English," he says. "Like this one. *Fuchsteufelswild*. It's like wild, animal rage."

I sip from the beer bottle, feeling the century between me and Dore evaporate, as though an invisible thread is weaving through time, connecting me to her lost and restless soul.

Diego continues, reading about a moment of Dore's anger toward Friedrich. My hands twitch with a sudden chill in the warm night air.

Diego stops reading, and I can feel his eyes on me in the dark. "What is it?"

"I was just . . . thinking."

"About what?"

"I don't know." I turn toward him. Right now, there is something about the dark, about us not knowing each other, that frees me, that makes me want to talk instead of hide. "Have you ever felt that way? A rage like that?"

His head nods so automatically I'm taken aback. "Really? When?"

"A couple of years ago," he says. "I was out with my uncle on his boat, and in the distance we saw another boat. We assumed it was tourists, since no fishing is allowed where we were, but when he looked through his binoculars, he could see what they were doing. Finning sharks." He looks at me. "Have you ever seen what they do?"

I shake my head.

"They haul the shark on board and slice off the dorsal fin," he says. "Then they toss the shark back into the water. It can't swim anymore, so it sinks to the bottom of the ocean and dies. Horrible suffering—just for a bowl of soup."

I look toward the ocean as I pass Diego the beer bottle. "What did you do?"

"They could see us coming, so by the time we got to them, all the evidence was hidden away. They denied everything. The word *Fuchsteufelswild* didn't enter my mind, but that's exactly what I felt—I wanted to board the ship, to prove what they did. My uncle grabbed his radio, and that's when they pulled their guns on us." He takes a long drink of beer. "We had to turn around and get out of there."

"They never got caught?"

"We reported them when we got back to Puerto Ayora," he says, "but these poachers are impossible to catch. They're everywhere, in small boats so they can sneak around, move quickly. Then they bring their haul to the mother ships. They keep their AIS off so no one can track them. The navy and the park service just don't have the resources to keep up with them. And to top it off, they leave their nets in the ocean, where so many sea animals get caught up in them and die. 'Ghost nets,' they call them." Diego hands the bottle back to me. "What about you? Have you felt *Fuchsteufelswild*?"

I grip the bottle in hands that feel unexpectedly clammy. "I never knew there was a word for it."

He's quiet, but he seems to want me to continue—the way he leans back, propped up on his elbow, waiting as if he has all the time in the world. I wonder how I can choose just one moment of helpless anger to share with him—one moment of so many.

"I have this makeshift art studio in my garage," I say finally. "It was a gift from my husband—nice on one hand, but it was also his way of telling me not to be such a helicopter mom with our daughter and her food allergy. He wanted to give me something else to focus on. He thought I was too obsessive a parent."

Scott had bought me a series of local classes in stained glass and then hired a contractor to build a workbench, a sink, storage shelves, cabinets. He'd remembered how much I'd loved visiting Sainte-Chapelle in Paris, years earlier; I'd been pregnant with Emily and had joined him on a business trip, knowing it would be harder for me to travel once she arrived.

The stained-glass windows of the chapel suffused the entire hall and the two of us with rosy light. *You look gorgeous,* he said. *You're glowing.* I laughed and said, *It's just the hormones.* But he'd looked at me with something like awe, and we ended up spending hours within the chapel's intricate bones, its perfectly controlled light.

I'd never been particularly artistic, but years later, once Emily was in school all day, the studio gave me a respite from the constant worry—and something about it was exactly what I needed, as if the medium itself was tasking me to embrace the shifts, the unknowns, the what-ifs, the way stained glass interrupts and changes the properties of light.

"My daughter used to join me sometimes," I continue. "She'd paint or draw while I cut the glass. After polishing and foiling the edges, I let her hold the pieces—she liked the way they sounded, rattling like poker chips."

I nudge the beer bottle into the sand. "Anyway, one day Emily was at a friend's house, and she ate something with peanuts. I had talked to the family a hundred times, sent Emily over there with her own food—still, something happened, and she had a reaction."

I pause, remembering how I'd arrived home later that night, after hours in the emergency room. Emily was safe, the crisis over, but what had happened was the thing I constantly feared—that no matter what I did, it wouldn't be enough. Emily had fallen asleep, but I couldn't leave her room. *You don't have to watch her sleep, Mallory,* Scott said. *She's okay.* I knew he meant to be reassuring, but it sounded cold. I thought, in that moment, of Gavin—and I resented what I saw as a similar detachment in Scott, whom I'd chosen because he was the opposite, and suddenly I worried I had turned him into someone different. When he nagged me to leave her alone, telling me it was ghoulish to stand over her bedside, I went out to the studio to cut some glass.

It was late spring, the night cool and breezy, a few leaves rustling under my feet and skittering in the bright blue light of my phone. The garage door yawned open in front of me, and I looked at the workbench, layers of glass piled atop one another, the lighter shades together creating new, darker colors.

The studio had been my refuge since Emily's first bad reaction, the first time I knew we'd have to be vigilant for the rest of our lives. The first time I realized I couldn't control everything—in fact, anything. And working with stained glass was surprisingly satisfying—the minor violence necessary to create something provided an outlet for much of my angst.

"I went into the studio that night and picked up a plate of clear glass," I say to Diego, then pause again. "I lifted it up and let it drop. The sound was so gratifying, I did it again, and again, until I broke every piece of glass I had."

I feel my throat close up against the details: reaching down for a shard, bumping into the hanging light over my head as I hurled the glass. Watching the gem tones, the deep greens and bright blues and solid blacks, the beveled jewel, the glue chip, all of it becoming a mosaic of glass on the cement floor—a chipped, feral Sainte-Chapelle laid out before me, coruscating like an ocean in the swaying light.

Diego is looking at me in a way I don't expect: serene, unblinking. I feel the tightness in my throat loosen up. His silent calm makes me feel as though I can tell him anything, and the thought is both freeing and terrifying. I compromise and tell him something safe.

"I can't seem to make myself contact the park service," I say. "I know it's the right thing to do. I just can't."

"You'd rather see this cat eat the penguin babies you're working so hard for?"

"Of course not."

"Then it needs to be trapped."

If only death weren't necessary to preserve life.

Then I have a thought. "What if *we* set the trap? Maybe you know of someone who could adopt? Someone back home?"

"Are you joking? You know it is illegal to take animals from island to island."

"Maybe someone here, then. Maybe the owners of our lodge. Or a family in town."

"I don't know."

"You think I should call the park. Even though it's a death sentence."

"It's more humane than letting it fend for itself," Diego says. "It has to be suffering in this heat, with no water, hardly any food."

I'd only gotten a glimpse of the cat, but I'd noticed the thickness of the fur around his face, a wide, jowly look that meant he was unneutered—not that there'd been much doubt about that. But despite his fluffy face, he had also looked thin, and his fur was scraggly and unkempt. Diego is right—the cat has to work so hard just to stay alive, hungry and desperately thirsty, hunting on paws that burn and bleed from the sharp, hot lava.

And he is living off an endangered species, the very birds I'm trying to protect.

"And it will just breed more cats," Diego adds. "More predators."

"There's no veterinary care on this island at all?"

"The vet on Santa Cruz did a clinic here a few years ago, but that's it."

"I hate having to choose," I say.

We get up and begin walking back toward the casitas. When we see the dim, flickering lights of the lodge ahead, I remember the night with Gavin on the South Island—how he'd led me out to the glowworms, his face alive in their light, a reminder of what nature can do when given the chance. *That's why we're trying to make it right again.*

Dore

Friedrich's hunting continues to torment me. He claims the inferiority of animals as justification for using them for labor and killing them for food—but I wonder if it is the other way around. I am beginning to believe the land and the animals are superior to us—and in my bleakest moments I fear we shall destroy Floreana.

When we first landed here, Friedrich pointed out that we'd be living in the shadow of a volcano—and, sure enough, when I listen I can hear the island breathing. If we humans do not destroy this island, I fear Floreana will one day reject us all, avenge all our violence. That we are at its mercy in more ways than we know.

Though Friedrich keeps hunting, now he does so only when others come to the island for the wild cattle. I find it cowardly that he will not hunt on his own, man versus beast, giving the cows a fighting chance—but he ventures out only in the company of other men, guns in arms. Lately their work is made easier with the drought; the animals have less to eat, little to drink, and they are weak enough to be easy prey.

I had a glimpse of hope one strange morning when I thought Friedrich's hunting might be stayed—if not forever, at least for a time—thanks to the Baroness, of all people. She and her companions are well armed, and she has taken Heinz's place as the most avid hunter on the island.

I'd gone along with Friedrich to Post Office Bay, with the hope of picking up our mail—I did so whenever possible, since I could not trust the Baroness or her entourage—and Friedrich and I were both shocked to find her there, holding a group of Ecuadorian hunters at gunpoint, refusing to let them past the beach. Rudolf Lorenz and Robert Philippson were close behind her, with rifles in their hands—but it was clear that it was the Baroness who commanded the show.

She spoke to them in Spanish, a bit of which Friedrich and I had picked up over the years, and I understood enough to know that she was claiming the island as her own, telling them that if they wanted to hunt "her" animals, they needed her permission—which, clearly, she was not about to give them.

In the group of seven men, most of them looked aghast and stood unmoving. Yet two of them laughed out loud and, ignoring the Baroness and her revolver, began to walk up the beach, toward the pampas where they did their hunting.

A warning shot pierced the air, and the two men froze, standing as still as the rest. The Baroness began to shriek at them, flailing her arms around, the revolver in her hand spinning dangerously in the air. I struggled to comprehend what she was saying, her words now a frenzied mix of Spanish, German, and French.

As I watched in horror, I realized that, for once, the Baroness wore no makeup, and perhaps it was this, as well as her actions—the raving that contorted her face, that exposed the yellow of her protruding teeth—that made her seem suddenly so much older. And yet, though I saw she could be ten, even twenty years older than I, she was no less frightening to me. I was reminded of the drunken Irish pirate who'd ruled over his prisoners with his fearsome temper and machete—and it seemed as though his spirit was still among us, right here, in the form of a madwoman with a revolver.

One of the two men who'd moved forward waved a hand toward Friedrich and me, asking, as far as I could tell, why Friedrich is allowed to hunt when they are not. She replied that she was in charge and that anything we did was only with her permission.

Dismayed, I turned to Friedrich, whose face looked quite stern, though he neither said nor did anything to contradict her outrageous lies.

I looked at Rudolf Lorenz and Robert Philippson, who stood by, seemingly unfazed by the Baroness's outburst. I realized I was waiting for them to bring her to her senses—but they acted as though her utter madness was quite usual.

The Ecuadorian and the Baroness exchanged a few more heated words, but by then my mind was elsewhere, wondering what we were going to do. We'd known the Baroness was creating ridiculous stories for readers abroad—but would she be content merely to believe she owned us all? Or would she one day need to fulfill this fantasy of hers?

At last the Ecuadorian group returned to their boat, and the Baroness, Lorenz, and Philippson left the beach and headed up the trail toward the Hacienda.

I waited long enough to avoid them on the trail before I started my walk back to Friedo, alone. I learned later from Friedrich that the Ecuadorians had returned to shore that afternoon and found a campsite, far from the beach, so the hunt would continue as planned the next day, without the Baroness knowing.

This particular hunting trip brought me both terrible grief and new joy. I am grateful to have received a blessing—but, as usual, it came along with a tragedy. Why is this always the case on Floreana?

When Friedrich returned to Friedo from the hunt, he led by a rope a young donkey, less than a year old. My heart leaped at the sight of him but then sank almost immediately because I had never received a gift from Friedrich and knew immediately that something must be very wrong.

Indeed, as I took the rope and stroked the fur of this darling creature, Friedrich told me what happened. Out on the pampas, the animals all congregate together, and Friedrich recognized Viktor, his companion, and their foal. Friedrich aimed for a boar very close by and instead shot my Viktor, wounding him so badly he had to put him out of his misery. (The image this conjures in my mind is so horrific I cannot bear to think about it.) Viktor's lady companion fled, but the baby couldn't keep up, getting tangled in some thorny bushes, where he cried pathetically and got more stuck the more he tried to escape. The hunters took pity on him, knowing that if they left him there he would surely die, and they freed him from the bushes so Friedrich could bring him to me.

The shooting death of Viktor was devastating and unforgivable, and would have been unendurable were it not for this little foal.

I have named him Max, and he has settled in well in his father's former pen. Though it is not my wish to imprison him, I keep him enclosed when I am not walking him around on a lead; I do not want him to disappear on me as Viktor had. I weep for Max's mother, who no doubt still searches for him and feels her milk for him heavy in her body.

Friedrich does not like little Max any more than he likes my other pets, but—out of guilt, perhaps—he rarely says anything cruel about him.

I have noticed, however, several occasions on which the gate to Max's pen was not properly latched. I, who am obsessed with Max's safety and continued presence here at Friedo, would never make such a mistake. It had to be Friedrich, but when I asked him about it, he laughed and said he never goes near the stall of that "filthy animal" and implied that I was dim-witted or losing my sanity.

I wanted to fling myself at him, tear out his hair, his eyes. Yet what could I do? Instead of growing stronger, I have become more physically weak since being here. I could no more attack Friedrich than defend myself if he fought back.

Then I thought of something. I knew Friedrich was lying but had no way of proving it—not in words, anyway. And for some reason I needed to be right—for once, I needed to win one of our hopeless arguments. So one night, in the darkness after sunset, when Friedrich was finishing dinner, I made an excuse to visit Max, to give him some leftover greens. While I was there, I took out the acacia thorns I had gathered and used some sticky clay from the wet ground near the spring to place them around the latch to the gate. In the dark, or if not paying close attention, anyone who tried to unlatch the gate to let Max out would be stabbed in the hand.

It was my only chance at revenge.

In the following days Friedrich said nothing to me, though I noticed a deep red gash in one of his hands, along with a few smaller scratches. As I watched him work around Friedo, I could tell he was favoring his noninjured hand. And never again was Max's enclosure left open.

Finally I felt I had won, but the feeling was short-lived. I knew that—as it would be with the Baroness—this was but one skirmish in an endless war.

Mallory

The night is clear and cool, and I cover up with a loose long-sleeved top to avoid putting on more bug spray. Before heading to the beach I go to the kitchen to pick up one of the bottles of Pilsener I'd bought to replenish Gavin's supply. I turn away from the fridge to find Gavin there, leaning on the breakfast bar.

"So you're the beer thief."

His tone is playful, and I force a smile as I hold up the bottle. "This one's new, and your replacement beers are in the fridge. Along with a couple extras."

He takes two glasses from the cupboard and puts them on the counter, then reaches for the bottle. He opens it and begins to fill the glasses.

I put a hand near the closest glass. "Just a little for me."

He looks at me. "Really? Then where were you headed with that bottle?"

I hesitate. Diego must be at the beach by now, waiting for me, but Gavin has half filled my glass and is watching me.

"My eyes are bigger than my liver, I guess," I say. "I just wanted a little something before bed."

He hands me the glass. "Having trouble sleeping?"

"A little." It's a good excuse for my weariness, my hooded eyes.

"Is it different from what you expected?" Gavin says, taking the bottle and the glass and sitting in the dining area.

I follow but don't sit down. Before finding the journals, this is what I'd been waiting for—a chance to sit down with Gavin, talk things through. And if Diego weren't waiting, perhaps I would.

I know that Diego and the journals are just an excuse, just another distraction. But distractions are easier.

"It's late," I say. "I should go."

He nods and stands. He tops off his glass once more, then hands me the half-empty bottle. We part ways at the casitas, where I wait for him to close his door before I turn toward the beach. I hesitate for a moment, feeling guilty, then walk away.

On the beach, a streak of light from the moon shimmers on the water, and in the near-dark I hear the high-pitched bark of a sea lion pup begging to be fed. When my eyes adjust, I walk to where Diego is sitting, hand him the beer and the journals, and sit next to him on the sand.

He smiles at the weight of the bottle. "You started without me."

"It's been that kind of day."

I watch him take a long drink, then pick up one of the journals and begin reading. "Hmm," I murmur absently, at the mention of Dore's cat.

He looks up. "What is it?"

"Oh, nothing," I say. "Johanna was my grandmother's name. I'd totally forgotten until now."

"She was German?"

I nod. "She died before I was born, so I don't know much about her. My mother says she was born in Germany but came to the States during the war. She was just a child, an orphan, apparently, and had no family until she married my grandfather."

"I thought you looked like you have German heritage. Despite your Irish name."

I laugh. "I'm definitely a mix. My mother always told me, 'You look German, but you act Irish.'"

I'm startled by a voice ringing out in the relative quiet, coming from the direction of the casitas. The voice—shrill, calliopean—grows louder and more insistent.

"Diego! Are you out there? Diego!" It's Callie.

Diego holds a finger to his lips and shoves the journals under the towel. Then he turns and waits, looking in the direction of Callie's voice.

Callie stops in front of us and looks from me to Diego. "What are you two up to?"

"Just having a beer," Diego says.

Callie notices that there's only one bottle between us. "Well," she says. "I guess I should've brought my own if I want to join the party."

She's standing close to Diego—and the journals. Diego doesn't move a muscle, his body so immobile that he looks like a street mime. Sitting close to him, I feel the tension in his body and wonder if Callie can sense it as well.

After a long few moments, she sighs and says, "Fine. I guess I'll get out of your way, then."

Neither of us tries to dissuade her, and after a pause, Callie turns and begins to make her way back toward the casitas, calling out over her shoulder, "Remember, early morning, Diego!"

He doesn't answer. Once Callie is out of sight in the dark, he takes another drink from the bottle and picks up the journal again.

But I'm still making sure Callie is gone. "Did you tell her about the journals?"

He shakes his head.

"So, she's just out here looking for you for no reason?"

He laughs. "It's not the first time. It has nothing to do with the journals."

"Maybe you can skip ahead a bit," I suggest. I'm not sure whether to believe him, but Callie's interruption reminds me that our time to read may be limited or derailed at any moment.

And it's more than that. I wouldn't say this to Diego, but something about Callie evokes the Baroness, who, from what I remember, was always interfering in the other settlers' lives. Always looking for her next conquest, sexual or otherwise. Always finding ways to elevate herself at the expense of others.

Diego looks at the journal, open to the page where he'd left off the night before. "How far ahead?"

"It doesn't matter. I'm just curious."

Dore's and Margret's published memoirs already feel different from what's in the weathered pages in Diego's hands, and I'm becoming more hopeful that there is something historically significant in these journals. Something that could be life-changing, career-changing. Something that could free me from my wish to return to the past and, instead, look toward an entirely different future.

As Diego continues reading, I lean over his shoulder so I can see the journals, and it's a pleasant distraction: looking at the elegant handwriting, the crinkled pages. Eventually, I lie back and focus on the sound of his voice drifting toward me in the dark. The way he pauses between sentences, between words, makes the story more dramatic, though I think he's simply looking for the right words as he translates in his head. I find myself relaxing a little; something about these diaries allows me to shed my anxiety—this setting, the foreign language, the gap in time, the sense that something that exists in one culture has no translation in another.

Next to me, Diego stifles a yawn. I check the time on my phone; it's nearly two.

"What time is it?" he asks.

"Late." I sit up again and look past Diego toward the water. "I think I'll go for a swim."

He, too, looks out over the black water. "Now?"

"Why not?"

"I'll come with you."

I want to assure him I don't need protection, but then I realize I wouldn't mind his company. The moon is tucked behind a cloud, and it's dark enough that I don't feel self-conscious as I take off my shirt and step out of my shorts. I can see only the silhouette of Diego's body as he takes off his own shirt and kicks off his flip-flops. We walk slowly to the water's edge, avoiding sharp rocks and sleeping sea lions.

Without the sun's heat, the water is unexpectedly icy; I've never been swimming here at night. Diego plunges straight in, no hesitation. I follow haltingly, the cold taking my breath away.

I hear him laughing. "And you are from Boston?" he says.

"I'm a native Californian," I say. "I've always thought the Pacific is too cold." I swim closer to him, trying to breathe normally. "Thanks for doing this. The translating."

He doesn't respond, and I strain to see his face in the dark.

"There's something I need to tell you," he says.

"What is it?"

"Callie is not here to get footage of the local flora and fauna," he says. "She's hoping to solve the murder. Like Hannah said."

A current flows toward the shore, its wave splashing my face in a smack. I cough out water as I take in what Diego has just told me, the revelation rippling through my nerves. So perhaps she is not so different from the Baroness after all—but what does this mean about Diego, about sharing these journals with him? I'm about to ask why he didn't tell me earlier, but instead I say, "Why'd she lie about it?"

"She doesn't want to talk about it until she does more research. That's what she told me."

I can't see him clearly in the darkness. "And you haven't told her what I found? Honestly?"

"No. I haven't," he says. "But she's looking for more records."

"Where is she looking, exactly?"

"She's talked to the folks at the Wittmer hotel," he says. "They haven't given her anything new, so now she's talking about searching Post Office Bay. And the caves."

My arms are growing stiff with cold, making it hard to tread water. I can't remember how well I concealed that loose bit of stone that had revealed the journals, and I won't have an opportunity to go back to check anytime soon.

"That's why she hired you, then," I say. "Because you speak German."

"Yes."

The clouds have shifted, revealing the moon again, and I can see Diego's face more clearly. A glint of moonlight on the water clings to his eyelashes. "How do I know I can trust you?"

His eyes meet mine, and I hold them there, wanting to see the truth, and I realize he's searching for the same thing. "Your teeth are chattering," he says. "Come on, let's go."

Dore

It can be difficult to access this journal, my true diary, for to extract it from its hiding place takes time, and then I have to write without Friedrich seeing or knowing. Right now, I am huddled on a rock, far from Friedo, writing as quickly as I can so I can hide it again and return home before he knows I have gone. As I write, I can feel the volcano's hot breath—the dry season is behind us, the air humid and windy, and I know that if I do not hurry I will soon be drenched with rain, these words washed away as if I'd never written them.

We continue to struggle living among our new neighbors, namely the Baroness, though fortunately she and her manservants live far enough from us to avoid seeing them daily. Still, life on the island requires that we welcome visiting ships, to retrieve our mail and supplies—and on these days, all of us trek to the beach for the bounty we hope to receive.

Of late, the Baroness has been the recipient of most of the visitors' offerings; she is the newest and most demanding inhabitant. From visitors who come bearing gifts for all of us, the Baroness takes her pick of shoes, clothing, and bedding; sugar, flour, and cooking oil; tools and building materials—while the rest of us end up with only the supplies we'd requested and paid for, and nothing more.

After one ship's visit in which the Baroness was lavished with goods and supplies, I stood on the beach at Post Office Bay, staring wistfully as the ship faded into the horizon, wishing I were on that deck, watching the island disappear and not the other way around, watching civilization disappear.

No one noticed me standing there on the beach. The ship had stopped here only briefly, and already Friedrich was on his way back to Friedo with our few meager provisions: seeds, oil, a few tools. The Wittmers had not been here for the ship's arrival, and the Baroness, Rudolf Lorenz, and Robert Philippson now seemed to be arguing over what to do with the remaining supplies.

I looked away from them, back to the sea. The ship had vanished.

A short while later, I noticed movement in my periphery. I glanced over, expecting a bird, and nearly jumped when I saw it was Rudolf Lorenz.

"Good morning, Mr. Lorenz," I said, straining my voice in an attempt to sound pleasant. I hoped what I felt didn't show on my face: a mix of girlish awe—for he was so very handsome—as well as disdain, for he was a willing servant of the Baroness.

"Please call me Rudy," he said, taking a step closer. "Is everything all right?"

I looked at him sharply. "Why do you ask me that?"

"I'm wondering why you didn't leave with Dr. Ritter."

"Why are you here with me and not with the Baroness?" I gestured toward the stack of supplies that she and Robert Philippson were still sorting. Her donkey stood by, the poor dear creature, waiting to be saddled with what looked like an onerous load to take back to their homestead.

"I wanted to make sure you were all right."

I studied him for a moment: his thick blond hair, eyes as blue as the ocean, a thin face that makes his ears and nose look bigger. Just then, I felt a strange and overwhelming desire to fall into his arms, to be held and comforted. It had been so long since anyone asked how I was feeling.

But then I remembered why he was here: his devotion—or was it servitude?—to the Baroness. And I turned away.

My gaze fell on the Baroness and Robert, and that's when I saw Heinz and Margret Wittmer walking toward them. I watched as they began to talk, as their conversation became animated. Heinz pointed angrily at a large sack, and when he attempted to reach for it, the Baroness planted herself in front of it.

I glanced over at Rudy. He was watching, too. Without a word between us, we began walking toward the others.

"It's our rice," Margret was saying. "We paid for it weeks ago."

"I don't see your name on it," the Baroness said innocently, pretending to inspect the sack, which must've contained at least ten kilos of rice.

"You took the label off, that's why," Heinz said, fury leaching into his voice.

"I did no such thing," she said. She looked at Robert and then back at Heinz, as if she were momentarily deep in thought. "If it means so much to you," she said, "I might be willing to sell it to you. A fair price, because we're neighbors."

Margret let out a sharp, incredulous laugh. "Buy our own rice? Hardly!"

And then, the Baroness reached into her riding jodhpurs and pulled out her revolver, holding its polished wooden handle near her face, as if she were posing for a photograph. It was an oddly jolly gesture, given what she was threatening.

I heard myself gasp out loud, and both Margret and Heinz took a step backward. Rudy and Robert were unfazed. Both the metal and the dark wood gleamed in the sunlight, and no one dared to move.

"Okay, then." The Baroness shrugged and put the gun back into the pocket of her jodhpurs. "Come on then, darling," she said to Robert. "Let's go."

He began to load the provisions onto the donkey's back. The Baroness glared at Rudy. "Well? Don't just stand there. There is work to do here."

Rudy met her glare, and his slender frame seemed to straighten a bit. "We should give the Wittmers what belongs to them."

I held my breath as the Baroness stepped closer to Rudy. I thought she might pull out her gun again, hold it to his head or point it toward his chest, but instead she bent her mouth to his ear. She uttered words I could not hear, and I saw a blush creep up Rudy's cheeks. Without looking at me or the Wittmers, he silently began to help load the supplies.

My heart sank as I watched him pack all these items onto the donkey's back, and I had to look away. By the time I turned around, I realized the Wittmers had apparently bought their rice back—Heinz had the bag over his shoulder and was slouching toward their home, Margret close behind, her rigid posture and stomping footfalls revealing her anger. I have no doubt that the Wittmers were right in this matter, for they are nothing if not organized, and they ordered rice at every opportunity to supplement their diet. I don't know how they will negotiate such challenges in the future.

The Baroness and Robert had already gone ahead, leaving Rudy and the donkey behind. I watched Rudy lead the donkey from the beach, both sinking under the weight of their burdens.

Mallory

After less than four hours of sleep, dawn arrives far too soon. As I dress in a sluggish haze, I'm reminded of the complete exhaustion, of body and brain, I felt when Emily was an infant.

From the time I realized how much I wanted to have a child, I began to imagine myself pregnant, to imagine becoming a mother, but when I found out I actually *was* pregnant, I felt a sense of panic, as though it was too soon. But Scott made it all seem doable, even easy, with his big, rambling family in New England—a brother and sister, nieces and nephews—and he'd always wanted kids of his own.

Becoming pregnant with Emily was unexpected, though, and I'd wanted to be more ready. Even my body seemed to be in denial. I was sicker than I'd ever been, getting dehydrated and losing so much weight during the first trimester that I spent three days in the hospital. Afterward, I gained thirty pounds and lumbered around during an early-summer heat wave, nervously counting the days past my due date. Emily being late, as if unwilling to take her chances on the outside, only seemed like further proof that I wasn't yet ready—and later, I couldn't help but wonder what I'd done wrong, how I've never been allergic to anything but had somehow given my daughter a life-threatening allergy to a childhood staple.

Yet the day Emily arrived, after eleven hours of labor, nothing else mattered. "Well done, mama," Scott murmured in my ear. At home, I slipped easily into my new role. I especially loved the late nights when

Scott was traveling, when it was just me and Emily and I didn't worry about waking him up when I nursed her. The quiet of the house, the rustle of my thin cotton nightgown around my thighs, the comfort of the newly upholstered rocking chair, a gift from my sister. The warmth of Emily's body, a deep, enveloping heat that sank into my bones. The creak of the hardwood floor under the rocking chair's long legs. The clock's rhythmic ticking and the knowledge I had nowhere to be but right there, exactly where I belonged.

Whatever lingering qualms I'd had about the career I'd given up disappeared. While at first I missed my penguin work, I found that motherhood was hopeful in the same way—even more so. I was helping a living being grow and thrive.

I still missed Gavin at times; I missed our work together. He had made it possible to believe I could save the penguins, and this, in a way, helped usher me into my journey into motherhood. But I could never tell him such a thing; I hardly spoke to him after moving away with Scott. I'd left him abruptly and horribly, but I did it with the echo of his voice in my head: *I can't contribute to a species that is our planet's biggest problem, that is the sole reason these penguins are disappearing.*

Scott inhabited a different world—a world that didn't hinge on life or death—and it became a relief to live there.

Until Emily. Who, like Gavin, filled me with the bittersweet anxiety of knowing you aren't really in control of anything at all.

∼

From the panga, I see a flash of movement on shore. Hannah sees it, too; I feel her turn to look at me. I reach for my binoculars and feel a sick sensation in my gut when the glasses confirm what we'd seen: the cat, roaming along the tide-washed shore, all too close to the nests we are building and the nests that already exist.

"I thought the park took care of it," Hannah says.

"I guess they haven't." I glance at Darwin, who is looking for a spot to land, and hope he isn't listening.

I take another look through the binoculars—the cat has stopped hunting and is crouched in a tiny spot of shade under a prickly pear tree. He's definitely a tom, I can see now. Through the magnifying lenses, I see his bones, the sharp angles of his shoulders, his wasted hips. I lower the binoculars as the boat heaves in the waves that crash against the rocky shoreline.

On shore, we work as a trio, identifying suitable nest sites as Darwin helps us carry and place the heavier pieces of lava. My head throbs from last night's beer and the lack of sleep, and thinking about the cat is creating a new, persistent nausea in my stomach.

Hannah has been learning well, and I let her and Darwin take the lead. They enjoy working together, and I feel I'm hardly needed, except when Hannah asks the occasional penguin question and Darwin the occasional logistical one, punctuated by a joke or a wildlife pantomime.

Hours later, when we're ready to stop for lunch, I say, "I'll be right back," leaving Hannah and Darwin to cart the tools back to the panga.

Yesterday, too, I'd snuck away from them to visit the occupied nest. Kneeling down and inching forward on padded knees, hands against the searing rocks, I'd been relieved to see that past the dry brown dirt around the entrance, beyond a few twigs, the penguin's calm, protective posture told me all was well.

Now, I'm nearly at the nest when I notice Hannah behind me, close at my heels in that quick, silent leporine way of hers. I lean over to peek into the nest; the egg is still there. The male is standing between it and the small entrance. I press a hand against my forehead, against the ache.

"What would happen if the cat attacked him?" Hannah asks.

"That's not very likely. The cat would go after the chick, worst case. The egg itself has a thick shell, so there's no real worry until the chick is born."

Hannah shakes her head. "You'd think the park would be all over this."

I say nothing as I turn to walk back to the landing. After only a few steps I trip over a loose lava rock and barely catch myself. I look down at the sharp ground at my feet and pause to regain my balance. A fall on this terrain, even a stumble, means cuts and bruises at best, infections and stitches at worst.

How soon I've forgotten how precarious every moment can be, how quickly things can change.

"You okay?" Hannah asks.

"Fine."

"Hmm," Hannah says, and I look at her. "I heard you come in at, like, two in the morning," she adds.

"I was out for a walk."

Hannah jumps as a nearby marine iguana spits seawater fiercely out of his nostrils. Skin dark and wet from the ocean, he ambles toward a large group of other iguanas spread out over the rocks, like dozens of tiny dragons, warming up after their time foraging at sea.

Hannah says nothing more, but as we continue toward the panga, I think about the distractions I'm embracing, as if the work isn't enough. The cat, the journals, Diego. The things that have come up to remind me that trying to impose order on anything in life is futile. To remind me I can still find newer ways to escape.

Dore

Everything on Floreana has become a battle. While things between Friedrich and me were not perfect before the Baroness came to the island, I cannot help but blame her for the tensions that consume us.

I have been quite unwell, and Friedrich becomes very annoyed with me when I'm ill and unable to help him work. The heat has been relentless and exacerbates my limp, making getting around ever more difficult. Friedrich has fashioned a cane for me out of black mangrove, which helps me walk on the uneven terrain so that I can help with our daily tasks and the clearing of brush, a constant chore around Friedo. We work every hour of daylight, our skin black with dirt, red from heat, scarred by the slashes of thorns and stings of insects through tender, sunburned skin.

I often have stomach pains and lack any appetite, and suffer from headaches that come on so strong I feel them in my entire body. Exhaustion overtakes me long before nightfall.

"You are weak," Friedrich said to me one day. "If you were strong in mind, you would be strong in body."

By now I am used to his lack of empathy, and I feel as weak as he believes me to be.

Yet in that moment—perhaps in response to the strain caused by our island's new inhabitants—my only response was anger. "You can't really believe that," I told him. "You're only accusing me of weakness because I'm the patient you couldn't cure."

"Have you forgotten everything we talked about?" he said. "You have the greatest power there is—the power of your own mind—to make you well, and you do not use it."

"Don't you think I would be well if I could?"

"It's a matter of will," he said. "You had so much potential. But you gave up. Instead of making yourself well, you are making yourself sick. Making yourself unavailable to work. Hiding behind these animals."

"Potential?" I repeated. "Is that all I am to you?"

"It is all any of us are."

"But what about who I am now? Can you not love me for who I am," I asked, "instead of who you hoped I might become?"

"You are proving my point," he said. "By asking this, you're making an excuse for refusing to try to be better."

"How much better do you expect me to be, Friedrich?" The words explode from me in a shrill cry. "I left my home and traveled all this way with you. I do backbreaking work no matter how much I'm hurting. I ask for so little, and you hardly grant me anything. I've given up everything, and you still expect me to be *better*? Why am I not good enough as I am?"

For this he had no answer. His reply was to turn from me and walk away.

Helplessly I watched him go. I loathe myself for being so passive, and sometimes I believe this is the reason for my ailments. I have noticed that I often fall ill after witnessing the Baroness's repugnant behavior, as if the energy I've used to suppress my rage and unhappiness finally overcomes me, and I can do nothing more than collapse.

If the power of my mind can make me well, I wonder—can it also make me ill? Am I making myself sicker each day with the battle that truth and lies wage every day within my own body?

Perhaps this was on my mind when the next ship anchored off Floreana. We were all—the Wittmers, Friedrich and I, and the Baroness with her men—on the beach awaiting the crew's arrival.

On this day, it was the Wittmers who received the biggest prize—two crates' worth of gifts from their friends and family. As Friedrich looked over the letters we'd received, I found myself watching the Wittmers, a little envious that their people back home had been so generous; our own families never sent us anything. Though we did stay in touch, they'd remained quite unsupportive of our journey here.

The Wittmers were ecstatic as they ripped open the crates, so delighted by receiving the items they'd longed for that they shouted over everything as they tore through the crates: books, curtains, chocolate, oats. A razor for Heinz, kitchenware for Margret, clothing for Harry.

The Baroness, who had not received even a letter, hovered over the Wittmers' gifts as if she were at a market, deciding what she wanted. Feeling protective, I walked over and stood near young Harry, who was already poring over one of his new books. "What fabulous treasure," I said to him, and he beamed up at me from where he was sprawled in the sand.

"This material looks perfect for covering the pillows on my divan," said the Baroness, leaning down and picking up a bolt of colorful fabric from one of the crates.

Margret Wittmer took it from her hands. "This is for Harry's room."

The Baroness peered at the fabric as if looking for a label. "I don't see it marked as such."

Margret laughed. "It doesn't need to be. It's a gift from his grandmother. If you'll kindly step back, we need to pack these things to take home."

"But I haven't decided what I want yet," the Baroness protested.

Heinz, who'd bent down as he examined the contents of one of the crates, suddenly straightened up. "It doesn't matter what you want," he said, "because these are gifts to us. You shall receive nothing."

"How can you prove these things are meant only for you?" asked the Baroness.

Margret laughed again, a harsh sound that showed she wasn't amused. She held up a batch of letters. "Everything in these crates is expressly for us, and you'll not touch a single thing."

The Baroness patted her hip, as if to remind them of her revolver—but it seemed she hadn't brought it with her or she'd have been waving it in the air already.

It was then, in the freedom of knowing she wasn't armed, that words burst from my lips: "You are not a real baroness."

She turned from Margret to me, fury in her heavy-lidded eyes. "What did you say?"

I continued: "A real baroness would not need to beg for gifts belonging to others. Or steal what is not hers."

I was keenly aware of the Wittmers turning quiet, of Friedrich's unsupportive silence, of Rudy and Robert Philippson standing motionless behind the Baroness, as if waiting for their next command. I felt both strong and frail at once, and I stood my ground.

The Baroness stared at me for a long time, and again I was grateful she did not have her revolver. At last she spat out, "At least I am not common, like you."

With that, she turned and walked off the beach, with Rudy and Robert behind her.

When they'd disappeared, Margret burst out laughing. "My goodness, Dore! I didn't think you had it in you."

Heinz patted my shoulder in a friendly way, and I caught Harry smiling as he began to help his father pack up their donkey for the trip to their home.

"Let's go," Friedrich said, brushing past me, and I followed him back to Friedo, as obedient as the Baroness's servants. Yet for once, my body was absent of pain, and I felt a lightness in my step I had not experienced in years.

Mallory

I'm wearing my wet suit, and though it's not zipped up, the air is still warm, heavy with clouds, and I'm beginning to swelter underneath its thick skin. I've brought a bottle of wine and two plastic cups from the kitchen. I've set a precedent in offering beverages, and it works: adding the diversions of drinking and late-night swims helps me avoid thinking about home.

When I see Diego on the beach, I zip up the wet suit. "I came prepared for the cold," I say. "How about a swim first?"

We walk into the ocean in silence. When I feel my toes leave the sand, I begin to tread water. In the wet suit, the temperature feels just right, and the air surrounding my wet hair feels cool. The sea is as dark as oil, and I feel the brush of invisible creatures all around me.

"I hope I'm not burdening you," I say as Diego leans backward to float. "Translating these journals when you must be exhausted."

"Working for Callie is exhausting," he says. "This I enjoy."

"You still haven't said anything to her? About the journals?"

He slowly rights himself in the water but doesn't look at me. "I told you I wouldn't."

"Does she wonder what we do out here every night?"

"Let her wonder."

So this is how he's playing it: let Callie believe we're fooling around so he doesn't have to feel guilty about hiding the journals from her. I take a couple of strokes toward shore, feeling the sudden need to ground myself, to feel my feet against the sand again. I wonder what Callie would think is a bigger betrayal.

I feel as though I'm cheating, too, somehow. By being here. By letting myself escape, forget. And then, as I find myself filling Diego's ears with the things I've avoided thinking of, let alone saying, this, too, feels like a betrayal—to talk to Diego instead of Scott, instead of Gavin. Yet something about being out here in the water, with someone who knows so little about my life, frees up the part of me that has been silent for too long and finds relief in finally being able to voice so many regrets—about my marriage, about my parenting, about coming here. With the space between us obscuring our faces from each other, the words flow like the water around us, dark and swirling, without beginning or end, and Diego is silent. He only listens, wading slowly toward me until we're a couple of feet apart.

"Do you have a partner?" I ask him. "Someone you had to leave behind?"

"Not at this moment."

I smile at the phrase *not at this moment*, which he's used many times before. I like this charmingly formal translation of *ahora*; he always seems to say *at this moment* instead of simply *now*. It may be an odd thing to pick up on, but it makes me feel close to him, somehow, recognizing this small habit that probably goes unnoticed among everyone else.

"What do you mean, not now?" I ask.

"There was a woman in Quito, but we are broken up. Because I am always leaving."

"You don't believe in long-distance relationships?"

"I don't know," he says. "She's the one who doesn't."

"Oh." I pause, then offer, "Well, most of my marriage was long distance. It's definitely not easy."

"You have only one daughter?"

"Yes. Just Emily." I look at him, his face close to mine in the dark. "Do you ever want to have kids? What would it be like, raising them here? It must be so different now, from when you grew up."

"In some ways, yes," he says. "In other ways, not enough. Everyone thinks it's paradise—the tourists, mostly. They don't know the reality. The kids here don't see what the tourists see. I mean, Puerto Ayora is a small town, but it's still . . . how do you say it, a concrete jungle? Kids spend their time in classrooms, at home, on the streets, watching *fútbol* on TV. We have all this"—he lifts his arms toward the sky, water dripping from his fingers like raindrops—"but they don't have access to it. They have recess on asphalt, not on beaches or out in nature."

"Why?"

"You can't go into the national park without guides," he says, "and ninety-seven percent of the islands belong to the park. But even the places locals are allowed, like Tortuga Bay on Santa Cruz, people don't visit very much. We need to work harder at educating the community, especially the kids, about nature. We need to get kids out on the water, out to all the islands. But there's no money, no supplies, no environmental studies. We need to change this. But change is very slow here."

"What's the holdup?"

"Politics, corruption. And a lot of people—like my parents and their friends—are suspicious of scientists. Scientists were foreigners who got money to come here to study the animals, while we had empty shelves in the grocery stores and not enough drinking water. The animals mattered, but the people didn't."

"I didn't realize. I should have."

"You work with other scientists," he says, "but you don't interact with the locals, right? Except to stay at their hotels, eat at their restaurants. And that's good for business, but it doesn't change things long term. People need to see that we're all connected—foreigners and Galapagueños. We need to get the kids involved. Get them into all the places the tourists go so they can appreciate where they live."

"How did you end up getting interested in nature, then, if you weren't exposed to it?"

"I was lucky," he says. "My uncle was a tour guide, and he took us around to places that most locals don't get to visit. I went to Tortuga Bay more than most kids, and even Las Grietas, which is a popular spot for tourists but hard for local kids to get to because you have to take a boat."

"What's Las Grietas?"

"It's like a swimming hole," he says. "A big crack in the earth where the river and ocean meet. Green water, black cliffs. It's like being in a pirate cave of emerald jewels. That's what I thought as a kid, anyway."

I spread my arms wide, then bring them together, sending a small wave cascading toward him.

"There are a couple of pools there," he continues, "with little caves you can swim into. Lots of fish. We didn't have snorkeling gear or anything like that, but you can see the color of the water change when you swim deeper. When you look up you see the cliffs and the ferns hanging down." His face stretches into a smile. "Sometimes you look up and see the feet of tourists. But it's okay. As long as there's always room for the local kids. They're the ones who need to see it more than anyone."

"Do you think you'll work with kids at some point? You'd be good at it."

"Maybe. I do want to create opportunities for them. It made all the difference for me. Volunteering with turtle research when I was in school. Helping at the vet clinic in the summer."

"Was that when you wanted to be a vet?"

"It was after that, actually. I did it because of all the stray dogs and cats in the street, getting hit by cars or starving. I just wanted to do *something*. I went around Puerto Ayora trying to convince people to get their dogs fixed. No one wants to do it." He gives a short laugh. "I had to explain to them: I am talking about the dog's balls, not yours!"

I shake my head. "It's like that in the States, too." As the thick clouds part in the sky, I can see his face more clearly. "I still haven't contacted the park about this cat," I add. "I know it's important, I know it has to be done—but I just don't want to get him killed."

"It's understandable, how you feel."

I've been mulling an idea about the cat, and I move a little closer to Diego. "Will you help me with something?"

"With what?"

"We need to get that cat away from the penguins."

"That's what the park service is for."

"He doesn't deserve to die." I think of the cat's bones, showing through his rough fur. "He's just trying to survive, like everyone else."

"Like all of the endemic species, too. You remember what happened with the goats?"

I let myself drift away from him. Another tragic part of Galápagos history: The goats that settlers brought with them to the islands, and largely abandoned, had multiplied like crazy, and they devoured the tortoises' food—the grasses and ferns, the leaves and vines, even the mosses on the trees—until the few remaining tortoises that hadn't been taken by sailors ended up starving. Decades later, multiagency projects set out to eradicate goats from the islands. One campaign killed one hundred thousand goats on Isabela alone.

"How could I forget?" I say. "They hunted them with dogs. Sharpshooters nailed them from helicopters. And then they sent in Judas goats to round up the others."

To be sure that they killed every last one, sterilized "Judas goats" with radio collars were sent in to lead hunters to the remaining herds. Even as an attempt to return to the natural order of things, it was barbaric—but was there any other way to restore the habitat, after we humans had ruined it?

"You know it's the only answer."

"This isn't hordes of goats we're talking about. It's one cat. Why can't we find him a home?"

"Who's going to take it?" Diego says. "The cat is feral, and no one needs another mouth to feed, especially an unfriendly cat."

"But if we get him fixed and he has shelter and mice to catch, at least he won't be roaming the park. He'll stick around."

"This is a nature preserve. He shouldn't be here at all."

I let myself drift back toward Diego in the water. "Can you just talk to a couple of people? That's all I ask. I would do it myself, but I won't get anywhere. People will listen to you."

He sighs. "I'll try."

Then he reaches out and puts his hands on my shoulders, turning me gently around. "Let's go," he says. "We have a lot of reading to do."

Back on the beach, I shed the wet suit and put on shorts and a T-shirt over my swimsuit. We sit together on one of the beach towels I brought. There's another towel in the sand nearby, which Diego uses to dry his hands before he picks up the journal. I pour wine into the plastic cups and hand one to him.

I take a few sips of wine as Diego pages through the journal, looking for the place where we left off. After listening to him read for a few minutes, I say, "You're reading faster tonight."

"I was dreaming in German last night," he says. "Like I used to back in school. I was even thinking in German when I woke up."

I take another drink of wine, savoring the lightness in my head. A line from the journal swims through my mind. *The more I see of them, the more I must confess to a particular longing* . . . Dore, the Baroness, her two lovers. Like me, she was eager for distraction from the troubles in her life.

As Diego reads, I keep sipping wine, losing myself in the intoxication, in the story. I forget I barely know him and can't be sure I trust him. Ever since Scott left, my physical senses have become more dulled than ever, and now, on the sand in the night drinking wine, I let myself focus on being a body on the beach, nothing more. I want to enjoy this time in Diego's *ahora*, in this moment, in which everything else so easily disappears.

When he reaches the end of a long section, he gazes at me for a moment, then closes the journal. When he moves to stand up, he leans forward and holds out his hand. I give him mine and let him pull me up in a single, fluid motion of seemingly effortless strength. My head spins from the wine.

"Thank you," I say, my voice a whisper, his face a silhouette with the emerging moon behind him. "For reading. For the cat. For all of this."

As we walk toward the casitas, I stumble in the sand, wishing I was less drunk but not wanting to lose the fuzziness that has set my mind temporarily free.

The casitas are dead silent, and we tiptoe across the wooden planks of the deck. Diego sees me to my door and waits as I fumble it open. "Tomorrow," he says, and I nod, closing the door as quietly as I can and leaning against it for a long moment before stepping over to the bed and falling into it.

Dore

Another year has begun, and despite the many ordeals we face, there is a glint of happiness: the new year has brought new life to the island. Margret Wittmer gave birth to a baby boy, whom they named Rolf.

When the Wittmers first arrived, Friedrich had been clear he wanted nothing to do with Margret's medical care. I, too, felt certain she would call upon Friedrich when the time came—but to my great surprise (and no small amount of admiration), Margret delivered the baby on her own. We heard from Heinz that her labor lasted three days, yet it wasn't long after the birth before Heinz did come for Friedrich, for Margret had not shed the afterbirth, and Friedrich had to perform this procedure for her. He did so with good and generous spirits, and the Wittmers were very grateful.

Once Margret recovered, we all went to visit. It was a happy occasion, and for once everyone acted like true neighbors, bringing gifts and food. I was filled with a flurry of emotions—envy and joy, respect and a bit of heartache—and held the baby in my arms for a few precious moments. Even the Baroness, though she did not wish to hold little Rolf, told the Wittmers how handsome he was, with his bright eyes and fluff of light hair.

Harry was smitten with his baby brother; he held him effortlessly while Margret prepared tea and a snack. I stood next to him and ran my hand lightly over Rolf's tiny soft head. "You'll be a good brother," I told him.

Harry smiled at me. "Do you mind," he asked rather shyly, "if I keep your stories and read them to the baby?"

The question brought tears to my eyes, which I blinked away. "That is exactly why I wrote them," I said to Harry. "They're yours now—yours and Rolf's."

It seemed a cruel twist of fate that of all the humans on Floreana, my two favorites were the youngest, and they were not my own family.

Although we enjoyed this momentary celebration, life grew challenging yet again. The storms have brought rain in torrents, broken soon enough by sun and blue skies, as if the capriciousness of the weather mirrors the new unpredictability of life with the Baroness.

How did we believe it necessary to give up civilization to become our best selves? Indeed, with the Baroness we are living no differently than we had back in Europe, with neighbors and conflicts and angst—all the trials of daily life we'd hoped to escape. The Baroness continues to behave as though we are the intruders on her island. Soon after our celebration of baby Rolf, she came to Friedo—with both Rudy and Robert Philippson, as ever—to talk about making movies! She wants to turn our lives into some sort of Hollywood spectacle. We discouraged her, of course, saying that her plans are unrealistic, that there is not enough here on Floreana to interest filmmakers. She was not convinced, of course—perhaps because she brings so much of her own drama, and because she is confident in even her most outlandish ideas.

We shall never be able to trust her. A few days earlier, the Baroness was able to meet a ship before any of us could get to shore, and she took everything—even the supplies clearly not meant for her. Heinz stopped by Friedo to complain that she'd taken a whole case of condensed milk and some gifts that had arrived for little Rolf. He'd found out from the captain of one of the yachts, learning that, apparently, the Baroness sends one of her manservants to wait at the beach every day in hopes that they will be the first to intercept visiting ships.

"She wants to take everything," Heinz told us, anger sizzling in his voice. "She probably took supplies and gifts meant for you as well. We must do something."

Friedrich told him that he expected the island's governor to arrive soon from the mainland. "We must keep track of all of her misdeeds," he said. "We need to have evidence if we want to get her off this island."

"She's acquired more guns," Heinz warned. "And she's asked for someone to come help her hunt."

"For what?" I asked, alarmed.

Heinz shrugged. "Food, I suppose."

I have never stopped worrying about the Baroness's plans for a zoo, but whether she shoots animals for food or kills to steal the babies for her own menagerie, I couldn't stand the thought of it.

It did not matter; until the governor's visit, we had no choice but to let it go. On a positive note, I feel less alone, as we have much more contact with the Wittmers now that we are aligned together against the Baroness. Unfortunately, we're bonded in feeling more than action; for now, there is not much we can actually do.

And yet . . .

The more I see of the Baroness and her men, the more I must confess to a particular longing, one which I cannot yet define. Though both Rudy and Robert are young, handsome, and wholly devoted to her, she treats them so wretchedly, even when she's speaking in endearments. I wonder how long it will last. She said to me once how much she likes variety when it comes to sex—are two men enough in numbers to be considered variety?—and hinted that she would soon grow bored of them.

On an island so very sparsely populated, who will she move on to next?

Do I even care that my own partner is likely her next target?

It's ironic that in this tropical paradise Friedrich has become so frosty. His obsession with Nietzsche and his need to reject all things human—including love, especially love—has destroyed us. Friedrich's idea of himself as an *Übermensch* disgusts me, and perhaps it is the idea of Rudy Lorenz and Robert Philippson as ordinary men that attracts me.

Robert is the most objectively handsome—tall, with thick, curly hair—yet I am even more drawn to Rudy, for reasons I cannot fully understand. There is about him a certain grace, and a certain vulnerability, something lost and aching to be found, like the formerly domestic animals left behind on the island.

I am feeling sensations that are quite foreign to me now, little flutters of awakening I have not felt inside me in a very long time. I cannot say what these murmurs might be, but I wake each morning without my usual dread, my eyes opened now to a new sense of promise.

Mallory

The morning sun is a glowing orb behind the clouds. In the panga, I scan the shore for the cat as we approach, but I don't see him. Gavin is back at the casitas, being interviewed by Callie for her newfound project on the Galápagos penguins. When I left, he was sitting in front of a reflective light screen, while Callie, holding up a light meter, barked out instructions to Diego, who was behind the camera.

Now, I sense Hannah watching me look for the cat, and I force myself to keep my gaze forward. As we clamber out of the panga, the shadow of a frigate bird passes over us, and I look up to see her soar past, her jet-black wings spanning more than six feet on either side of her white-feathered breast, her hooked beak ready to pluck fish from the sea.

Our first stop is the occupied nest, and when we get there, we still see only the one egg, half-hidden by its protective mother, who gazes at us warily. "They're supposed to have two, aren't they?" Hannah says.

"I was hoping to see another," I say, "but it might've fallen, rolled into the water." I look around, as if I might see the little white orb nearby. "Often they only have the resources to raise one chick—the second chick may not survive anyway. But we like to see two eggs, just in case."

"Just in case what?"

I point toward the dirt-strewn egg. "If this little one doesn't make it, that's it for the season. If there were a second egg, that would double their chances of success." I kneel down next to the nest. "We need to measure it." I pull out my field notebook and calipers, feeling a bit of the old thrill of seeing a new generation on its way. "Will you get me the egg?"

Hannah takes a step away from the nest. "What if I drop it?"

"You won't. Put your gloves on. Reach in slowly. Take the egg firmly, but don't squeeze too much."

"Will she bite me?"

"She might. Don't dawdle once you're in there." I recognize Hannah's expression and can't help but laugh; I must've looked the same way—terrified—the first time Gavin gave me these instructions. "You can do it," I tell her, smiling.

Hannah kneels near the cavern's entrance, then reaches in under the belly of the penguin. I hear the penguin's protesting squawk, then see the egg in Hannah's hand. "Well done." I take the egg, carefully. "Now, write this down." I push my field notebook toward Hannah. "Length 61.8 millimeters." I maneuver the calipers. "Width 48.5."

I gaze down at the thick white egg filling the palm of my glove, thinking of the miracle of life, of all the magical timing that led to this penguin finding her mate and creating this egg—and also of the precariousness of life, of how this little chick growing inside is safer now than she'll ever be again, and how I wish she could stay in her protective shell forever.

I stretch my arm past Hannah into the cavern and gently push the egg back under the penguin's belly, feeling the bird's beak peck angrily at my glove. Hannah and I step back as the penguin turns her head to the side and fixes an eye on us, and I smile again at her fierce-mom protectiveness.

I turn to Hannah. "Great job. You're getting the hang of it."

She's still watching the penguin, but she smiles. "Will it hatch while we're here?"

"I hope so."

A sharp, high-pitched cry pierces the air, and we both look skyward. Above, a Galápagos hawk floats on the wind, her marbled brown-and-white wings spread wide, her lighter tail feathers fanning out behind.

She alights on a rock about twenty feet away, and even without binoculars I can see the hawk's sharp, hooked bill, black morphing into lemon yellow as it meets the feathers. Her mottled light- and dark-brown and cream-colored feathers. Her serious amber eyes.

Hannah asks, "Is she going to go after the penguin egg?"

"Maybe. But it's safe for now."

As we make our way back toward our worksite, I pause to look back at the hawk, who gazes at me calmly. I think of the penguin in her nest, her egg tucked safely underneath her, and somehow I feel they both will be okay.

~

"I found someone to take the cat," Diego says.

It's midday, and we're standing in the kitchen, where I'm making a pot of coffee to get me through the afternoon. The news jolts me out of my weariness.

"Darwin's brother, Jorge, from the restaurant?" Diego continues. "He says his wife used to have a cat, and he says she would enjoy having another one around, even if it's not friendly. I warned them he might not be. Jorge has a shed where he can stay while he gets used to his new home."

"How will we trap him?"

"Come with me."

We walk to town, to the restaurant, where Diego shows me a tidy-looking contraption—a wooden box with mesh on the front, back, and both sides.

"It's called a 'guillotine door,'" Diego says, maneuvering the wooden slide, "but that sounds much worse than it is. The door is actually very gentle, and when it closes, the cat won't be anywhere near it."

I stare at the trap. "Where did you get this?"

"I built it."

"When? How?"

Diego smiles. "When? Yesterday. How? Third-generation carpenter. I worked in my father's shop for years."

Diego walks me through the details. "The cat comes in here," he says, gesturing toward the front, "and he will go for the bait at the back of the box. As he does, he'll push past this trigger."

He points to a piece of wood coming up through a hole in the top, and I peer into the box to see the stick of wood skimming the floor of the trap. "It's pretty loose," Diego says, "so it won't take much. Then, when he hits the trigger, the door comes down."

The trigger is attached with rope to a long stick of wood suspended with a rod between two wooden stakes—it looks like a seesaw—and on the other side, another piece of rope is affixed to the door.

"Try it," he suggests, handing me a long two-by-two stick. I reach into the trap and nudge the trigger. The door slides down so fast it makes me jump, but it doesn't land as hard as I expect.

"What if he just takes the bait and runs?"

"He can't. He'll hit the trigger before getting to the bait. Which reminds me, I'll need to sneak some of Callie's chicken from the fridge."

"Do you think it'll work?"

"Depends on where the cat is now. If he takes the bait, it'll work. But if he's not around—"

"Or if the park service already has a trap of its own?"

Diego shrugs, then brushes his hands on his shorts. "I'll take the trap over now," he says. "You can check it tomorrow morning. If we caught him, let me know."

I look at my watch, realizing I'm running late, and head back to the lodge. Despite how tired I'd felt earlier, something in me has awakened—a new energy, new fuel. It takes me a few moments to recognize it—hope. Such a long-lost feeling I barely know it anymore, but it's there, as if having nearly drowned and finally resurfacing for air, and, for once in a long time, I find myself able to let it breathe.

Dore

The day finally came when the islands' governor came to visit, accompanied by an interpreter named Knud Arends, a dark-haired Danish man whom we'd met before during one of his brief island visits. He used to be in business with one of the fishing boat captains, who'd recently drowned, and I suppose that is how he ended up working as an interpreter.

The two men visited Friedo first and assured us of our right to live here as long as we wanted. But, as Knud Arends translated our list of grievances against the Baroness, the governor listened with such a placid demeanor I wondered whether Mr. Arends was being accurate—shouldn't they both have been outraged? But I knew the governor would hear the same from the Wittmers when he went to visit them, so I didn't worry myself about it.

It was days later that the governor gathered us all at the Baroness's Hacienda—and it was a meeting we attended with foreboding. Why there, and not at Friedo, the island's first permanent settlement, or at least someplace neutral?

We were shocked to learn that instead of deporting the Baroness and her entourage, the governor granted her a title to more than twenty-five hundred acres of land on Floreana! Friedrich and I, and the Wittmers, were each granted fifty acres. This was plenty for our uses but so much less than what the Baroness received we could hardly bear to imagine what she planned to do with all that land.

And how had she accomplished this? We later learned that the governor invited the Baroness to go away with him to San Cristóbal Island on a "holiday." We'd all have enjoyed this three-week reprieve from the Baroness's antics if we hadn't been so crushed by the governor's decisions.

During her absence, Rudy has taken to visiting us at Friedo. He says that with the Baroness away, there is much tension between him and Robert, which is his excuse for getting away from the Hacienda. I also think he is curious about us, though I suspect he is most curious about me. Or perhaps that is only a wish.

I always enjoy his visits, if secretly so. If Friedrich is here when Rudy shows up, I join him in acting put out by his company, and Rudy doesn't stay for long. But when Friedrich is away, I long to see Rudy's face at our gate, to see the bright mop of his blond hair.

He is so very nice to me, and he complains often that he is not happy with the Baroness and with life at the Hacienda. It appears that while he had been in her favor before, Robert next became the favorite, and now she treats Rudy as merely a servant. Rudy suspects Robert may soon suffer the same fate, now that she is vacationing with the governor. I confided that Friedrich and I are no longer intimate ourselves, and he did not seem terribly surprised. "I do not believe people were meant to live like this," he said.

"Then why did you come to Floreana?" I asked him.

"I met her in Paris," he said, "where I owned a small shop. She charmed her way into my life, into my business, and the next thing I knew I had lost everything. I came here because I had nothing left. I stay because I have nothing to return to."

I was quiet, but my heart ached—for him and for myself, for we were so very much alike.

"Is that why you speak French to one another?" I had noticed that the Baroness often spoke in French to Rudy, though he is German. "Because that's where you met?"

"She speaks French with me and Robert so no one else can understand. I much prefer German, but she likes to have secrets. She'll only speak in German if she wants everyone else to hear." Rudy shook his head. "She is a good actress," he said bitterly, "a better one than even she can know. The world is her stage, and we are all her players."

Of course, I knew exactly what he meant. "Have you ever thought of rewriting the play?" I asked him.

He looked at me, surprised and intrigued. "What do you mean?"

"I mean, why do you have to do what she says? You are a free man, are you not?"

He looked hopeful for a moment, and then his shoulders sank, his head falling nearly between them. "I am not free at all," he said.

I thought about that day at Post Office Bay, when he tried to stand up for the Wittmers and the Baroness shot him down. I reminded him of this and asked, "What did she say to you? To keep you quiet?"

"She threatened to reveal something," he said. "Something very private."

"What is it?"

"I can't say."

"Please tell me." I wanted to know more than anything. I wanted him to trust me with his secrets.

But he only smiled sadly and shook his head.

We were sitting on the front porch at Friedo, and I went to him then and touched his hair; he seemed to me like a child in need of comfort. And then, at that slight touch, he flung his arms around my waist, pressing his face into my body, as if he might never let go. I sank down to my knees so I could look him in the eyes, and this is when it happened—his lips upon mine, that sweet and tender pressure, a flow of warmth throughout my body that I had not experienced in so long.

Rudy immediately pulled away, and we both stood, flustered. Then, without a word, he turned and fled.

I felt as though my head was not attached to my body. I fell back into one of the chairs, the one Rudy had been sitting in, and I could feel the heat of his body as if he were still there.

~

The next day, Rudy appeared as Friedrich and I were finishing our breakfast. Friedrich made a point of saying we were very busy and surely Rudy would understand, and Rudy nodded but didn't leave. He busied himself with helping me with the breakfast dishes and accepting my offer of a cup of tea. My sweet donkey Max, who follows me around like a dog, even in the tiny space of our kitchen, nuzzled Rudy for treats. Rudy is his second-favorite person, after me, and I'd noticed immediately how they took to each other. How Rudy always pets him, talks to him, brings him some leaves or fruit when he visits.

Today, however, Rudy must've been distracted, for he had brought nothing to give to Max. Max eventually turned away and inspected the table, finding a papaya rind to nibble on.

When Friedrich finally went out to pick some fruit, Rudy turned to me. "I am sorry," he said in a desperate whisper. "About yesterday. I know you are a married woman."

"Friedrich and I are not married," I told him.

He seemed stunned by this. After a moment he asked, "Then why are you with him?"

"I came here believing in the dream he had for us—for Friedo. But it turns out Friedrich and I have different dreams. And now, like you, I am stuck."

He did not say anything to that, and I told him I didn't regret the kiss. I could see his lips move toward a bit of a smile, but still he said nothing.

The euphoria I'd felt the day before vanished, and my heart sank, nearly dragging the whole of me down with it. "I do not compare with the Baroness, then?" I asked, trying to keep bitterness from my voice. "She is so much more experienced than I—"

He flew to my side, taking my hands into his own, on which I could feel the cuts and scrapes from all his manual labor. "She is an actress," he said, "even when it comes to the act of love. She is empty of interest in anything other than herself."

"How am I different?"

"You are beautiful and kind," he said. "You are not bossy or self-involved. You are everything she is not."

We heard footsteps then, and we immediately parted. Rudy left with a quick thanks for the tea, a friendly rub over Max's delighted face, and a nod to Friedrich. I finished cleaning the kitchen and went to collect the eggs from my chickens, with Max trailing behind. At no point during the rest of the morning did Friedrich speak to me, and at no point did my thoughts wander far from the memory of Rudy's lips on my own.

Mallory

After dinner I pull on my wet suit, still damp from the previous night's swim. It rained that afternoon, a hard, drenching rain that caused steam to rise from the lava. The storm cut short our nest building, but though I returned to the casita to sleep, I could only lie there, my thoughts drifting, caught up by the wind outside my window, whirling further and further in distance and memory and time.

I remember snippets of something Dore had written—*we are not entirely alone out here in our shared darkness . . . there are indeed souls all around us . . . seeking tranquility but do not know where to find it*—and I wonder if she was right, if the spirits of the island's inhabitants still surround us, and if this is why past and present are colliding in my mind. Why I think of the cat and see Emily. Why I think of Scott and see Gavin. Why I think of Gavin and see Diego. Right now, each memory that lights somewhere in my mind flickers off someplace else, and, for the moment, nothing can take hold.

The sky is clearing now, the full moon glowing behind a scattering of clouds. When I get to the beach, Diego is already there. I sit next to him and present a bottle of sparkling wine, which Callie—apparently to commemorate the footage she'd gotten of the penguins and her interview with Gavin—had left sweating on the countertop after dinner. I turn the bottle in my hand until the cork lets forth a loud pop. "I forgot to bring cups."

"We'll drink from the bottle," Diego says. "Like pirates."

I take a drink and hand it to him. He holds the bottle in one hand while flipping the pages of the journal with the thumb of the other. "We're almost done with this one," he says.

I move closer to have a look. The two journals are small, comprising about fifty unlined pages, and Dore's handwriting varies quite a lot. Sometimes her letters are small and compact, as if she'd been writing slowly; other times the writing is large, scrawled across the pages, as if she'd been writing in the dark, or in a frenzied state.

The past few days' weariness invades my bones, and I stretch out on my belly, lowering my head toward the sand. Diego shifts onto his side, propping himself up on one arm as he holds the journal with the other. As he continues reading, I turn toward him, my head so close to his arm that I can feel the gentle twitch of his muscles as he turns the pages.

Again I lose myself in Dore's story, in the timbre of Diego's voice. I stop him when I hear German. "Wait—what was that word you just said?"

"Honigkuchenpferd," Diego says. "In German, it means grinning like a fool, like when you're very happy. I think the best comparison would be the smile of the Cheshire Cat. Does that make sense?"

"It does."

I look up at him in the cloud-veiled moonlight and feel a sudden burst of synesthesia—a mix-up of the senses in which you hear colors, taste words, see sounds—a rare phenomenon in humans but not as much in animals. I think of butterflies, the way they see heat with their eyes, and as I look at Diego, all I see is heat and light. And I realize that all along I have been tasting wine in his voice, seeing indigo sky behind the moon in his every word.

He leans toward me. "This section is hard to read. See the change in handwriting?"

I turn toward the journal and see the words overlapping, curving over one another like waves on a stormy sea. "Maybe she was writing in the dark."

"Or in a hurry." Diego thumbs through the remaining pages. "We don't have far to go."

"Let's finish tomorrow?" As much as I want to see what happens next, I suddenly don't want to be moving so quickly through the journals. Through these nights in which, with Diego, I'm free of everything I used to be.

I look toward the water. "I'm going for a swim before turning in. Come with me?"

The glint of the moon on the water looks like a thousand shattered mirrors, and swimming through it, I have the odd sensation that I might get cut. But the water is smooth and cool, and I feel my mind calm as we swim out, side by side.

Past the break, we stop, floating and treading water. The bright beauty of the full moon illuminates the clouds and the lava rocks on shore. Diego's hair, in the moon's glow, looks as though it's streaked with silver, and I feel a glitch in time, as if I'm seeing what he might look like in twenty, thirty years.

"Do you think—"

Then there's a searing pain around my ankle, shooting up my leg. I instinctively reach down—then feel the same stinging pain in my hand. "Oh shit," I say. "Jellyfish."

In a few quick strokes Diego is next to me. "Come," he says, taking my good hand. He guides me through the water until I can stand, then helps me half wade, half walk back to shore. Once there, he puts his arm around my waist, pulling me close, holding me as I limp up the beach.

"Wait," I say. "The journals." I bend down, stretching my throbbing foot behind me, to pick up my backpack, shoving the journals and the empty wine bottle inside.

We continue on toward the casitas, pain flaring with every step. "Dammit," I say. "If this swells up, I'm fucked." I hold up my hand, trying to see it in the dark.

"Are you allergic?"

For a moment, the pain ceases to exist altogether. Was I allergic? I had no idea. I'd never been allergic to anything. I still can't understand how I—who'd never put any credence into allergies and despite my own seasonal sniffles never took a single antihistamine—had to witness my own child's body, time and again, release a flood of chemicals so overwhelming it sent her into shock.

The question hangs in the air between us as we hobble toward the casitas, dark and quiet. He walks me to my door. "You need to soak your foot in the bathtub," he says. "I'll go see if there's some vinegar or baking soda in the kitchen."

"Bathtub? I don't have a tub. Just a shower." I wince as I try to put weight on my foot.

"Come with me," he says. "I have a bath in my cottage."

I tiptoe on my good foot as we cross the creaky wooden deck, past Callie's door at the other end of the row. Diego pushes the door open and helps me inside. I take a quick look around—clothes strewn about, books piled on the bed—as he leads me to the bathroom. He turns on the faucet, and I sit on the edge of the tub and swing my injured foot into it.

The water is very hot, and I watch his hands on my bright-red and puffing foot as he bathes it of salt and sand, using a washcloth and checking for any lingering stingers. He reaches for my stung hand and turns it over and back again.

"I think I have some calamine," he says, and I hear him rummaging through a bag in the other room. He returns with a bottle and, after toweling off my hand, begins to rub in the pink lotion. His touch is so gentle, so reassuring, and I haven't been touched in so long, and the next thing I know I'm leaning forward, pressing my lips to his.

I feel his surprise, the sudden stillness of his mouth. After a moment's hesitation, he's kissing me back. He lifts me from the side of the bathtub, my foot dripping water as he carries me toward the bed. He holds me with one strong arm as he shoves off the books with the other, then lays me down.

Streaks of calamine from my hand mingle with seawater around Diego's neck and shoulder, the only remnant of the now-forgotten pain. With my good hand I reach around for the long nylon strap connected to my wet suit zipper, pulling it down and freeing myself from this second skin. Diego slips the straps of my swimsuit off my shoulders. Intertwined on the bed, it's as if we are still underwater, moving so fluidly, our bodies wet and salty, coming together as easily as we'd slipped into the ocean earlier.

Later, as we lie together on the twin bed, in the dark but for the white glow streaking like moonlight from the open bathroom door, I feel my mind drift and soar, toward nothing for once, simply free-falling, everything beyond this bed, this room, this moment ceasing to exist.

∼

When I emerge at dawn from a deep, dreamy sleep, I'm wondering why Scott is sleeping so close, why we are nearly glued together when he hasn't touched me in months, and as I reach toward his shoulder, my hands connect with this new body—warmer, younger, and not yet familiar.

I pull away, and Diego stirs in the tiny bed.

"What is it?" he whispers, half-asleep himself.

"Nothing," I say.

I lean forward to kiss him, and I feel his hands on my back, his warm lips, the prickle of his unshaven face. The sun glows stronger outside the window, drenching us in its early heat.

I want to stay in bed all day, but Diego eventually gets up. "It's late," he says, and though I know he's right, I'm beyond caring. He keeps kissing me as he pulls his shorts on, interrupting only to pull on a T-shirt. Then he straightens and looks down at me. "I really do have to go," he says. "Do you want coffee?"

"No, I'll get some myself. Thanks, though."

I lie in his bed for a bit too long after he leaves. Callie's sudden appearance on the deck surprises me as I make my way back to my casita. I can't tell whether she's seen me emerge from Diego's room. I mumble a good morning and continue to my door, but she stops and says, "I'm looking for Diego."

My hand pauses on the doorknob. "I don't know where he is. Sorry."

She takes a step closer to me, tilting her head to one side. "Have I offended you in some way, Mallory?"

"Why would you say that?"

"Because you are conspicuously absent when I do anything penguin related."

"I have other things to focus on."

"Like canoodling on the beach with Diego?"

I look at her, trying to figure out what she knows. "We're just hanging out. Talking."

"Right. You two certainly have a lot to talk about."

I turn the knob. "I have to get going, if you don't mind."

"Wait," she says. "Gavin said you could take me to Punta Cormorant sometime in the next couple days."

"What?"

"I need to get some footage, and he said I'd need a guide."

"I'm sure Gavin would be happy to be your guide," I say. "Or how about Diego? He knows this island better than anyone."

"Diego's asked for some time off," she says. "So you're the only one available."

"Except that I don't work for you, Callie." I step inside my casita. "I'm sure you'll find someone to help you out."

I close the door, leaving her standing on the deck.

Dore

The air is oppressive, the sky on fire. I wonder if I would notice it so much if I were not burning up from within—my body dripping with its own heat, quenching its own thirst, seeking its own sweet relief.

Every day I longed for Rudy to return, but I did not see him again for weeks, until the Baroness invited us for lunch. I did not want to attend, but Friedrich accepted, and so we went.

I do not understand why he agreed to the luncheon, as Friedrich has expressed nothing but disdain for our fellow settlers. Perhaps he is trying to keep the peace. Or, perhaps he is thinking that it's necessary to keep an eye on her, with all her grand plans.

To our surprise, the Baroness had returned from San Cristóbal with the interpreter Knud Arends, who was now, according to the Wittmers, her new "hunting partner" and "gamekeeper." Yet surely it had to be much more: Knud was very handsome.

When we arrived at the Hacienda, I steeled myself to suffer through whatever she had to offer. Indeed, the lunch was tedious and long, with the Baroness bragging about her expertise in everything there is—medicine, art, painting, gardening, teaching, writing. I admit the food, which was prepared by Robert Philippson, was much better than I'd expected, a simple but nourishing meal of breads, fruits, and vegetables—they had killed a boar, but I ignored the slabs of meat on the table, which I noticed Friedrich ate with gusto, as if to impress the Baroness. As if to prove he was a real man.

The Baroness did all the talking, and she spoke almost entirely to Friedrich, as if I were not even there. I wondered, not for the first time, if she would become interested in Friedrich as a potential lover, once she moved on from the others. I felt certain she would—she seemed unable to resist any man—and I confess I did not care if he reciprocated her feelings. It's not as if he were mine to lose.

Then, later, when Friedrich went on a tour of the property with Robert and Rudy, my hunch was confirmed, in a strange way. The Baroness brought me on a tour of her own, into her bedroom, which was quite luxurious and appealing, I had to admit. The walls were covered with tapestries, and there was a mirror above the bed, which was sprawling and lush with linens and pillows. Light curtains fluttered in the breeze.

She spoke of hunting with Knud Arends every day. "He has a great eye, and he is such a good shot," she said with a girlish sigh. "I feel quite certain his skills will be equally impressive in the bedroom."

Then she asked me, quite directly, about my relations with Friedrich. I told her I could not possibly speak of this with her, putting on an act of being deeply offended by her question when in fact I was simply ashamed. Ashamed that I no longer captured the attention of Friedrich the way she commanded not one but several men, that this part of me had shut down so completely.

Until now.

For most of all I felt I could not speak of sex without thinking of Rudy, which set my skin ablaze.

But to the Baroness, my contribution to the conversation did not matter. She continued speaking, now of her own sexual prowess. I pretended that I did not care to hear about any of her talents and tried to busy myself with looking around the room.

Yet even as I looked around, I could not help but listen as she spoke of her charm and appeal, her insatiable desires, her power over her lovers. It had been so long since I had been loved that even though her boasting disgusted me, another part of me thought of Rudy and nearly melted with envy.

Finally, I closed my ears to her chatter, and that's when I saw, on her bedside table, a copy of the book *The Picture of Dorian Gray*. She had mentioned once before that it was her favorite book—seeking Friedrich's approval, I'd thought. I was surprised to see that she actually had the book, had perhaps even read it. I picked it up and leafed through it, and a phrase leapt out at me from the page: "To realize one's nature perfectly—that is what each of us is here for."

The Baroness snatched my attention from the book and my thoughts when she said, "There's only one way to ensure absolute loyalty."

"What is that?" I asked.

But instead of men, she spoke of dogs. "You shoot them in the belly," she said, "so they won't die but will be very sick. And then you nurse them back to health. They will be forever grateful to you, and dependent on you." Then she laughed. "Men and dogs are alike," she said. "If they don't come on their own, you take them down."

I did not know what to say to this appalling philosophy, and as I looked at her I saw that her headscarf was slipping back from her forehead, and the roots of her hair were dark and marbled with silver. She must have run out of hair dye, I realized, and was trying to cover it up. The ends of her hair, peeking out from under the scarf, were a faded blond.

But while she tried to hide this aspect of her appearance, she seemed no less confident in her abilities to attract men. She told me she is finished with Rudy and that her focus on Robert is waning as well. "I am eager to see what Knud has to offer, though I don't know for how long I can tolerate him," she added. "By then, I trust someone new will come along. Opportunity always does have its way of presenting itself."

Indeed it does, I thought. Indeed it does.

I did not mind that her "someone new" would possibly be Friedrich, for I had ideas of my own.

There are some things, no matter how carefully you plan, that will be completely unforeseen. During my time here, one thing I have come to accept is that people will surprise me. What is more unexpected is how much I surprise myself.

And so the day came when Friedrich went to Post Office Bay, and Rudy came to Friedo, and I knew we would have several hours before Friedrich's return. I filled a basin with water from the spring and set it out on the porch, next to my chair.

"Rudy," I said, "my feet are so dirty and sore from working in the garden. I don't have the strength to wash them myself." I hoped he would not think I sounded too much like the Baroness.

But if I did, he did not notice or care. Without another word, he knelt down and eased my feet into the cool water. He massaged the dirt from between my toes; he rubbed my soles until I felt my entire body relax deep into my chair. He ran his fingers up to my ankles, my calves, and when I looked up his eyes were on mine, and his hands continued upward, over my thighs, under my dress, between my legs. I felt a bolt, like lightning, a current so strong it nearly knocked me from my chair.

Rudy picked me up and carried me to my bed. We laughed as we became tangled in the mosquito netting—I was nervous, and our laughter put me at ease. How long *had* it been? I cannot even remember, don't even want to remember.

He pulled my dress over my head—I wore nothing underneath, as it was far too hot—and then I took off his shorts and shirt. He was lean, his skin pale despite the tropical sun, and I let my fingers trace his body as I'd never done with Friedrich. I had never wanted to; to Friedrich, such an expression of desire was unbecoming, and I had learned to suppress it.

But, oh, with Rudy . . . he woke this dormant part of me with such fervor it left me trembling. He caressed every part of me, as gently as he had washed my feet, and he guided my own hands where he wanted them. I felt a flicker of embarrassment for my lack of experience, and a spark of jealousy as I wondered whether he had done these things with the Baroness . . . but then all such thoughts vanished as he whispered my name over and over, matching the rhythm of our bodies, and I knew that it was all for me, for us.

We lay drenched on my bedding, our exertions nearly too much in the hot, unmoving air. I had lost track of time, and suddenly I worried Friedrich would return and discover us. I sat up and scurried to find my dress, and I gave Rudy his clothes, and he simply lay back and watched me, smiling the whole time, his eyes never leaving me as I raised my arms and put them through the sleeves of my dress. I was amazed that I did not feel shy. I enjoyed him watching me.

I admonished him to leave, and he finally donned his clothing and headed back to the Hacienda, but not before giving me no fewer than a dozen kisses. Once he was gone, I began to clean the house, rather frantically, to avoid any trace of what we'd done but also to distract myself. I was afraid, when Friedrich returned, he would find me giddy and smiling like a *Honigkuchenpferd*.

To realize one's nature perfectly—that is what each of us is here for. For once, I feel as though Floreana is exactly where I am supposed to be. Perhaps I needed to be right here, right now—wasted with passion, glowing inside and out—to learn what I could not ever have learned in Berlin.

Mallory

In the afternoon, while Hannah and Darwin are hauling lava to a big nest site, I follow Diego's directions to the trap. It's so well hidden amid the shrubs and bushes it takes me a while to find it.

No cat.

Disappointed, I return to nest building. As I strap on my kneepads, I notice odd tan lines; despite layering on sunscreen every couple of hours, most of my body is striped with varying shades of brown and red, my hands and knees nearly white from wearing gloves and kneepads. The jellyfish stings still smart, but the swelling has gone down, and I've been able to get by without anyone noticing.

I take a break to visit the penguin family, and when I reach the nest only the male is there, alone with the egg, waiting for his mate to return. I gaze into his dark, reddish eye for several long moments, and he stares back calmly, without moving.

I walk back along the edge of the water, a pool of faded emeralds breaking against the rocks. Under my feet, Sally Lightfoot crabs skitter, the bright blue and red of their shells stark against the wet black lava. A raft of penguins swims in the distance, floating on the waves, then diving back under to forage. When I get back to where we've been working, only Hannah is there. "Where's Darwin?"

She looks up from the dirt. "I don't know. He got a call on the radio and left in the panga. Said he'd be right back."

I look out toward where we'd landed and see the panga, coming toward shore. This time, Darwin has Gavin with him. Even from a distance, I recognize Gavin's mood, the way he stands stiffly, as if anchored, in the boat.

I stand where I am, waiting. He walks toward us with more speed than I thought possible on such crooked terrain, and when he's close to me, he says, "Come with me."

"What is it?" I ask. Out of the corner of my eye I see Hannah looking from Gavin to me and back again. Gavin doesn't answer.

I follow him as he walks a few yards away, until we're out of earshot. He turns to me, a mix of emotions on his face I've never seen before and can't decipher. "Mallory," he says, then stops. "I don't know where to begin. Did you think I wasn't going to find out?"

His words send my heart pounding. I try to see on his face what he's thinking, and when I can't, I attempt to change the subject. "I've been meaning to talk to you, too, Gavin. Why'd you sign me up to take Callie to Punta Cormorant? That's not my job. Especially when we have so many more nests to build."

His lack of reaction to this makes me wonder whether Callie made the whole thing up. He opens his mouth, as if he's about to speak, then sighs. "Take me to the trap," he says finally. "We're going to remove it. I've already called the park service."

Is this all? Bathed in relief, I begin walking, having no choice but to show him. When we get close, I stop. "Who told you?"

"Jorge. When I went to the restaurant."

"I'm sorry, Gavin. I just couldn't let them kill him."

He's standing close, his eyes concerned. "What happened, Mallory?"

"What do you mean?"

"You know what I mean," he says, and the softness of his tone surprises me. So there is more after all. In the day's unforgiving light, I see, in the lineaments of his face, traces of regret, and I wonder if they were always there, now deepened by age.

"To us?" It's the only thing I can think of to say.

He shakes his head. "I'm talking about—"

Just then, a sharp, ear-splitting crack reverberates through the air. Instinctively, I duck.

And then I know what it was, not so much with my mind but with a sudden sick feeling in my stomach, and I rush ahead, stumbling over the rocks, arms flung out in an attempt to keep myself upright as my ankles twist and wobble on the uneven terrain, as pain soars through my injured foot.

I stop when I see the body, a few feet ahead, splayed out over the rough rocks, a red stain spreading beneath him, eyes open as if watching me. From behind the lifeless tomcat comes a uniformed *guardaparque*, shouldering a rifle.

The ranger kneels to inspect the cat, a hand on its chest to feel for a heartbeat, then rises. He introduces himself in English and asks if we were the scientists who called.

By now Gavin is right behind me. "Yes," Gavin says. "I called this morning."

"Have you seen others?" the ranger asks.

"Just this one."

The ranger nods, then asks Gavin to call if we see any more. I notice Diego's trap, now disarmed, a few feet behind him, and then I turn to look down at the cat. As the ranger continues to examine the body, Gavin takes my arm. "Let's go, Mal," he says softly. "We have to talk."

But I don't move, letting the gentle weight of Gavin's hand hold me steady.

I'm thinking of the tawaki, of the Galápagos penguins, who lay two eggs but rear only one chick.

I'm thinking of quokkas, the small Australian marsupials who mate twice a year but give birth to only one joey.

I'm thinking of humans, of the absurdity in expecting our little humans to survive. I'm thinking that for all our so-called wisdom, we know nothing, and our nonhuman counterparts know everything.

Take the quokkas: After the first joey is born and growing up in the pouch, the female produces another fetus—but this one will remain inside the body, in a sort of limbo, and will continue to grow only if something happens to the first. If the first baby survives, the second fetus will disappear—but if the first joey dies, the second baby will be carried to term.

It's astonishing—admirable, even—the practicalities of the animal kingdom. And yet it's unthinkable, as a human, to ponder what I'm thinking now: what life would be like if Emily had had a sibling. Even to imagine wanting another child in case something happened to the other. And for the first time I wonder: When a female quokka loses her joey and brings the second fetus to term, does she mourn the first or simply move on? Would having had another child, all things considered, be a blessing or a curse?

"I talked to Scott this morning," Gavin is saying. "I know everything."

I snap back to the moment. To Gavin, his hand on my arm, my body trembling, both of us sweating in the equatorial sun.

"No, you don't," I say, my voice cracking. "You don't know."

He lets go of my arm, as if freeing me to speak. "Then tell me. Please."

I open my mouth, but words don't come—I feel that synesthesia again: where words should be, I see shattered glass, sharp edges, a fractured life.

"I wish you could talk to me," he says.

I wish I could, too. Even now, I feel paralyzed.

"I'm sorry if I've made it difficult for you," he says. "If I've been working you too hard—"

"It's not that, Gavin." I try to laugh, but it sounds more like a sob. "Mallory."

I hear our past in his voice, what we shared long ago, and this makes it harder to say even as it makes it possible. He waits.

"You want me to say it? I'll say it. Emily's dead. She died."

By then my voice is nothing but a whisper, those words together sounding so wrong, a terrible combination of light and dark colliding in the air, the merging of her name and any iteration of the word *death* an explosion, a heart-stopping alchemy.

Gavin is still waiting. Off to the side, I see the ranger pull out a bag, laying it near the cat. I step forward. "We'll take him," I say. "We want to do a necropsy."

"Mallory," Gavin says again.

But the ranger relinquishes the bag, and I kneel next to the cat, aware of Gavin standing over me.

After the ranger is gone, Gavin says, "We don't have the instruments."

"Just leave him to me, Gavin."

Gavin goes quiet, and I look down at the cat, his mouth slightly open. I run my hand along the bloodless part of his back, feeling his rough fur, his bones, the evidence of his short and difficult life.

He's still warm, and I kneel there not wanting to put him in the tiny body bag, as if there's a chance he might still be alive. At the hospital, I'd kept leaning close to Emily, as if I might feel her breath against my cheek again—as if, despite the coldness of her hand when I grasped it, despite the bluish tinge to her skin, she wasn't really gone.

Finally I ease the cat, impossibly light, into the bag. Cradling him as gently as I can, with my arms shaking and him rolling limply in the plastic, I turn and walk back to the landing. I hear Gavin behind me. He doesn't speak or try to stop me, and I'm grateful, but I keep quickening my pace, as if to outrun him.

Hannah and Darwin are moving a large, flat strip of lava, and they don't see me. Wordlessly, Gavin climbs after me into the panga. We ride back to Puerto Velasco Ibarra in silence.

Dore

I did not expect what happened over these many weeks, the awakening I felt deep within me. I do not even know exactly what it is, but it feels like hope.

Are we different people depending on whom we are with? Depending on where we are?

I feel as though I became a new person with Friedrich, and then I became someone else when we arrived on Floreana. And now, I am reborn yet again, here, with Rudy. One touch, and I have been transformed.

I lie awake at night, inhabiting my body in a way I never have before. Just as I felt myself grow sicker under Friedrich's waning affections, I now feel myself grow stronger with Rudy's every visit. Is love, is passion, powerful enough to heal? I feel my body singing and know that it must be true.

We meet as often as we can. We make love at Friedo, when I know Friedrich will be gone for hours, or we sneak off to the Hacienda, if the Baroness and Robert are away. The relative opulence of the Baroness's large, plush bed makes me feel as though I could be anywhere in the world. I think Rudy likes to make love to me in her bed, and I admit I relish the excitement of yet another forbidden act.

We lie together and talk. He tells me about Paris, and we dream of escaping there together, one day. How ironic, to have escaped to so-called paradise, only to dream of escaping to another.

I feel alive, fully alive, for the first time in my life. And I never imagined that to be so awake would mean living with so many conflicting feelings. I'm filled with bliss and with fear, satiated physically and still yearning emotionally. I am so afraid someone will discover us—but not enough to stop what we are doing—and I am content and restless at once, enjoying every minute with Rudy but always craving more, wondering about the future and whether one is possible for us.

One afternoon, as we lay in bed at the Hacienda, he finally confessed to me what the Baroness had said to him at Post Office Bay. "She threatened to tell everyone on the island that I could not make love to her," he said.

It took me a moment to understand what he meant.

"She thought it would embarrass me," he continued. "Back then, it would have. But now I know the real reason. I could not be with her because I can't stand her. You've proven that I'm a man after all." His voice softened. "You've given me that."

I held his face in my hands and kissed him. "We need to get off this island," I whispered in his ear. "Both of us. Away from the shackles of Friedrich and the Baroness."

He covered my hands with his own, then pulled them down between us, as if in a shared prayer. "We'll go together," he promised.

"But how?"

"I'll find a way."

I looked into his eyes, which gazed unwavering back into mine, and wanted to believe him. But I did not know how he could find a way to achieve the impossible.

Mallory

On my knees, digging into the dirt, I feel as if I'm at Emily's grave all over again, though it's been nearly a year. The soil dark and damp, the sky cloudy and gray.

The tabby cat is curled up in his grave, cupped by the earth, as if he's sleeping. I look at his markings and think of Dore's cat, Johanna, and how many litters she must've had since the 1930s, and I realize how likely it is that this little cat came from her bloodline. I reach down to touch him one last time.

I'd gone to the restaurant to borrow Jorge's truck and had driven up here to the caves. As I cover the small body, my heart lurches and twists, and I lower my head to the dirt, muddying my face as tears fall.

There are no rules for grief, I was told when Emily died, but I felt that I was breaking them anyhow. That I didn't cry enough, and when I did, I couldn't stop. That, eventually, I forced myself to stop feeling altogether.

I still can't remember details I should—the words spoken by Emily's friends and teachers at her funeral—and I remember details I shouldn't, like her EpiPens on the floor of Scott's car.

Scott and I had been a team once, especially when it came to Emily. When she had her first severe attack, the day before Christmas, sneaking cookies Megan had brought and stowed up high but not high enough, Scott and I sprang into action as though we were one. I scooped up Emily, her face pink and splotchy, wheezing, barely able to breathe, and Scott was beside me with the car keys, his face as pale as Emily's was red. We rushed to Children's Hospital in the shared rhythm of love and panic, so connected in that moment I can hardly believe we are no longer talking.

But then I was alone again. In the days and weeks and months and years to come, Scott would travel and work while I learned how to use an EpiPen, while I pored over books and websites and food labels, while I explained to everyone who came into contact with Emily that she couldn't even breathe peanuts. Even the tiniest contact would require a rush to the hospital, and because of this, I convinced myself that life could be normal only when Emily was in my sights, when I could watch her every move.

Though the malady belonged to Emily, I had the steepest learning curve. Emily grew up knowing no other way of life, but I'd entered a singular new world, one that spun around a growing library of books on the nightstand, immersion into message boards, subscriptions to blogs and bulletins and e-news. I carefully counseled the parents of Emily's friends, arranged playdates that didn't correspond with mealtimes, and provided all of Emily's meals and snacks.

As Emily got older, she didn't want to be different. She hated having her own food, being unable to eat everything her friends and classmates could eat. I'd given her what freedoms I could; I let her select her own clothes and things for school, pick out our new sofa, choose our family cat at the shelter. But there was one rule I couldn't give up: every day, I would check her backpack for the EpiPens. And the one time I didn't was her last day alive.

∼

I wake at five the next morning without having slept at all—or at least I can't remember sleeping. The fog in my head that had hovered for weeks and months following Emily's death has returned, along with the numbness of not knowing or caring about anything.

I barely remember returning to the casitas after burying the cat. I don't remember washing the dirt off my hands and face or changing my grubby clothes, though I must have because everything is clean.

I remember lying in bed, feeling the shape of the room, thick and moody, hearing the air-conditioning whirring. It could easily have been our bedroom in Boston, in the roomy old house Scott had grown up in, where we'd moved after his parents passed away and where we lived until Emily died and he moved out.

And I remember the day I left to come here, stepping out the front door, an Uber on its way, to catch my flight to Dallas and then to Quito. Pausing on the front steps, wondering when I'd be leaving forever, this home that's his, not mine. Not ours, not anymore.

I'd looked up at the house—Scott's childhood home as well as Emily's—and felt as I always had, as if I'd ended up in someone else's life. First it had been Gavin's, and then it was Scott's—and now I was on the brink of yet another, wondering whose life it would feel like this time.

I thought of a day not long after we'd moved in, when I'd dropped Emily at her preschool in the Back Bay and gone shopping, eventually maundering into the North End, catching lingering scents from Italian bakeries, their windows fogged up from the warmth inside. I found my way to Copp's Hill cemetery, which I thought was a neighborhood park until I saw the gravestones. By then I'd already opened its wrought-iron gate, so I walked the brick path and meandered among the thin, weathered markers, which were sinking into the ground, the earth claiming them slowly, century by century. Tree roots grasped the headstones in gnarled fists, twisting them into one another, making me want to straighten them. It was a bitterly cold day, and I was alone.

A house across the street caught my eye—a skinny green building wide enough for only one window on each of its three stories. One side of the house abutted the home next door, and the other side overlooked an alley so narrow that two people couldn't walk through it side by side.

"Checkin' out the spite house?"

Startled by the voice, I looked over to see the cemetery's groundskeeper watching me.

"Coupla brothers inherited that real estate there," he said, nodding toward the house. "One of 'em was off in the army, so the other one built himself a nice big mansion, leaving nothing for his brother but a sliver of land too small to build on. 'Course the brother came back to find only that little slice of his inheritance left, and he decided it wasn't too small to build on after all. Built that house for spite, so his brother'd have no view and no sunlight and no use of the alley to get to the back. No more'n ten feet wide, that house. People living there now."

When my Uber arrived, I was still standing on the steps of our house—Scott's house—immersed in the memory, thinking of the skinny house near the cemetery. Our house was huge by comparison—two thousand square feet, flooded with sunlight, rooms wide and ceilings high—but it felt like a spite house just the same.

∼

It's starting to rain, the light drops mixing with the sweat on my face. I'd convinced Darwin to bring me here alone, and time has passed without any true awareness of it.

When I finally look at my watch and see that two hours have gone by, I have to retrace my steps to count the number of nests I've done—four, on my own, a record—and it's only then that I feel the ache in my muscles.

I'm relieved no one has shown up to join me—maybe Gavin agreed to let Hannah take the morning off due to the threat of rain—and I'd left behind my phone, with a half dozen missed calls and voicemails from Scott. I haven't listened to them. I can't imagine how I'll begin to explain myself, how to answer his inevitable *why?*

I think of a card game Scott and Emily and I played every so often, designed to get kids talking about their thoughts and feelings. You drew a card and finished the sentence printed on it: *I worry about . . . I feel embarrassed when . . . I wish my family would . . .*

The only rules of the game were simple—to be honest, and to listen. One of the last times Emily and I played together, she said, "I wish my family would stop worrying about me."

"Okay," I said, biting my tongue, and as we played on, I continually broke the game's most important rule as I finished my sentences with faith, trust, optimism—all the things I knew I owed Emily but that I couldn't yet feel myself.

I finish two more nests, working slowly in the increasing heat, my arms barely able to move, my knees throbbing despite the kneepads. I toss down my tools and go to visit the nesting penguins.

When I arrive and bend down to peek into the nest, I catch my breath. The egg has hatched.

I kneel down and watch the tiny, trembling body, flailing awkwardly against the ground, the female penguin hovering over her baby protectively. Nearby is the broken shell, brown with dirt.

The newborn is covered with soft charcoal down, with a little white on the chest and chin. I've left my gloves behind, so I don't reach in, but the little chick would fit easily in the palm of my hand—no bigger than a week-old kitten, about five inches long, shaking and wobbling, flippers splayed, shiny black beak resting on a stick of wood. The flippers are still a light, pinkish white, covered with brown dust.

"Well done, mama," I whisper to the penguin, who stares back with unblinking eyes.

Dore

It is, as ever, so difficult to write—to sneak back to my hidden journals, to steal the precious time to put pen to paper. I loathe that so many of these days will go unrecorded, but whatever minutes I can purloin from this busy life I am determined to record, even if only for myself.

We are now into yet another new year—it is almost impossible for me to grasp that it's been nearly five years since we moved to Floreana—and life with the Baroness is more perilous than ever. I am beginning to fear for our safety.

Knud Arends is in a hospital in Guayaquil.

What happened was this: A group of visitors came to the island, and the Baroness insisted they all go hunting together. The group had also visited with the Wittmers—they were planning to come to Friedo for supper—and they got a late start, with just a couple of hours of light left in the day.

I was working hard at Friedo to get ready for supper, and when no one showed up, I knew something was wrong. The hours went by, and at last Friedrich and I had no choice but to go to bed. At that point I was more cross than anxious—I suspected they'd killed some animal and had returned to the Hacienda to eat it. The Baroness often mocked my vegetarian meals, and visitors often showed up at Friedo with no appetite, having already eaten at the Hacienda after hearing her lies about my food.

But it was far worse than I imagined. The next morning, we learned from the Wittmers that Knud Arends had been shot by a member of the hunting party. Heinz told us it was unclear who'd shot him, but as he described the incident, I knew immediately who had fired that bullet. Knud had been shot in the stomach.

She wounded him on purpose, I realized as I recalled our conversation at the Hacienda. *If they don't come on their own, you take them down.*

Heinz and Margret heard about the shooting from Robert Philippson, who had witnessed the whole event and told them the Baroness had fallen to her knees at Knud's side and promised to nurse him back to health.

I felt a chill so deep come over me that I struggled not to shiver in the midday heat.

I said nothing, however, for despite the wickedness of the incident, it seemed that this would surely lead to what we'd all been hoping for—the removal of the Baroness from Floreana.

Friedrich was dispatched to treat Knud's wounds as best he could until a ship arrived. And then, we waited several days for news. At last we had a visit from Robert, who stopped in at Friedo to let us know a ship had come to take Knud to Guayaquil, where he would, we all hoped, recover.

Yet when Friedrich asked about the Baroness's fate, Robert seemed confused as to what he meant. He insisted it was not the Baroness who'd wounded Knud but one of the visitors, though he declined to say which one. No one was questioning him, or the Baroness herself. And with that, the one tiny bright spot in the entire debacle was extinguished.

As if to mirror our misery, the rain has forsaken us, and the drought is horrendous. The heat is so fierce it steals our breath, and the sun is closing in, burning the vegetation with nothing more than a glance. It is hard on everyone, but I fear it is worse for those at the Hacienda. Since Knud's injury, we have not seen or heard from any of them. As I write this, Rudy has not shown up for more than a week, and I've begun to worry—with Knud gone, is he back in the Baroness's bed? Or has something even worse happened? He usually comes by every few days—rarely would this much time go by without hearing from him.

As ever, I turn to my animals for comfort, though, as with Rudy, my time with them has to be stolen behind Friedrich's back. Johanna is as affectionate as she could be, and I suspect she has had other litters of kittens but that she has wisely chosen to raise them far from here. Max has grown into a strong and happy donkey; he is free to roam and often does, but because I feed him at sunset, he returns to me most evenings and spends nights in his enclosure. My chickens have had children and grandchildren of their own, and I have named them all.

Despite the peace I find with my animal children, I worry about and long for Rudy. One afternoon, when the Wittmers stopped by, I asked, as casually as I could, what they hear of the Baroness. Margret Wittmer told me that, according to the Baroness, Rudy is no longer welcome at the Hacienda.

"What does that mean?" I asked, with alarm. "Has he nowhere to go?"

Margret shrugged, making it clear it was not her concern. "She will change her mind in a week," she said, "if what she says is even true. She wants something different every time I see her. How can one keep track?"

Yet I feared the Baroness would not share her scant supply of water with Rudy, or even her food. For the next several days, I desperately tried to think of a reason, an excuse, for Friedrich and I to make a trip to the Hacienda.

Then, Rudy finally showed up at Friedo.

I was alarmed to see the state he was in. He looked exhausted, and so much thinner than when I saw him last—I could see his ribs through his shirt. Friedrich was there, so we didn't have a chance to talk privately, but even Friedrich could see that Rudy was suffering and asked if he was ill. Rudy said that he has been working very hard at the Hacienda and that he has also been feeling sick with stomach pains and could not keep food down.

I walked him to the gate and gave him some vegetables and fried bananas, making sure Friedrich couldn't see. I was worried for his safety and whispered to him that he should stay here, at Friedo, but he refused. "I would be too tempted to sneak into your bed," he said.

"Come back soon," I said. "I can't bear not seeing you."

But the next time he returned, two days later, he looked even worse. His eyes appeared small and sunken into his face, and his skin was sunburned, perhaps from the Baroness working him so hard outside in the heat, or maybe he was sleeping out in the sun without shelter. Again, Friedrich was there, so it was a very short visit with no chance to talk.

After Rudy left, I turned to Friedrich with a sudden memory—an awful afternoon I had nearly blocked from my mind.

I had invited the residents of the Hacienda to lunch at Friedo in reciprocation of their hosting us, and the Baroness had come with only Robert, as she claimed Rudy was ill. I tried not to show my concern, but I found the luncheon to be unbearable, and I took every opportunity I could to tend to my animals to escape the Baroness's prattling on and on about her life in Paris. But I did catch one interesting—and perhaps, now, important—question she'd asked Friedrich.

"Do you remember," I asked him now, "when the Baroness asked you about the antidote to arsenic?"

Friedrich shrugged.

"Do you think the Baroness could be poisoning Lorenz?" I was careful to refer to Rudy by his surname, as Friedrich always did.

"I would doubt that," Friedrich replied. "And anyway, I do not want to be involved in their business. The next time Lorenz shows up here, I will send him away."

I couldn't bear the thought of anything happening to Rudy, and I tried to convince Friedrich that we should invite him to stay at Friedo. "She is dangerous," I told him. "Do you want that on your conscience?"

He shrugged it off and said, "What they do is not our concern."

He could not have been more wrong, but I was powerless to change his mind. He did not live with the same fear—that the Baroness's venom would one day hurt us all.

She destroys everything. She works her poor donkeys to the bone, and they are tired and dull-eyed and wretched. The Wittmers had a little boat that Heinz and Harry would take out to go fishing, or to meet the big ships—and one day, the Baroness ran it up against the reef, breaking it into splinters and blaming it on Friedrich and me. The Wittmers knew better, I think, and believed us when we vehemently denied it—but this is what she does. She poisons people. And I fear Rudy is her next victim.

∽

Finally, one day when Rudy came to Friedo, we had a few moments alone to talk—Friedrich was out in our orchard—and I told Rudy about the arsenic. "Do you think this could be why you're ill?"

His face registered agony, and then a look of calm and understanding seemed to wash it away. "I will look for it," he says. "I remember she said she was using something to kill the rats." He left straightaway, as if to investigate immediately.

That afternoon, mimicking the darkness hovering in my mind, the sky turned black in the middle of the day. Later, the heavens glowed red, and we could see, to the north, great clouds of smoke and flame. A volcano had erupted on another island—likely Fernandina, though we did not yet know for certain—and it rattled me to my core. Though we've always lived among volcanoes here, and I should have known to expect this, this explosion felt quite ominous to me, given my concerns about Rudy, about everything falling apart.

I haven't seen him for three days.

Mallory

The next morning, when I open my door, Gavin is sitting outside his casita, just a few paces away. I step out slowly. After having left alone for fieldwork the day before, I'd returned in the afternoon, showered, and gone straight to bed in the sticky heat. I slept deeply, dreamlessly, through the whole afternoon and night.

When Gavin looks up, his face is calm. "Scott contacted me," he says. "He was concerned because he'd tried to get in touch with you and hadn't heard anything."

"I'm sorry." I sit down in the chair next to his. "I should've gotten back to him."

"Why didn't you tell me? I mean, it's been almost a year . . ." Another pause. "You never said a word."

"It's so hard to find the words. I've been trying, ever since I got here." I stare down at my hands. "After the first couple days, it seemed weird that I hadn't told you, and then it became easier not to. To forget for a while."

"And Scott?"

I don't want to admit how much Scott and I had begun to unravel even before Emily's death. I look up but focus my gaze around Gavin's chest, unable to raise my eyes to his face. "He left. I deserved that."

"No, you didn't, Mal."

But I did. When Scott and I met, I felt we could be together as seamlessly as Gavin and I had been. And for a long time, we were—until

I decided that I was the only one who could care for Emily properly. I sliced our jobs neatly into two, embracing my role as the conscientious parent and forfeiting to Scott the role of the fun one. I'd made it my responsibility to prepare her food, to counsel her friends' parents, to be sure she had her EpiPen; even when Scott took her out, it was with snacks I'd made, with a little backpack I'd filled with everything she needed. I hadn't let him play an equal role in her daily life, to fully know her many needs. And it's taken me an entire year to realize that this—my having done this—was part of what led to her death.

Emily had gone to a sleepover, and Scott hadn't checked that she had her EpiPen. We'd argued about it hours earlier. I insisted she still needed our help; he believed I was suffocating her. So, for once, I'd backed off, let him have his way, not thinking about the things he didn't know because I hadn't given him the chance to learn.

Late that night, at her friend's house, Emily must've gotten hungry; she opened a packet of cookies someone had brought. She knew to read the ingredients, but the cookies contained trace amounts of peanuts, from being produced in a facility with nuts, and it was enough. She didn't have her medication. By the time one of the girls awoke and figured out what was happening, they got Emily to the hospital—too late. She was gone before Scott and I got to her.

She looked so small in the adult-size hospital bed, tubes and machines everywhere. I climbed into the bed and cradled her, unbelieving, unwilling to let go. I buried my face in her hair and smelled strawberries.

For weeks, months, afterward, I would hear a sound in the house and turn to find no one there. I would make too much food for dinner and keep the kitchen nut-free, as it had been for years. I would lie on her bed, surrounded by her stuffed animals—among them, the creatures of these islands—and watch the light move across the room as the hours passed.

Scott took time off work, but soon I faced the long days alone: no making lunches, no carpooling, no dentist appointments or ballet classes or birthday parties. Eight years earlier, I'd changed careers, from science to parenting, and again my work, my reason for getting up in the morning, had abruptly disappeared.

And Scott—I blamed him. Not secretly but aloud, horribly and irreversibly; the things I said could not be unsaid. In the days after Emily's death, grief and exhaustion made my brain feel black around the edges, fried like old wires gone bad; I tasted burned metal in my throat, between my teeth, and thought I might be going crazy. I couldn't think, couldn't get out of bed—and while I remained there, Scott did the unthinkable: calling his siblings, my sister, my mother; calling friends; arranging the funeral.

I have never thanked him for doing all that, and I have no idea how he did it, and how much it must've shattered him every time.

Back then, I needed someone to blame, and Scott became my target. I think some part of me wanted him to leave, because even I knew there could be no other outcome after the way I treated him. And Scott being gone gave me a reason to leave, too. Somehow I hoped that, despite all my regrets, seeing Gavin would confirm I'd made the right choices, that there was nothing I could've or should've done differently. Instead, being here has made me realize that choices can take you only so far. That life unfolds in a certain way no matter how much you try to plan your way through it.

"Why didn't you tell me?" Gavin asks again.

I stand up. "I need to get back to work."

He looks stunned. "You don't have to do that right now, Mallory. In fact—"

"Yes, I do," I interrupt him. "Where's Hannah?"

His expression is filled with so many questions that I have to look away. "In the kitchen, I think," he says finally.

I find Hannah, and when I tell her it's time to go, she pours coffee into a thermos, pockets a banana, and follows me without asking questions. During the panga ride, I tell her about the new baby penguin.

After Darwin drops us off, we go directly to the nest. Hannah leans over my shoulder as I pull out the chick, the mother snapping at my gloves.

"Write what you see," I say, cradling the chick.

Hannah narrates as she scrawls in her notebook. "All black around the eyes. Black beak, with a bit of pink. Gray, fluffy. No feathers."

"Good, good."

"White on the chest. Black eyes, half-open."

"The pattern he'll have as an adult isn't formed yet," I tell her. "But see that little spot of white on his cheek? He'll grow into it."

I hold the chick gently by the neck so Hannah can measure the bill. From this angle, the chick shows off his pear shape, and we admire the big, round belly. He weighs in at fifty-six grams.

"Healthy baby," I say as Hannah writes it down.

I hold the chick for a moment longer, admiring his awkward, fluffy beauty. It will take six months before he's ready to forage for himself, and his parents will stay close for up to a year. And then, he'll be on his own—and if all goes well, he'll live another fifteen to twenty years.

At last I return the chick to the nest, and his mother bends her body down as her baby snuggles into the space between the ground and her feathered chest.

~

I knock on Diego's door before dinner. I haven't seen him since being in his bed. Maybe he regrets our night together—but I still want to see him. To keep reading the journals. To leave this world for another. To get some answers in a world where answers seem impossible.

He appears, wearing shorts and a white T-shirt. As usual, he looks cool in the sticky heat.

"There you are," I say.

He seems to be studying me. "Are you okay?"

"Gavin told you?"

"Told me what?"

"Never mind." I feel a cool rush of relief. "I haven't seen you for a while."

He leans against the doorframe. "Remember I talked to my friend at the veterinary clinic?" he says, and I nod. "They were already planning a trip to Floreana, and they'll be here tomorrow. They'll do spays, neuters, and any other treatments they need to do. I volunteered to help. Callie's giving me the day off."

"That's . . . incredible." I've tried not to think of the cat, let alone the island's other cats, and I'm not even sure Diego knows what happened. I quickly change the subject. "I just . . . I wanted to see if we could read tonight. But if you have an early day . . ."

He shakes his head. "No, it's fine. Let's meet later."

∼

I wait on the beach, journals in hand, and when Diego arrives, I hand him the books right away, not wanting to talk. I feel him looking at me, and I'm relieved when he silently takes them and finds the spot where we left off.

"Look," he says. "The handwriting changes here."

I glance over at the pages. The ink is a slightly different color, and the hand is neater, not as messily scribbled as the previous paragraphs.

"'It is amazing to me,'" Diego reads, "'how completely such a pervasive anxiety can vanish, how rapidly a slate can be wiped clean, how immediately a woman can become free.'"

I envy Dore in this moment, the mere fact that she wrote these words—the notion that such freedom may be possible.

As Diego reads on, the waning moon disappears behind a cloud and turns the night dark and muggy. Even if he weren't on the last pages of the second book, I can tell Dore's story is reaching an end. It's suspenseful, riveting—and yet I know that, like life, it's the end of only one chapter.

And, as he reaches the end of the journal, I find myself stunned by its revelations. For the first time, I wonder what became of Dore after what happened here on Floreana. But this is a question these books cannot answer.

Diego stretches out next to where I'm lying in the sand. Though my mind reels with what Dore has written, he doesn't say anything, and while a part of me wants to talk, to unpack everything that happened and to consider what might've happened next, I realize that letting go is an option I rarely take, and it's no wonder I'm exhausted.

And so I turn my thoughts outward, listening to the lap of the waves, the humming of insects in my ear. I let my head fall toward Diego's in the sand. "I have something to tell you," I say.

I tell him about the cat, about the park ranger confiscating the trap. I tell him about Emily. About Scott. I tell him about the first night at home, without Emily—Scott seeking to comfort me, seeking comfort from me. I wouldn't touch him, or let him touch me—not that night, or since.

What I don't say is how much I needed to be touched but that I didn't want it to be the man who'd helped me raise Emily—that I had to start over, and Diego had breathed life back into me, almost like getting a shot of Emily's epinephrine: alleviating the damage and bringing me back to myself.

It's during this pause that I see a shadow in the distance and nudge Diego. "Guess who," I whisper. He doesn't have time to cover the journals.

Callie emerges from the dark. "We've got to stop meeting like this," she says.

As she stands over us, I force myself not to look toward the journals.

Callie's face is strikingly pale in the clouded moonlight. "I'm glad you're both here. Mallory, when do you want to go to Punta Cormorant tomorrow?"

"I'm building nests tomorrow. Sorry."

She doesn't answer but turns to Diego. "Since you're taking the day off, I need to talk with you about the footage we still need so we can jump back into it. Let's head back so we can brainstorm a bit."

I hold my breath; she doesn't seem to have glimpsed the journals, but I can't tell.

"How about in the morning," Diego says.

"How about now." It's not a question but an order, given through lips nearly clamped shut, as if holding back much more. She lets the words hover around them for a few moments, then turns and walks away.

I sit up and watch her disappear. "She knows something." I reach across Diego and pick up the journals. "Did she see them?"

"I don't think so." Diego looks at me. "What will you do with them?"

"I don't know." I can't read his face in the dark. "The truth changes everything, doesn't it?"

I'm thinking of something Dore had written, about why women have children—*how can we depend on men to return the abundance of love we have to give?*

And yet what of women who don't have children, or don't have them anymore?

Dore gave her love to her animals, and I suppose I'm doing the same. And maybe I'm here not only for the penguins but for Gavin, whose eyes are a window into the past. For Diego, who has turned me toward the future.

"Maybe I should put them back where I found them," I say. "It seems strange to know all this. Especially if she didn't want it known."

But even as I say the words, I'm thinking about another possibility. With these diaries, the history of the islands is forever changed—and this means publicity. And money. Exactly what Gavin needs to give the penguins a chance at survival.

As Diego and I walk back to the casitas, I remember an article I'd read on the flight here, in a stack of scientific journals I'd brought with me to catch up on my years out of the field. Scientists who study Darwin's finches have discovered that, despite the eradication of predators on many of the islands, the finches, even though they're now safe, still behave as though they're in danger. Generations later, no longer under threat, the birds still act as though they're being hunted.

Perhaps, I'd thought, leaning my head back against the seat and closing my eyes, it's not possible to recover from something that has threatened to kill you. Perhaps, as nature is proving, there are things we never recover from, and a part of us will always be afraid.

Dore

I am not sure how I can justify what I have done—but I have done it, and there is no going back.

They were going to kill me, he said. I had no choice.

I had to do it first, he said, or I would have been their victim.

Rudy had found the arsenic. He knew then that the Baroness and Robert had been poisoning his food. He knew they thought he was taking up too much space, too many resources, too much sacred water. That they wanted to be rid of him altogether.

He waited for his chance—for the day the Baroness ordered him to cook for them. She was always ordering him to do things at the Hacienda, from clearing brush to cleaning up after her and Robert. He knew the day would come to cook, and soon enough, it did.

She had no idea he'd discovered the poison. She and Robert didn't even notice that Rudy didn't eat with them. They didn't care if he starved.

I knew nothing of any of this until he showed up at Friedo, in the middle of the night. I lay in a state of half sleep. Friedrich lay snoring in the other bed; it had taken him a long time to fall asleep, and even so I felt resentment that sleep had come to him when it eluded me. I yearned for escape so badly and had not been able to find it anywhere, not even in sleep.

I was startled out of my stupor to find Rudy at my side. He put his finger to his lips and motioned for me to follow him. I stepped very slowly, very quietly across the long planks of our floor so as not to wake Friedrich.

Outside, a safe distance away, Rudy whispered, "I need your help."

"What are you doing here?" I hissed at him. "You are a fool to come here at this hour."

"I need you to bring Max to the Hacienda."

"What? Why?"

He did not answer, and I said, "I will not take one step until you tell me why."

Then he confessed.

And now, he said, the only way to be rid of the bodies would be to take them to Post Office Bay, to feed them to the sharks. The Baroness's animals had all fled, and he could not ask the Wittmers.

I stood there in the dark, the night buzzing and swarming all around us, hardly able to believe what he'd done. I felt myself shiver in the muggy night air, and as Rudy watched me, waiting, I felt a burst of anger toward him. He knows how much I love Max—I thought he loved Max, too—and he knows I have vowed not to use Max for work. The bay was hours away from the Hacienda, I pointed out, and Max was still so young. He had no experience carrying such weight and probably wouldn't tolerate it. "We'll never make it all the way to the bay," I told him.

"Please, Dore," he said. "I wouldn't ask you if I wasn't desperate."

I reminded him that no one ever travels in Floreana after dark; not only is it treacherous and impossible to see, but this is when the ghosts roam the island.

"You should not be afraid of ghosts when there is real evil about," he told me.

Real evil? I could never argue that the Baroness was not evil at her very core—but what did murdering her make my Rudy?

He saw my hesitation, my confusion, my fear. He said, "The donkey will find the way, and look, I have made it here in the dark, haven't I? We will be fine. I have a lantern at the gate, and the moon is out."

Still I did not move or speak, and he pleaded, "If you don't help me, I will never leave this island alive. We will never have the chance to be together."

He pulled me close and whispered the things we used to talk about in bed—the two of us, in Paris, running a shop together, a bookstore perhaps—and I finally relented, if for no other reason than to keep our frantic whispers from waking Friedrich.

At the Hacienda, Rudy had wrapped the bodies in cotton sheets and secured them in a wheelbarrow, and he had a harness ready to attach to Max. I talked softly to my pet, ignoring Rudy, as we began the slow journey down the path.

It was still early, I realized, probably not even midnight, which gave us more than six hours to make the trip. Rudy led the way, keeping up a manic pace, as Max and I followed breathlessly.

As we walked, I grew very tired, my limbs weakened, and I leaned on Max, apologizing to him for the added burden. I thought of the island's ghosts and wondered: Will the spirits of the Baroness and Robert haunt this place forever?

Finally we reached Post Office Bay, with no more than a half dozen words passing between us during the journey. And then, with the same hands that had caressed my body, Rudy unwrapped the corpses and nudged them into the lapping water at the shore. I kept my gaze high, toward the sky; the moon was higher now, and I did not want to see the lifeless faces of either of them.

Then I saw the glint of silver and glanced down. Rudy reached over with a pocketknife and cut the throat of the Baroness before shoving her into the sea. He did the same to Robert Philippson, then stepped into the ocean, dragging them out a couple of meters before returning to the shore, rinsing the blood from his arms and legs as he did.

He stood next to me and put his arm around me. "It will be high tide soon," he said. "They will be long gone by daylight."

He had planned very well. I had to admit that much.

I wanted to shrug away from him but didn't dare move. "We have to go," he said at last, and we turned back to Max. I gave my donkey a treat and removed the harness, letting Rudy pull the wheelbarrow himself.

By the time we arrived back at Friedo, my muscles and joints ached as much as my heart, and I could barely walk. The sky was lightening, but the sun was still down. Rudy and I had not uttered a word to each other, and I left him at the gate without speaking. I silently returned my exhausted body to bed. Friedrich never stirred.

∼

A few days later, Margret Wittmer and Rudy came to Friedo with a story.

Apparently Rudy had convinced the Wittmers that the Baroness had left on a fancy yacht with Robert Philippson. "They wanted to go to the South Pacific," said Margret. "Imagine that!"

"Imagine," I said.

Because the yacht was leaving right away, Rudy said, they had packed up their things quickly. He added that the Baroness had put him in charge of all that remained at the Hacienda.

Friedrich did not say much, and Rudy chattered on nervously. "Good riddance," he said. "I'm glad they're gone. I am planning to sell what I can so I can leave the island also. Surely there are some things you might wish to buy."

I remained completely silent as Friedrich spoke to the two of them, and they agreed on a time to visit the Hacienda to go through the Baroness's things. After they left, Friedrich said to me, "You're as good an actress as the Baroness."

"What?"

"You don't really believe that story?" he said.

"What do you mean?" I tried not to show that my heart was beating madly.

Friedrich sighed, as if I were slow. "Isn't it obvious?" he said. "The Baroness and Philippson were murdered."

I could not move with the shock. How did he know? Had he heard me leave Friedo that night? Had he heard our whispers?

He continued talking, and it took me several moments to realize he did not think I was involved. He was saying that he'd heard no ships come to the island, and he noted that we'd received no mail—surely we'd have known of a visiting yacht, which meant there hadn't been one. He seemed to believe the Wittmers and Rudy had done something to the Baroness and Philippson, that they were all in on it together. I did not say anything.

Even though Friedrich did not suspect my involvement, I was still brimming with anxiety. I soon began to worry less about the bodies and more about Rudy himself. I thought perhaps he was going too far in selling the Baroness's things, that his desperation to get off the island made him look guilty.

And then, when he and I leave together—everyone will know.

The following week, Friedrich and I took lunch at the Wittmers' place before we all went to the Hacienda. When we arrived, I felt my breath stop—it did not look at all as if the Baroness and Robert had packed and left. How could Rudy be so careless? Everything was tidy, in its place—their luggage, the Baroness's hat, and her beloved copy of *Dorian Gray*. Wouldn't everyone know she would never leave it behind?

Rudy seemed especially casual, as if he hadn't a care in the world. He was eager to sell as much as possible. I tried not to look at him and instead pleaded with my mind and my body to calm down so I would not look as anxious as I felt.

As the others began to choose what they wanted, I wandered away, outside and into the useless, parched garden. As I walked aimlessly through, my foot struck something, and I leaned down to see what it was—a small wooden cylinder whose label, beige with red lettering, had been mostly torn away. I opened the top of the container and saw inside a grayish powder.

The arsenic.

I quickly closed the lid and slipped the container into the pocket of my dress.

Rudy had perhaps meant to bury it and had been interrupted, or perhaps the animals had dug it up during their foraging. I went back toward the house, but I did not have a chance to speak with Rudy, who was busy dealing with sales to Friedrich and Heinz.

I did not see Rudy again until after the rains began, when he came to see us at Friedo. A ship had come, he told us, and he handed Friedrich the mail.

A ship? Why were Rudy and I not on it? I now realized that our escape was not going to be as easy as I'd hoped.

The visit did not last long, and, as casually as I could, I offered to walk him to our gate. "When are we leaving?" I asked him. "Why did you let a ship go without us?"

"There was no ship," he whispered. "I made it up. So that no one will think I am too eager to leave."

"And when both of us leave together? How will that look?"

His eyes darted back and forth. "It won't matter by then, will it?" he said. "By then we will be gone. There are no bodies. What can anyone do?"

"Friedrich already suspects they were murdered," I said.

"He suspects us?"

I looked at him. *Us?* I thought. But he was right: I was as much a murderer as he was. "You should've burned her book," I said. "Her most treasured possession is right out in plain sight."

He laughed a small, bitter laugh. "Her most treasured possession changed from day to day," he said. "Hour to hour. Me, Philippson, Arends, the captain of every ship that moored here. Even Friedrich."

Before I knew what I was doing, my hand connected to his face in a loud slap. I backed away, quickly, hoping Friedrich hadn't heard anything. Rudy stared at me with a shocked expression, and I returned to the house.

I picked up the mail he had brought and saw that it comprised old letters, probably stolen by the Baroness a long time ago. And I knew then he would leave without me.

Mallory

The next morning, I get up early to go for a swim. The beach is empty, the water so cold it shocks me to the core even in my wet suit. I relish the feeling of every pinprick of pain, the shivering and chattering of my teeth. The feeling of being alive.

I didn't spend last night with Diego. Somehow I knew I wouldn't; somehow, I knew we were already over. Though we'd walked back to the casitas hand in hand, I said good night at the door to his cabin. Just before turning away, I stood on my toes to kiss him, a brief, tender kiss that felt like memory and nothing else.

When I return to the cabin after my swim, I shower off the salt water and get ready for the day's fieldwork. I lean down to pull the journals out from where I've been stashing them, under the bed.

They're not there.

I drop to the floor and, with the light on my phone, do a thorough search. I'm certain that's where I'd left them, but I check my duffel anyway. I check the drawers and shelves and under the sheets on the bed.

I'd had them in my hands when I left Diego last night; this much I remember because I only had one arm free for our quick embrace. Then I'd come into my casita, alone, and stowed them under the bed. Or had I? My mind had been in so many places, maybe I wasn't paying attention.

I step outside the cabin, looking on and under the chair outside my door. Seeing Gavin out of the corner of my eye, I ask him, "Have you seen any notebooks around? Leather journals?"

"No," he says, shouldering his backpack and taking a sip of coffee from a thermos. "Missing your field notebook?"

"Something else, actually. Something important."

"What could be more important than your field notes?"

I stop my search and look at him. "Gavin. I found something. That day in the cave. I was going to give them to you today, and now they're gone."

"Well, you can search for them later." He looks at his watch. "I'm going to help Hannah today, so you can take Callie to Punta Cormorant."

"About that—"

"I'd like for you to take a day off," he interrupts. "You need a break. A hike will do you good, and Callie needs a guide."

"Spending the day with Callie is not my idea of a break, Gavin."

Gavin puts his hands on my shoulders, forcing me to look at him. "I saw your nests from the other day, Mallory. They were already falling apart. We have to rebuild every one of them. I know you don't think you need a break, but you do. And it's not negotiable."

I feel my face flush; I try to picture the nests I'd built, what I'd done wrong, but I hardly remember making them. "I'm sorry," I say. "But—"

"No more arguments," he says. "I'm leaving now. We'll talk tonight."

I watch him leave, then return to my casita, where I pull everything off shelves, out of drawers, even out of my suitcase. Nothing.

I text Diego, asking him where they are. His text back is brief and unhelpful: ?

He's at the vet clinic; I'd forgotten. He'll be gone all day.

I go to his casita and stand in front of the door. No one else is around. Just in case, I knock—no answer. I open the door and close it quickly behind me.

The room looks very much as it had on the night I spent here—the bed unmade, the books scattered. First I look among Diego's books for the journals, but they're not there. I check the floor, the desk, under the bed. I see them nowhere, and I begin to open drawers—the desk, the bureau—not letting myself think too much about what I'm doing. I sift quickly through Diego's belongings: his clothes, his field notes, a few folders containing what look like PhD application materials. No journals.

There's only one other possibility. Callie.

At the door of her casita, I lean close and strain to hear whether she might be inside. It's nearly impossible to tell, so I venture a knock. A moment later she appears.

"You ready?" she says.

I'm caught off guard, with no other explanation for why I'm there.

"Darwin will be back to pick us up after he drops off Gavin and Hannah," she says. "We have time to get some coffee—I'm already in withdrawal."

She shuts the door behind her and shuffles me toward the kitchen. We each pour a cup of coffee and fill our water bottles. As she fits the bottle and some fruit into one of her camera bags, I look for the worn leather of the journals but see nothing.

Fifteen minutes later, we meet Darwin at the landing. Callie is unusually quiet during the ride to Punta Cormorant. As we approach the white-sand beach, framed by desiccated slopes of earth, I feel the missing weight of the journals in my pack and envision what we might've looked like if this were the middle of the last century: arriving by rowboat rather than motorized inflatable, dressed in simple clothing made of natural fabrics. And as I watch Callie disembark from the panga amid the rush of turquoise waves, she could be the Baroness herself; she waits for Darwin to unload her camera bags, waits for his hand to assist her off the boat. Head raised high, lips painted, she begins walking up the beach, knowing I'll follow dutifully behind.

Darwin hands me a radio and says he'll call when he's back, in about two hours. On the beach, sets of twin tracks reveal sea turtles' paths to the low, green brush among which they dig nests to lay their eggs. Beyond that, the vegetation blankets the landscape in a dry, grayish white, like old bones.

I take the lead from the beach along a sandy trail that winds around a lagoon. Flamingos stand elegantly in the water, the mirrored surface doubling the length of their thin legs. The lagoon is so perfectly calm and still that water and firmament meld into one.

After about twenty minutes, I glance over my shoulder. Callie, still close behind, raises her camera to photograph the lagoon. Then, without speaking, she walks past me to continue along the trail, a narrowing path of dirt among the thickening brush. I follow, watching her thin shoulders under the straps of her camera bags, her upright posture and steady gait. The trail's brown dirt becomes flecked with sand, and soon we're walking past large dunes to a small, curved beach of pristine sugary white sand. The beach is empty, and, just offshore, dome-shaped lumps bob in the water—Pacific green turtles floating in the waves, waiting for nightfall so they can come ashore to lay their eggs.

"Oh, that water," Callie says.

It's a crystalline, unreal shade of blue, with waves of light cyan lapping the shore, deepening to cobalt farther out. A sea lion pops his whiskered face above the surface, then dives back under. The thin, wafer-like bodies of rays rise and fall with the surging tide. A cool, steady breeze dilutes the heat of the sun.

I begin to walk along the shoreline, looking for swimming penguins, with Callie at my side. "I'm glad you decided to come along," she says. "This beats building penguin nests, doesn't it?"

"Not really."

Callie holds out her camera, giving me no choice but to take it. "Hold this for me while I get some video," she says, already bending down to take her video camera out of its bag.

"I'm not a pack mule, Callie."

"It's just for a second," she says. "I can't carry them both."

"Then put one away."

"I need them accessible. I don't want to miss anything."

"I'm not going to carry this around all day," I say. "It's heavy."

"It weighs twelve pounds," she says, a bit proudly. "I think you can handle that. And it's the least you can do. Diego would be here doing this if it weren't for you. You've been such a distraction."

I wonder how much she knows—about everything. "I'm not sure what you mean."

She lowers the camera to make some adjustments, then hides behind it again. "Don't play stupid, Mallory. I know what's going on."

"Which is what, exactly?"

"Fucking my assistant, for one," she says. "Two, translating Dore's journals. Is there anything else?"

I'm so relieved she doesn't mention Emily that it takes me a moment. The journals.

"Diego told you?"

"Of course he did. He tells me everything. He's on my payroll, not yours." She lowers the camera and looks at me. "I'm sure he made you feel very special, Mallory. It's one of his talents. But it means nothing."

So he didn't tell her everything. Nothing about Emily. I feel another wave of relief, so strong it makes me momentarily lightheaded.

Then, the realization sinks in. "You're the one who has the journals," I say slowly.

"That's right."

"He gave them to you? Just like that?"

She laughs. "You think he's such an innocent. I bought them. I mean, his intentions are noble enough—his grand plan is to put himself through school and save these islands—but I can't tell you I didn't pay a pretty penny for them."

I suppose I shouldn't be shocked, but somehow I am, and I can't help but feel a sense of betrayal—not so much because of the night Diego and I spent together but because of all the other nights.

Exploring the journals, discovering the island's lost history. The late-night swims and talks about our pasts and futures. He'd helped me move forward in ways he didn't even realize, and when I think of him stealing the journals and selling them to Callie, I recall something Dore had written—*Fuchsteufelswild*—and the word comes alive within me in a sudden rush of anger.

Callie shrugs. "It'll be worth it in the end, with the story I'll have to tell. An exclusive, no less."

"Those journals belong to me," I say. "I was going to give them to Gavin. For the penguin project. You have no right to them."

"Sorry, Mallory. At least you'll have my footage and interview. I'm sure I can get you guys a little screen time somewhere."

I'm still feeling light, woozy, as if I'm no longer in my own body, as though I could float away on the breeze. My mind whirs, ratcheting backward, trying to make sense of it all.

Callie lowers her camera and scans the beach, the look on her face so serene I almost think I'd imagined our conversation. "Such a beautiful spot," she says. "Let's go for a swim. The water's gorgeous."

"It's also full of stingrays," I murmur, half to myself, not sure whether she hears me.

Callie returns her cameras to their bags, then pulls off her T-shirt and steps out of her shorts, revealing a navy-blue bikini. "I'm not worried about a few little stingrays." She takes a few steps toward the water. "They'll get out of our way."

I remain on shore, watching Callie as the first waves splash into her legs. Once she wades farther in, I kneel down next to the closest camera bag and open the unzipped flap. No journals. I run my hands over the outer pockets, and when I find nothing I turn to check the other bag, taking my eyes off Callie and the water. I rummage through the bag but find nothing other than the video camera, a battery pack—and then I hear Callie's piercing scream.

I stand and whirl around to see Callie doubled over in waist-high water. By the time I reach her, she's back at the water's edge, and the rays have scattered. I see that she walked right into two rays, which stung her on the ankle and the thigh. Her right hand is red and beginning to swell, from trying to remove one of the barbs from her leg.

Though I've never been stung, from what I know of the rays' highly venomous sting, Callie is in excruciating pain, and there will be no relief until she gets to a hospital.

"Okay, Callie." I take her left arm and lead her away from the water. "One step at a time."

Callie can't walk more than a few feet, and we stop farther up the beach, where she collapses. I radio Darwin, who is not yet on his way, and ask him to come immediately and to meet us on the trail. While Callie's on the ground, I kneel down to examine her injuries, careful not to touch. Her ankle is red and swelling, and her thigh looks much worse; it's bleeding, and the stingray's serrated barb—nearly two inches long and about the width of a pencil—is still embedded in muscle and flesh, its poison unrelenting.

She's writhing in pain, her hand clutching again at the barb, attempting to pull it out.

"No, Callie." I grab her by the elbow to avoid touching her injured hand. "I know it hurts, but you need to leave it."

"I can't." Callie's breath is shallow, her words sobbed rather than spoken.

"It'll be okay." I pull on my backpack and sling Callie's camera bags over my shoulder. Then I take her by the arm. "Come on, we need to get you back to the landing. Darwin's on his way."

"Darwin," Callie mutters. "Theory of evolution. Only the fittest."

"You're going to survive this, Callie. Let's go."

We begin to walk, but Callie can't put any weight on her right leg. She leans heavily on me, each step slow and arduous. We haven't gone far before she doubles over and vomits into the bushes just off the trail, and her legs crumple.

"We're getting there." I try to sound reassuring. "Darwin will be here any second," I add, though the radio has been silent.

We keep moving, and after what feels like hours, I hear a crackle and grab the radio; Darwin has just landed at the beach. "Hurry," I tell him.

Five minutes later, Darwin arrives, uncharacteristically serious, and takes Callie in his arms, careful to avoid the protruding barb. It's a half mile back to the beach, and even though he's strong and Callie is light, she's thrashing about in pain, muttering words that warble together and make no sense.

"She keeps trying to remove that barb," I warn Darwin. "We can't let her."

Darwin nods and shifts his grip on Callie so that her arms are pinned to her sides. When we get to the beach, he sets her down, gently, and gets into the panga as I help her through a couple of feet of water to the bow. Darwin lifts her in and settles her on a towel on the bottom of the boat. I toss our bags in, then shove the boat farther into the water before jumping in myself. As Darwin starts the engine, I kneel on the floor of the panga, holding Callie's arms down and speaking to her as reassuringly as I can.

At Puerto Velasco Ibarra, Darwin helps Callie out of the panga. He must've brought back Gavin and Hannah; they're both coming toward the landing, Gavin lugging a large bucket and Hannah a lightweight plastic chair.

I step a few paces away and call Diego's cell, getting voicemail. I leave a terse message, explaining what happened. "She needs to go to Santa Cruz," I say.

Hannah helps Callie into the chair and wraps her in a blanket. Gavin eases her foot into the bucket. "Hot water," he explains. Using a large plastic cup, he pours some of the water over her thigh.

I'm behind Callie when she bends forward and again reaches for the barb. I seize her shoulders and ease her backward as gently as I can. She curses at me but is too weak to fight.

"We've got someone coming in just a few minutes," Gavin tells her, smoothing her hair back from her face, which is red and blotchy, streaked with tears and salt water.

I let my breath out slowly, watching Callie's increasingly labored breathing, watching Gavin pour water over her foot. I think of Rudy Lorenz bathing the Baroness's feet, and Dore's, and of Diego bathing mine, and I feel my own mind become fuzzy, as if Callie's delirium is catching, somehow—as if the journals have taken some hold over me, as if the century between then and now is blurring, or disappearing.

I consider all that has changed over the last hundred or so years—the tortoises are back, the penguins disappearing, the cats reappearing—and yet there is one species that has not died out or evolved. For better and for worse, we humans are exactly the same.

Dore

We burn under the sun. We thirst. Our crops are withered, and the stench of animals dead and dying in the drought chokes our breath.

It has been three months since the Baroness and Robert were cast off into the sea, and I still worry constantly that the bodies will come ashore, or parts of them. Or that a passing ship will see one of them floating past. How will we know for certain that the bodies are gone, or whether they have washed up elsewhere?

Yet by now they must be long gone. We have had few visitors, and when they ask about the Baroness, we tell them that she and Robert Philippson have moved on to Tahiti. No one questions this story, and no one has come to inquire about them.

It has become ever more difficult to see Rudy. Even though he is now alone at the Hacienda, it is an arduous journey in the heat, and I can sneak away only when Friedrich is busy. In this terrible heat, he spends more time lingering in the house than working, and when he falls asleep I never know how much time I have.

If I weren't so desperate to leave, I might forsake Rudy altogether. But I still hold within me some great hope that he will take me with him when he leaves. And so, despite all my conflicting emotions—all my anger for what he'd done, my shame for having done my own part—I continue to see him.

I wish I could say I have resisted his bed, but even in the smothering heat, even as my mind slows and resists and protests, I continue to draw him into me. Perhaps it is an attempt to hold on to something I lost so long ago—or never even had—or to convince him that we must leave the island together. Or perhaps it is as simple and instinctual as the mating of my beloved animals—a need so deep and so primitive we cannot resist it.

And because every time we come together feels like it could be the last, I savor every moment, every kiss, every breath. I do not have to love him to love this.

***

At last came the day I have dreaded. Rudy is gone.

I learned the news from Friedrich. Heinz Wittmer told him that Rudy left Floreana on a boat called the *Dinamita*. I did not know this at the time, but he had spent his last nights at the old hut at Post Office Bay, apparently so he would not risk missing a chance to leave.

I cannot say I am surprised he left me. Though I so badly wish to leave this island, once I suspected he would leave without me, I knew I should let him. Despite the ways in which I still wanted him, he had become too much like Friedrich—a man I once loved who turned into someone else. A man whose dreams I once shared before they became more his than mine.

Why is my one greatest gift helping men achieve their dreams while I watch my own disappear?

It was not a week later when we received the alarming news that the *Dinamita* had been lost. After leaving Floreana, the ship had stopped at Santa Cruz. It sailed for San Cristóbal a few days later, and it has not been seen since.

I think again of ghosts and wonder whether I would know if Rudy were still alive. I do not see him in my dreams; he does not whisper to me in the night. In my heart, if not in my body, I had already said goodbye—so perhaps I would not feel his spirit around me, as much as I long for contact, even if it is otherworldly.

I truly do despair of ever leaving this place. Without the pleasant distractions Rudy had brought, life is unbearable with Friedrich, and the Wittmers live their own lives, without much contact with us. Yet the shadows of the Baroness and Robert and Rudy hang over us all. Even Friedrich seems to have lost his enthusiasm for our work; he selfishly tends to his writings while leaving all the chores to me.

This island has consumed so many, and if I cannot find my way off this piece of rock, it shall consume me, too.

Mallory

Later that night, in my casita, I pick up my phone and begin to scroll through the numbers. It's nine thirty, two hours later in Boston. Scott is sure to be awake. I haven't heard his voice in months, and it's strange to think of Scott and Gavin having spoken to each other; it would have been for the first time ever. I put down the phone.

Earlier, Gavin and I had dinner with Hannah, going over the data and what more we could accomplish during our last days on the island. I watched as Hannah leaned over Gavin's shoulder, commenting on his notes, adding her own observations about the birds. While I'd been at Punta Cormorant with Callie, Hannah and Gavin completed nest number 150, including the rebuilding of my nests. We met our goal.

Now, as I pick up my phone again, scrolling toward Scott's name, something Dore had written comes back to me: *Can we ever forgive one another for not being who we each thought we'd be?*

For the first time since Emily died, I think of the last night Scott and I spent together, the last night of our former life. With Emily at her sleepover, we'd had a rare night alone in the house, and I realize only now the magic of our unspoken agreement to spend it together—for Scott to forgo his work, for me to let go of my anxiety and the ways I distracted myself from it: housework, meal plans, stained glass. Together we made a simple dinner, an avocado-pesto pasta, and opened a bottle of wine and lit candles as the winter night cloaked the windows. We did the dishes and finished off the wine, then watched half of a movie so mediocre we eventually abandoned it in favor of sex on the living room sofa. I remember thinking of how long it had been; I remember thinking of how lovely it was to have the house to ourselves.

We'd been asleep in bed when we got the call about Emily, and much later, when we got home, I looked at the sofa and knew that now we would forever have the house to ourselves. I went back to bed and didn't emerge for days.

Scott and I never recovered—and I know now that this was at least in part because I didn't give us a chance. I spoke very little because nothing seemed to matter. I ate very little because every meal was a memory of foods tailored to Emily's diet. Scott and I both needed comfort, but I refused to offer it or receive it. That last night of lovemaking, which had in the moment felt like a new beginning, had become an abrupt ending. His hands now felt wooden to me, as if they would no longer fit into the places I'd always wanted them, and I didn't let him try.

I've known all along none of this was Scott's fault, but I had to come to Floreana to understand that there could be no such thing as order—with children or with wildlife—and that there could be no such thing as a right or a wrong choice. There is only what is.

More than a decade ago, the Galápagos had prepared me for motherhood—and then, marriage and motherhood prepared me for returning to the world of conservation. It had not been easy, back then, for me to accept its challenges: the necessary hard choices that scientists make, like culling one species to save another, or the choices animals make, to sacrifice one child to save another. The challenges remain the same, and I'm not sure I'll ever get used to them. But I know now that I've already survived the most difficult thing, and that I'm not alone. Scott has survived it, too. And I think this means there is hope for us still.

As I hold my phone, a gust of wind hums through the casita's open window. Moving my fingers across the screen, I feel a tug, an irrepressible pull that stretches taut, then forms a tight little knot in my chest. I tap the words **Scott cell**, bringing up the photo of him that Emily took two years ago in Marblehead, his face suntanned, hair wind whisked, eyes smiling. The photo is blurred from Emily's small, unsteady hands, but what's clear is the joy in his face as he looked into the camera held by our daughter. I trace the lines of his face on the small screen, then press call.

Dore

It is amazing to me how completely such a pervasive anxiety can vanish, how rapidly a slate can be wiped clean, how immediately a woman can become free.

I have lost Rudy, and now I have lost Friedrich as well.

Like Rudy, I had an opportunity, and I chose to act—impulsively, perhaps—but it is now done, and there is no going back.

For these past few weeks, I felt something tugging at my heart, my mind—I was flushed and anxious, queasy and heartsick, as if my body was trying to tell me something my consciousness was not ready to accept.

It was when I was sitting with Johanna near the chicken coop one day, stroking the fur and whiskers of her sweet face, that I felt a twinge inside my belly. Just then a word flashed through my mind—*Regelblutung*—and I realized, with a shock, that I have not yet bled this month. That I had not bled last month.

Was it possible, after all this time?

I did the calculations in my mind and determined that yes, it was possible—but almost as soon as hope rose in my chest, it sank down again. I had been through this five times already, and my history did not bode well for a different outcome now that I was past the age of thirty. I knew I could not bear to suffer through a sixth loss. Especially to lose a part of Rudy—this child could belong to no one but Rudy—so soon after losing him and everything I'd hoped for.

I touched my stomach to see if I could feel anything inside. Johanna nuzzled me as if she, too, knew. And my heart broke to watch her, as I remembered what Friedrich had done to her own babies.

It was there that Friedrich found us—he'd come to suggest slaughtering one of our chickens for dinner. I was shocked. Despite providing them to others, he has never proposed killing one for us. He knows I will never eat one of my pets.

But they have all been sick—we have so little food for them due to the drought—and he said it would be humane to kill them, to give them a purpose, rather than let them suffer. I grew angry and we had a prolonged argument, during which I protested until my voice cracked—but he insisted we needed the protein, that nothing else was edible.

I told him I would have no part of any of it. I left, with Johanna trotting after me, knowing I could not be near whatever he would do.

But in my rage and despair, an idea was born.

When it came time to prepare dinner, I left Friedrich in charge—I could not bear to witness the little body in his hands, dead on our stove. He'd told me he would boil the meat to ensure that it was safe to eat, and I was so upset my fury alone could have made the water boil.

I stayed away from our kitchen until all traces of his cooking were gone, and then I prepared what little vegetables and rice we still had. I asked him to go out to the garden to see what he could salvage from our crops, which were fighting for life, and while he was gone I added the contents of the Baroness's little wooden box to our food.

Yes, I put the rat poison into both our meals. I saw no future for myself any more than I saw one for Friedrich, here or elsewhere. I saw pain and misery and loss—and the spilling of all my secrets in the worst way imaginable.

And yet, as we sat down to eat, I could not bring myself to go through with it.

I thought of the stroke of fate that planted this seed inside me and how unfair it would be not to give it a chance to thrive. It may wither and die, as this season's crops have—but we had planted them anyway. We had to hope for the best.

And so I would, too.

I picked at my food, and Friedrich thought my reluctance was due to distrust of his preparation, and he ate perhaps more of the meat than he wanted, as if to prove to me that it was perfectly safe. He was so busy holding up his ego he didn't notice I was hiding my own food in the napkin in my lap.

Meanwhile, I watched him eat. I watched every bite.

Not long afterward, he got very sick with a headache and severe stomach pains. Innocently, I asked if he thought it was the meat, and he said no, it couldn't be, he had prepared it properly. I read to him from *Zarathustra* as he moaned in pain and drifted in and out of consciousness.

The light of dawn is arriving now, and I need to go to the Wittmers—I may have waited too long already. Friedrich can no longer speak, and I have given him a pencil and paper, which he has not used; he doesn't seem to want me to leave, but I have told him I must go and seek help.

It is interesting to me, this reversal—Friedrich, helpless; I, the one in control. I have wondered often what caused Friedrich to change so drastically once we arrived on Floreana. Perhaps I didn't know him well enough before running away with him. Perhaps I was so eager to leave my own life behind I didn't see the other side of him, that dark hidden part we all have but rarely show. Or maybe I didn't know the dark side of my own soul, which I did not recognize until I helped Rudy with his grisly undertaking. Maybe that darkness was there all along, in both of us.

Now, in these moments with Friedrich I cannot not help but think of Zarathustra. Those who know Nietzsche's work will no doubt recall Zarathustra's exhortation to "die at the right time." I have always wondered what this meant. Now I know. But I wonder, and now I always will, what Friedrich believed it meant.

Here is what happened. When I arrived at the Wittmers', Heinz was not home, and Margret went to fetch him while I returned to Friedo with Harry on one of their donkeys.

We found Friedrich struggling for breath and still unable to speak. He twitched and kicked, the throes of death entering his body, and by the time Heinz and Margret arrived, I could not take any more and went out to the garden. I lay there for a long time, feeling my cheek against the ground, the heat in the air. I heard the mosquitoes buzzing in my ear, and a snort from Max not far away. Johanna came by and nuzzled my face before she moved on to her day of hunting and napping.

When I finally went back inside, the Wittmers left me alone with him. In the last motion he would ever make, he reached out for me before falling back on the bed with his last breath. At that moment, I felt a sense of calm wash over me like nothing I'd ever felt before.

We buried him in the garden. And I began to pack, not knowing how long I might wait for a ship to take me from here.

Mallory

I wake early, head aching, and can't fall back to sleep. I think of my talk with Scott the night before—painful, tearful—and the release of long-held emotions feels like a hangover now. Yet it feels good at the same time—to have started the long process of apologizing, to have talked about Emily, about coming home, moving forward.

The air-conditioning is struggling, and my casita feels hot and stuffy. I look at my phone and see that it's not yet five o'clock. It's still dark outside.

I open the door as quietly as I can and step out into the cooler predawn air. I'm about to sit down when I notice a slice of light across the deck, coming from one of the other cabins. It looks as though it's Callie's.

Before I can think about it, I hurry over to the open door. Inside is Diego, holding a stack of folders, trying to fit them into what looks like an oversize briefcase. There's a suitcase on the bed, a pile of women's clothing in a heap next to it. He glances up, startled.

"I'm just here to pack up Callie's things," he says.

"Her things? Like my journals?"

He puts down the folders and straightens.

"Why did you sell them to her?" I ask. "How could you do that?"

His shoulders drop, and he sits down on one of the beds, as if it's going to tire him to explain. I sit across from him, trying to maintain eye contact, but he's looking downward. "You mentioned putting them back where you found them," he says quietly. "All I could think was that they're far too valuable to stay hidden."

"That wasn't your decision to make. You stole them from me."

"I'm sorry," he says.

"You didn't even give me a chance to tell you I wasn't going to put them back—I wanted to use them to help the penguins. And now you've ruined that."

He looks up, and I glimpse what looks like genuine regret in his face. "I didn't know," he says.

I feel a wave of disappointment crash through me—and I remember Dore's word again: *Fuchsteufelswild*—and I shake my head, trying to clear it. "All your talk about saving these islands—it's just talk, isn't it? Because those journals could've done something good. And now all they're going to do is feed Callie's ego. And your bank account."

He says nothing more, and for a moment I picture myself pawing through Callie's things, throwing her belongings around the room until I find the journals—if they're even here.

"I'm sorry," he says again.

"I can't believe I trusted you." Again I think of our nights on the beach, the unearned faith I'd placed in his keeping our secret. And I wonder if part of the blame lies with me, for so blindly believing in his loyalty. One thing I've come to accept is that blame is easy to assign and so much harder to own.

He doesn't respond, and without another word I return to my casita and shut the door. I lie down on the bed, suddenly exhausted, and drift to sleep.

~

I'm woken by a knock at the door. It's almost seven, and I get up, expecting Gavin or Hannah, but it's Diego.

I stand in the doorway for a moment, still sleep dazed. Then, though I feel like shutting the door in his face, I open it wider to let him in.

He stands there for a moment, and I wait.

"Callie's feeling a lot better," he says.

"I'm glad to hear it."

"The wound in her leg is bad, though," he continues. "The spine went deep. She may need surgery."

"I hope it goes well. You should be getting back to her, right?" I move toward the door, to send him on his way.

"Hold on." He takes off his backpack and reaches inside. He pulls out two leather-bound journals—Dore's journals—and holds them out to me.

"What's this about?" I'm almost afraid to reach for them.

"I never should have taken them from you."

Now I do reach out and take them, afraid he'll change his mind. They feel warm, as if they'd been in the sun. "Will you have to give the money back?"

"Probably," he says.

I wrap my hands around the journals and look at Diego, who holds my gaze, as if awaiting further questions, another wave of anger—yet I'm surprised to feel my bitterness subside. Without Diego, I wouldn't even know the journals' value, and for a moment I can almost understand why he'd done what he did. And now, with the journals back in my hands, and amid everything that's happened over the past month, I find myself feeling unexpectedly indifferent as to why he took them. Perhaps it's that I no longer need to know what motivates Diego; perhaps it's that I've learned it doesn't matter—that truth can be a slippery, chimerical thing.

After a moment, Diego fills the long silence. "We got twelve cats fixed at the clinic," he says. "Five were strays. A couple of families agreed to feed them."

I know this is his way of asking for forgiveness, and I feel a slight loosening of the tension in my body. But then I think of the cats still unseen, of the journals, of Gavin, of leaving Floreana—of all the loose ends, dangling like ghost nets in the sea.

I drive slowly to avoid filling the air with clouds of red dust. Gavin is in the passenger seat, staring at the journals I've handed to him. During the forty-five-minute journey to Asilo de la Paz, I tell him the story they reveal.

From the corner of my eye, I see Gavin leafing through the pages. "What are you going to do with them?"

"The question is, what are *you* going to do with them," I say.

"I don't follow."

"They're yours. To raise money for the program."

I feel his eyes on me. "This is a career-making find, Mallory. Are you sure?"

I nod. "I want to support the penguins." I pause, then add, "I've missed this. More than I knew."

I glance over at him, and he's looking back at me, in a way both familiar and new. I feel a surge of hope—as if there may be a way back, not to the way things were but toward something different.

We're almost there. Gavin coughs and rolls up the window a bit higher, even though the truck has no air-conditioning and it's already stifling in the cab. I pull into the parking area, which is empty. I haven't told him why we're here, and he seems to know to wait instead of asking.

As we walk through the jungly landscape, I pull back the vines and branches in our path. It's late in the day, the sun about an hour from setting, and darker than it was when I was here before.

At last we reach the large cave, and as we stand in its entrance I tell him about the day I'd ditched nest building to come here. He listens in silence, his eyes scanning the cave walls.

"I can't believe you found them," he says at last. "These caves must've been explored a million times over the last century."

"I still don't believe it myself, really." I step inside and then look back at Gavin, a silhouette against the last bit of daylight outside.

"That's partly why I wanted to come back—to cover up the hole in the rock. To make sure I've left everything as I found it."

When I reach the crevice in the lava wall from which I'd pulled the journals, the severed rock doesn't look loose, only cracked. And when I nudge the rock, it doesn't loosen under my hands as I expect it to. I back up a few steps, thinking I'm in the wrong spot. I try again, pushing harder, then pounding the rock with the heel of my palm.

"What are you doing?"

"This doesn't make sense," I mutter. "I thought this was the spot, right here."

He comes closer and peers at the wall. Then he shrugs. "That's what you wanted, right? To leave it as you found it?"

I take a seat on one of the cave's benches, bemused. Maybe I'd forgotten the exact spot, or maybe I'd covered the hole up that day without remembering. For once, I find I'm okay with the uncertainty, with accepting that I can't fix everything.

I think of those who have lived in these caves over the years—and I think of Dore and whether a part of her hid her journals here knowing one day they might be found, whether she actually did want her story told. I think of how she'd nearly given up, how she'd poisoned Friedrich's and her food and then, at the last minute, saved herself with the wild hope that her unborn child might have a chance. And I think of Emily, of everything she taught me in her few years on Earth, and all that's left for her to teach me still.

I look over at Gavin and know it's time. I say his name, and when he turns around, I wave him over to me. "There's something I need to tell you. Or maybe show you."

I take out my phone and scroll to a photo of Emily, a recent one. I hold the phone out to him. He takes it, and his eyes lock on to the screen. He sees what I've been looking at for eight years. Those eyes, a light sea-glass green, unmistakably familiar. And, I can tell, by the look on his face, that he sees what I always have. That it's like looking into a mirror.

He steps backward, then turns, walking a few paces away, running a hand through his hair, over his face. Long, excruciating moments pass before he turns back to me. "*Why* didn't you tell me?"

"I'm so sorry," I say. "I can see how wrong it was not to tell you. But back then"—I pause, my voice breaking—"I just did what I had to do. What I thought was best."

"You didn't give me a chance," he says, shaking his head. "All this time—"

"You didn't want kids," I say. "And Scott did. You and me—this never would've worked. It would've ruined us."

He comes closer and looks again at the photo. I see his eyes redden. "It ruined us anyway."

The sharp ache that rises in my chest reminds me of a night not long before we fell apart, when I had recognized that we wouldn't last, and I'd begun mourning the loss of us that very night, in bed, both of us drifting toward sleep. I listened to him breathe, for the first time knowing that it wouldn't be forever, and I remember pressing my lips to the skin of his neck in the dark, in both a greeting and a farewell.

Now, as I look at him in the dim light of the cave, I realize that night was one of the last times I'd lived so completely in any given moment, unafraid of what might be ahead. I have that same feeling now, with the truth between us as he sits down next to me on the cool old stone: that I no longer have to fear what comes next. I feel that he and I are again evolving, but now, in the hazy ray of light from the mouth of the cave, in the history in the air around us, it feels more like a beginning than an end.

Dore

This will be the last time I write. I have not yet decided what will become of this record, whether I shall burn it or hide it again or keep it close to me. I don't quite understand the purpose of putting such things to paper, even as I write them down; the only thing I understand is the danger in it, and yet I am compelled to do it anyhow. I doubt I will ever forget what I've recorded here, and I doubt it shall be of use or interest to anyone else, or whether I want it to be.

Today I received the good news that an American yacht has arrived—and I know I will have my freedom at last when they take me on board.

As many times as I've dreamed of this day, it would not have been possible until now. I'd always felt I could not leave on my own, without Friedrich, with no home left to return to. And as much as I'd wanted to escape with Rudy, I know now that beginning a new life attached to yet another man would have taken me, somehow, to the same place I am now.

I came to Floreana to heal myself, to become the person Friedrich believed I could be. And it has taken me these years to see that I was already whole, that I only needed to step into my own being and breathe on my own.

To realize one's nature perfectly—that is what each of us is here for.

I do not yet know where the yacht is headed, but it does not matter. I am no longer alone; I carry my companion within me. I have a bit of money, which Friedrich had stashed away, and for everything else, I will rely on the kindness of strangers to a destitute widow and, perhaps, single mother. I will go wherever the yacht sails, and when I reach my destination, I trust I will know it when I see it.

I am ready to go but for a few final things. I will write these last few words. I will visit the Wittmers to tell them that Friedo is theirs. I am not so naive to believe they will not eat my chickens, but I will ask that they treat them with compassion and gratitude. I will ask Harry to tend to my flowers and my garden, to look after Max and Johanna. I will ask him to keep reading their stories to Rolf and to add his own tales after I'm gone.

The crew of the arriving yacht brought an answer to the question in my heart—Rudy is dead. He and his ship's captain were found on Marchena Island, where they had been marooned. They perished of thirst, the sun desiccating their shriveled bodies.

I learned that the captain died first, as he was found under a skiff, which Rudy must have placed over him. Rudy was found some distance away, lying as if asleep on the black sand of the beach.

The crew, who did not know of my relationship with Rudy, provided more details than I could bear. His mummified hands, all bones and taut flesh. His eyes, burned shut by the sun. His nose, half withered away. His mouth, wide open, as if still hoping for a drop of water. His blond hair, thinned out and bleached white, blowing in the wind "in quite an eerily lifelike way," said one of the crew. His skeletal legs. His wind-shorn clothes.

I cannot imagine what Rudy went through—alone, mad with thirst, devoid of all hope. I wonder if he'd thought of me, if he'd thought of waiting for me, if—in the end—he was glad he hadn't. My fate would have matched his had I gone with him that day. But I cannot dwell on such things.

As I write these last words, I feel a darkness within the light around me. Though Friedrich and Rudy are no longer here on the planet, I have the feeling that they are still with me, and will be always. One thing I know to be true is that those whom you have loved will never truly leave you. And those whom you have both loved and hated, whom you have loved and lost . . . they will stay closer than ever.

As ever, I feel as though this island has eyes, that its spirits are watching us all. I do believe that there are places in which souls find themselves roaming—perhaps of their own doing, perhaps not—in places that they can never leave.

I remember so clearly the moment when I first set my eyes on Floreana—and I wonder how I will feel as I watch the island disappear, leaving it all behind. This place has changed me, in ways far beyond what I imagined, and I have left my mark upon it as well, as we all do. I have created life and destroyed it here; I have made it better for those who come next, and I have made it worse. We are healed yet forever scarred. And we are awakened, never to sleep again.

Mallory

It's almost time for dinner—I've been packing for my early departure tomorrow—when I hear footsteps outside my open casita door. I look up to see Gavin standing there, holding the journals. He's quiet, watching me.

"Everything okay?" I put down the shirts I'm holding and walk over.

"I found something tucked inside one of the journals. You must've missed it." He holds out an envelope. "It's for you."

"What is it?" I take it, my eyes watching him.

He shrugs. "Open it."

The envelope has my name on it. Inside is a note and a high-quality copy of a photograph. The note reads:

> *Mallory—*
> *I found this photo in Callie's things and remembered your grandmother's name was Johanna. The photo is from a historical museum in Berlin.*
>
> *I should have known from the beginning that these journals have always belonged to you. I know you will do great things with them.*
>
> *I wish you the very best, Mallory. I hope we will meet again one day.*
>
> *Until then—Diego*

The photograph is of a child about five years old, with thick, curly dark hair. The woman holding her on her lap is unmistakably Dore Strauch. On the back of the photograph are the words *Dore & Johanna, 1940*.

Johanna, Dore's daughter. In 1940 she was the same age as my German grandmother, Johanna, who came to the US an orphan.

I hand the note to Gavin as I continue to study the photo, looking for familiar features, for some sign of resemblance.

I'm looking, I realize, not only for a part of myself but for a glimpse of Emily.

Perhaps I'm being too hopeful, too eager to believe that something in the world aligns and makes sense. Already I'm thinking of when I'll have the chance to call my mother to confirm the dates—but I know that even if those align, we'll have to do a lot more research to learn whether Dore's Johanna was my grandmother. Whether Dore was my great-grandmother.

But for now, it's enough to believe—that I'm on the right path, that I can bridge my own past with a future on Floreana—and it's a feeling I want to cling to.

I look up to see Gavin waiting, and again I think of the reverberations of what he's taught me, how penguin lessons can translate into real life. Act quickly. Hold tight. Don't let go.

I give him the photo, watch the knowledge cross his face. Then he holds it out, along with the journals. "You need to keep them," he says.

I shake my head. "They're yours. I want to support your work."

"Our work," he says.

I look at him.

"It's always been our work, Mallory. I think I'd have asked you back years ago if I thought you'd come. I should've . . ." He sighs. "Well, there were a lot of things I should've done differently. Anyway, I didn't want to interfere with your new life."

I let out my breath. "But now I'm starting over."

He nods. "I know. And I'm so sorry for the reasons why."

His hands are still stretched toward me. I take the photo and letter but not the journals.

"We've moved on, you and me," he says, "but would you consider coming back? Working with me next season?"

I think of Dore—*This place has changed me, in ways far beyond what I imagined, and I have left my mark upon it as well, as we all do*—and I think of Johanna, and I think of Emily, and I say, "I would love nothing more."

We go to the dining area to make dinner, and it feels the way we used to be but different, less charged but more comfortable. Afterward, we linger in the kitchen together, sipping wine, talking about Emily, about everything, the hours disappearing along with the years we've spent apart, until finally we stand up and return to our casitas in the gently stirring salt-stained air, new clouds filling the sky.

∼

Dawn is breaking when Gavin, Hannah, and Darwin accompany me to the landing. The three of them will stay another week to build more nests, while I head to Santa Cruz for my flight.

We exchange hugs and goodbyes. I wave until they're out of sight and keep my eyes on the island as the boat circles it just offshore. I see the bright-blue feet of the boobies against the dark lava, penguins floating in the sea as they come up for air. As I look beyond to the gray-brown *cerros* above, I think about Dore leaving this island forever, leaving so many secrets behind, carrying one more within her.

I wonder if she'd felt more guilt or more relief, more regret or more freedom—or maybe she felt it all, and maybe also a sort of hopeful longing, which is skipping through me right now, like stones on the water. Finally I turn away and look ahead, into the clear blue deep of what comes next.

AUTHOR'S NOTE

The story of Dore Strauch in *Floreana* was inspired by real people and events, but I've taken many fictional liberties in this imagining.

When it comes to "the Galápagos affair," as the human drama on Floreana Island in the 1930s is known, the truth of what happened remains elusive because what we know of the events during that time are all subjective, based on the memoirs of Dore Strauch and Margret Wittmer, articles by Friedrich Ritter, and observations by visitors to the island.

Dore's published memoir, *Satan Came to Eden*, is filled with contradictions: her partner, Friedrich, is the love of her life on one hand, and on the other he is a harsh, unsympathetic companion. In addition, Margret Wittmer's chronicle of events on the island, including the disappearance of the Baroness and her lovers and the death of Friedrich, are nothing like Dore's telling of these same events.

Here's what we know: Dore Strauch and Friedrich Ritter (though they never married, they were known as "the Ritters" on Floreana) arrived first, in 1929. They'd left their spouses in Berlin to escape civilization and build a life together on an isolated Pacific island; they also arranged for their spouses to meet and, they hoped, form a life together in their absence.

A few years later, another German family, Heinz Wittmer; his pregnant wife, Margret; and his teenage son, Harry, arrived to start a new life on Floreana. The Wittmers were independent and capable, and they all might've lived harmoniously on the island if it weren't for the third arrival: a woman who called herself the Baroness, and her two lovers, Rudolf Lorenz and Robert Philippson.

One day, the Baroness and Robert Philippson disappeared from the island. Margret Wittmer claimed they had left for Tahiti, whereas Dore believed an act of violence had occurred. Rudolf Lorenz, at that time, behaved as though a burden had been lifted. The truth remains unknown, as the Baroness and Philippson were never seen or heard from again.

Rudolf Lorenz left Floreana on a boat that later became marooned on an uninhabited island, where he and the captain both perished.

Not long afterward, Friedrich grew mysteriously ill, apparently from eating bad poultry, and Dore and the Wittmers witnessed his death, though Dore's and Margret's accounts of this event are completely different. After Friedrich's death, Dore left the island; she died in Berlin in 1942. The Wittmers stayed on Floreana and to this day have descendants on the island. The mysteries of these deaths and disappearances have never been solved.

Dore's story in this novel is based loosely on this timeline of events, but I've taken liberties with the order and timing, as well as embellished or created the scenes in Dore's narrative; the dialogue and other details are fictional. I have kept the actual names of several of the main players—including the Ritters, the Wittmers, and the Baroness—but other names, and some characters, have been invented. While in her memoir Dore Strauch refers to having kept a diary, the hidden diary in this novel is entirely invented.

There are only a handful of sources on the Galápagos affair, and they include Dore Strauch's memoir, *Satan Came to Eden*; Margret Wittmer's memoir, *Floreana*; the book *The Galápagos Affair* by John Treherne; and the documentary *The Galápagos Affair: Satan Came to Eden*, directed by Daniel Geller and Dayna Goldfine.

The science in Mallory's story is based on real penguin conservation work and research taking place in the Galápagos Islands.

Dr. Dee Boersma, one of the world's leading penguin experts, has been studying Galápagos penguins since the 1970s, and her penguin nest-building project inspired Mallory and Gavin's work in the novel. The nest-building work, so far, has not occurred on Floreana Island, where conservationists are still in the process of eliminating invasive species; this aspect of *Floreana* is fictional, and any mistakes in the science of penguin conservation are mine alone. Visit the University of Washington's Center for Ecosystem Sentinels at www.ecosystemsentinels.org to learn more and to support penguin conservation in the Galápagos.

ACKNOWLEDGMENTS

I learned of "the Galápagos affair" while visiting the islands in 2016, a trip I'd taken in part for the chance to travel with Dee Boersma, whose real-life penguin nest-building project in the Galápagos inspired Mallory and Gavin's work in the novel. I'm grateful to Dee for teaching me so much about the penguins of the world, and most of all to her and her colleagues for working so hard to protect them.

I'm also grateful for the sources that gave me insight into the Galápagos affair, which include Dore Strauch's memoir, *Satan Came to Eden*; Margret Wittmer's memoir, *Floreana*; the book *The Galápagos Affair* by John Treherne, and the documentary *The Galápagos Affair: Satan Came to Eden*, directed by Daniel Geller and Dayna Goldfine.

Tod Emko, president and founder of Darwin Animal Doctors, generously provided information on domestic animal care in the Galápagos Islands.

I'm incredibly grateful to Kathy Schneider for championing this book and for such terrific editorial insights, enthusiasm, and support. I feel so lucky to be working with you. And big thanks to everyone at JRA for supporting this book in so many ways.

Thanks so much to Carmen Johnson for believing in *Floreana* and for your guidance, and to Ronit Wagman for helping to bring this novel to the next level. Big thanks to Jon Ford for keen eyes and a brilliant copyedit.

Thank you, Kate White, for being a wonderful matchmaker and all-around magnificent human. Thanks to Susan McBeth for bringing readers and writers together through your fantastic Adventures by the Book.

A million thanks to the Raymonds—Jack, Caroline, Rebecca, and Jacky—for endless support and enthusiasm, and occasional material. And a million more to John Yunker, for reading, listening, and brainstorming with infinite patience. *Floreana*—and so much more—wouldn't be possible without you.

ABOUT THE AUTHOR

Midge Raymond is the author of *My Last Continent*, the short-story collection *Forgetting English*, and, with coauthor John Yunker, the mystery novel *Devils Island*. Her writing has appeared in *TriQuarterly*, *Bellevue Literary Review*, the *Los Angeles Times* magazine, *Chicago Tribune*, *Poets & Writers*, and many other publications. Midge has taught at Boston University, Boston's GrubStreet Writers, Seattle's Hugo House, and San Diego Writers, Ink. She lives in the Pacific Northwest, where she is cofounder of the boutique environmental publisher Ashland Creek Press. For more information, visit http://midgeraymond.com.

12/24